Helena and Forrest kept closing the gap.
Five yards now . . . Four . . .

The people stayed put, glaring at the agents. They still looked as human as Forrest and Helena. "I thought that old lady was crazy," Forrest whispered to his partner. "Guess I was right."

At two yards, the people still stood there wearing vaguely impatient expressions. Forrest began to relax, that tingling in his fingertips fading away. These were people, that's all—they somewhat fit the description the old woman had given them, but how hard was it to find a bearded guy accompanied by a woman? He wanted to find out what they were doing here at this hour, but he didn't expect either of them to leap to the top of the twelve-foot wall. All that was left now was to play the UV lights over them and see if they burned.

At five feet away, he was bringing the light up to train its beam on the guy's face when the woman lunged.

Only *woman* was no longer an operative term.

She had dropped her human disguise, and came at him with claws out and fangs gnashing and a terrible tongue lolling from her open maw.

Enter the terrifying world of

30 DAYS OF NIGHT

Novels available from Pocket Books

Rumors of the Undead

Immortal Remains

Eternal Damnation

Graphic Novels/Comic Books available from IDW Publishing

30 Days of Night

Dark Days

Return to Barrow

Bloodsucker Tales

30 Days of Night: Dead Space

Spreading the Disease

Eben and Stella

Beyond Barrow

Annual 2004
(featuring "The Book Club," "The Hand That Feeds," "Agent Norris: MIA," "The Trapper")

Annual 2005: The Journal of John Ikos

"Picking Up the Pieces"
(featured in IDW's Tales of Terror)

30 DAYS OF NIGHT™

ETERNAL DAMNATION

STEVE NILES & JEFF MARIOTTE

Based on the
IDW Publishing graphic novel series

POCKET STAR BOOKS
New York London Toronto Sydney

Pocket Star Books
A Division of Simon & Schuster, Inc.
1230 Avenue of the Americas
New York, NY 10020

First Pocket Star Books paperback edition August 2008

POCKET STAR and colophon are registered trademarks of Simon & Schuster, Inc.

For information about special discounts for bulk purchases, please contact Simon & Schuster Special Sales at 1-800-456-6798 or business@simonandschuster.com.

Cover design by Alan Dingman; cover art by Justin Randall

Manufactured in the United States of America

10 9 8 7 6 5 4 3 2 1

ISBN-13: 978-0-7434-9653-7
ISBN-10: 0-7434-9653-1

AUTHORS' NOTE

In the *30 Days of Night* mythos, *Eternal Damnation* takes place shortly after the events depicted in the novel *Immortal Remains*.

BEFORE

I

FOR DAYS, smoke, steam, and the plaintive cries of the dying issued from the hole.

From ground level, it looked as if someone had built a new opening to hell. Norwegian authorities wisely stayed far away. The few travelers who noticed the smoke from the highway and tried to approach were dissuaded by the immediate stink of death, the electric madness that coursed through the air and set their teeth on edge and made their hair stand up, even the sight of the occasional filthy survivor, with matted hair and ragged clothes and open wounds.

Everywhere was blood, blood, blood.

So nobody bore witness to the ones who pushed through the wall of stench.

They drove as far as they could on a road made impassable by heavy snow, then got out and walked, carrying their equipment and supplies.

Approaching the hole, their booted feet broke through red snow. They stood at the hole's rim for a while, shoveling through snow and debris, talking about the sight in soft voices, making notes, one taking digital photographs to document the scene. They swallowed hard, chuckled, patted each other's shoulders with gloved hands, and stamped their feet against the cold—whatever it took to remind them that they were still upright, their bodies more or less whole, and that they wouldn't see anyone like themselves inside the gaping pit.

Then they went inside.

2

THE NEIGHBORHOOD was one of those built in the twenty-first century by developers with more money than imagination. Houses were crammed onto lots so small that an adult could almost stand between two of them and touch both with outspread arms. They were all brown, although some had a little red mixed in, others leaning toward ocher or tan. The dark roofs slanted identically toward the streets, like the bills of officers' caps at parade rest.

Forrest Tilden had been an army officer before he chucked it for six months in Iraq as a private security contractor. In those six months he made as much money as in three years at his previous salary. He also made contacts, and one of those contacts had recruited him for this latest assignment. The pay wasn't as good, but he had money in the bank, and he mostly stayed stateside, mostly slept in his own bed at night, and he believed in the cause.

That was the important thing—he didn't mind killing, but when he pulled the trigger he liked to know the reason why.

Forrest scanned house numbers as he drove. Next

to him in the Hummer was Helena Bair, who had not served in the armed forces but rose up through the ranks of the FBI until she too was recruited for this assignment. She was reading through the contents of a file folder spread on her lap, one he had already memorized.

Finally, Forrest pulled up in front of one of the identical brown houses, the one with the number 1407 on the front door. As a token of individualism, the owners of this house had wrapped the columns flanking the door with orange Halloween lights, but it was daytime and nothing, Forrest believed, looked quite as pathetic as holiday lights during the day.

"That's the place," Helena said. She had short black hair, a wrestler's build, and a knack for stating the obvious. But she also was smart and fearless, so he enjoyed working with her.

"Let's get it done," he said.

They strode to the door with the confidence of people who know they'll be allowed inside. Helena knocked twice. Standing back from the door, Forrest saw through a picture window as a woman walked toward it, wiping her hands on a kitchen towel. It was after six—dinner hour for some.

The woman opened the door about eight inches. She was slender, maybe thirty-five, freckled, wearing jeans and a rust-colored wool sweater that almost matched her hair. She probably thought they were selling something. *Not hardly.* "Yes?" she said. "I'm sorry, but we're about to sit down to dinner."

"This won't take long, ma'am," Helena said.

"Is Weston Beale your son?" Forrest asked.

Weston Beale. The kid fancied himself some kind of web genius. He ran fan sites for TV shows and movies . . . sites that looked pretty damn good, Forrest had to admit. But he also ran a tribute site to a woman named Stella Olemaun. The same Stella Olemaun who claimed that vampires were real. Recently Weston Beale had been posting new information about Stella . . . vampires . . . things a sixteen-year-old kid living in Norman, Oklahoma, should have no way of knowing.

This made him a person of interest to Operation Red-Blooded.

"He—yes, but . . ."

"We need to see him."

A man approached from behind the woman. His teeth were clenched as if gripping a pipe, and he tried to fold a newspaper as he walked. *Don't these people put anything down?* Forrest briefly wondered. The woman still clutched that limp towel like some kind of lifeline.

"What's going on?" the man demanded. He wore glasses that magnified his blinking, curious eyes. Forrest thought he looked like a cartoon owl.

"They want to see Wes," the woman said.

"Who are you?"

Forrest and Helena drew back nearly identical navy

blue blazers to display the badges they wore on their belts. These badges said FBI, but they had others, as needed, back in the Hummer.

"Do you have a warrant?"

"We're wasting time," Forrest said. "Ever heard of the Patriot Act?"

"I'm calling a lawyer," the man said, backing away from the door.

Helena bulled past the woman, and Forrest entered through the opening she made. "Go right ahead. Call a priest if you want," he remarked as he started upstairs, Helena at his heels. "Call your senator."

Only one of the rooms at the top of the stairs had its door closed. On that door was a hand-lettered sign that said KEEP OUT. Below that the circled A for "anarchy" symbol had been scrawled with a black Sharpie.

Forrest caught Helena's gaze, nodded, and went to that door.

The knob was locked. He stepped back, raised his right foot, and kicked sharply just below the knob. Wood splintered and the door burst open, slamming against the wall behind it.

The room's walls were plastered with posters: Kurt Cobain and Steve Jobs and Bono, buxom women advertising beer and power tools, centerfolds from *Playboy,* Obey the Giant, and the Clash, and an Elvis poster Forrest kind of liked, showing fat Vegas Presley on one side and nerdy young Costello on the other peering through his Buddy Holly glasses, with punkish letters above them both spelling out SHUT UP OR I'LL EAT YOU AGAIN.

The bed was unmade, sheets tangled like a whirlwind had slept there. The desk was a mess, too. The computer monitor (it wasn't even a Mac, which Forrest had expected when he saw Steve Jobs on the wall) canted forward, its glass smashed with the five-pound dumbbell that remained half-wedged inside. Cables from the monitor and keyboard dangled toward the floor, but the tower they had been plugged into was gone.

So was Weston Beale's head.

His body sat in his black padded desk chair with his arms on the armrests. A skinny kid wearing a black T-shirt with gray writing that said CHICKS DIG ME. The knees of his jeans were blown out. His black Chuck Taylors were untied, and he'd written on them with Sharpie, black on the white parts and silver on the black parts.

He'd had an irrepressible urge to communicate, Forrest guessed. The late Weston Beale had a BlackBerry and a blog, too. Now this final messy correspondence with the world.

Blood oozed from his neck, where the skin was torn raggedly, bone shards sticking up. That blood hadn't been oozing for long—it still dripped from the ceiling and coated the desktop and soaked his T-shirt and jeans. But his heart had stopped beating so the force of the jetting blood had slowed, then stopped, and now only a little stream trickled from the open veins of the neck.

Downstairs, Mr. and Mrs. Beale were still fussing, arguing with each other about who to call or what to do.

Forrest turned to Helena. "Figure we have another three minutes before they call the police. Five- to seven-minute response time."

"Let's get busy," she said.

They tossed the room, a quick, professional job. The computer tower didn't turn up. Neither did backup CDs. Neither did the boy's head.

They were driving away before the first siren sounded, before Weston Beale's parents stormed up to his room to ask him who those people had been and what they'd wanted with him. It was a good thing they hadn't followed Forrest and Helena upstairs in the first place, because it was always harder to conduct an efficient search when people were screaming and crying and beating on you with their fists. Not impossible, but harder. And some days, Forrest thought, his job was hard enough.

Andy Gray sat in front of a computer, bathed in the monitor's soft glow, trying to will an instant message to pop up on the screen.

It didn't work.

He checked e-mail again, for the hundredth time, even though his mail program alerted him whenever one came through. Nothing.

This was what he had, these days. This had become Andy's life. The War Room, the nerve center of his private network of acquaintances and supporters. Outside, the temperatures of Barrow, Alaska, hovered around zero but the inside was climate controlled, kept cool so all the computers could run at once (and they did, nonstop) without overheating. He had the War Room and he had those people who communicated with him electronically, texting or e-mailing or IMing, and he had the satisfaction of sometimes seeing results when they posted the information he fed them on their own websites and blogs.

And that, pretty much, was that.

He didn't have a social life to speak of. Oh hell no. Not anymore. He rarely left the War Room these days—a few hours to sleep, now and again, in one of the building's other rooms. He knew it didn't speak much for his creativity or his roundedness as a human being that the room he slept in had a bed and a wall heater and that was all. His few clothes hung in the closet or were piled on the closet floor. He took his meals in his kitchen or sitting in the rolling chair, scooting from one monitor to the next. He couldn't remember the last book he'd read that wasn't about vampires, let alone the last movie or TV show he'd watched.

Since he'd left the Federal Bureau of Investigation (in what seemed now like a lifetime ago) to chase after Paul Norris, the former partner who had murdered

Andy's family—or to put it another, slightly more accurate way—since he'd learned the terrifying truth that vampires were not only real but all over the place—Andy Gray had built his body into a tightly muscled, capable machine. He had developed his intellect. He had immersed himself in the world of the undead, becoming as expert as any mortal could be in their ways, their habits, their conflicts, and their community.

Vampires, and those who hunted them, had become the closest thing he had to friends.

But, ironically, it turned out when you shunned the sun and let the darkness embrace you, when you forgot about things like traffic jams and birdcalls, summer sunsets and waves lapping the shore, deli sandwiches and new music and celebrity gossip and the price of gas . . . well, maybe your heart still pumped blood and the synapses in your brain still sparked, but you had left humanity somewhere in your past, and reclaiming it wasn't as easy as right-clicking a file on the desktop of life.

Andy had befriended vampires—*vampires,* the beings he had dedicated his life to destroying, once he knew what they really were—and in doing so had lost touch with the human race. Rather than despising them for what they were, Andy actually found himself liking the (un)living legends Eben and Stella Olemaun . . . he had kind of liked Dane . . . had been thoroughly charmed by Ferrando Merrin, and they . . .

They saw him as a tool.

He was handy. He knew a little about computers. He understood law enforcement. He could handle himself in a fight.

He was a hammer, a screwdriver. On his best days, maybe a Swiss Army knife or a multifunction tool.

But he was also human, mortal, a fleshy bag of blood, and in a pinch any of them could tear his head half off and drink deep, and there wouldn't be a damn thing he could do about it.

They could eat him, but he couldn't eat them. He was like a smart, occasionally helpful, ultimately harmless pet.

Andy sighed and pushed back from the screen. He'd fallen into depression lately—*who wouldn't have?*—and it was getting to him. Not just about the general state of his life, which he would have described as shitty going on worse, but about things he'd been hearing from his network of contacts.

And things he wasn't hearing. People he wasn't hearing from.

For example, he had expected Weston Beale to get in touch today, or at least to update his Stella site. Neither one had happened.

Andy had sent his tenth message of the day to Weston, looking for a response, an excuse, an explanation. But nothing came through.

In college, Andy had taken an entomology course from a professor who had refused several lucrative offers to work in South America—refused them because he knew what the insects in South America could do to a person. Andy now felt like that professor. Most people knew about the usual dangers—traffic accidents, secondhand smoke, various cancers and STDs, the very occasional encounter with a violent criminal, a gangster, a madman.

Knowing what Andy did, though, opened up whole new realms of speculation, and he tried not to think about what might have become of Weston Beale that would have kept him out of contact for so long.

Just like he'd tried not to think of Sara Purcell or Steve Bent or Li Minh when they had suddenly gone off the radar over the past two weeks.

Something was up. Something bad. Maybe something terrifying. Revolutions started small: a whisper here, a thrown rock there, but soon enough there were bodies everywhere and the streets ran red with blood.

Andy didn't know if what he feared was coming was indeed a revolution, but he couldn't think of a more apt word for it.

The blood, though? He was pretty certain about that.

Had he been awake, and had he been the kind of kid who tended toward self-assessment—and in their early teens, not many were, not even precocious geniuses like himself—Marcus Kitka could have interpreted his dream, could have understood where it came from and what it signified. But he was asleep, and not particularly self-insightful at the best of times.

So instead of understanding it, he was just scared shitless.

He stood on a snowy plain, somewhere outside Barrow. Fir trees in the distance smudged the horizon. Above them was endless sky, just a little too gray to be white. Crusted snow crackled beneath his sneakers. He wrapped his shirtsleeved arms around himself for warmth, but the effect was minimal.

From the unbroken whiteness, figures appeared, pushing the pale mist aside like a moth-eaten shroud.

Marcus spun around, gazing back toward where he thought town was, but there was nothing there except more of the figures, even closer. The trees had been blotted out, too—now, nothing in any direction except more of them, those almost-human shapes, and they were coming for him. As they got closer he could see yellowed claws and long teeth and eyes the color of his pee when he drank nothing but Red Bull and Dr. Pepper for three days straight. They didn't say anything, but he didn't need them to tell him what they wanted.

They wanted him.

He was still human—an adolescent, a computer hacker, socially backward, not bad-looking but no casting agents would be calling anytime soon. But he was human—and that could not stand.

Marcus had accompanied his father, Brian Kitka, to

Barrow when his dad had been offered the job of sheriff for the little town. Neither one had known at the time how dangerous the gig was—or the town, for that matter. His uncle William had lived and died in Barrow. The previous sheriff, Eben Olemaun, and his wife, Stella, had been caught up in the first vampire attack on Barrow, during the long winter's night of 2001. Eben had saved the town only by turning himself, becoming a vampire so he'd have the strength to fight off the invaders. With the first light of the new day, he had sacrificed himself, but Stella had brought him back from the ashes, only to have him turn her as well. Now they were both undead . . . and they had saved Marcus's hide during Barrow's second attack.

That about summed up life in Barrow. Especially during the winter, but really all the time, even when summer's long day made the threat of vampires seem laughable. Especially when your dad was the top cop. Brian Kitka was overprotective, almost smothering, except when he was absent altogether.

"Stay by the UV lights. Don't walk around by yourself in the dark. Remember, nothing lives without a head." Most kids got "Don't talk to strangers," and "Don't go into adult chat rooms," and "Keep away from that house on the corner," but Marcus got "Try not to sweat, because they can smell you if you do." Barrow was probably the safest town in America, maybe the world, when it came to vampires, but in spite of that, everyone lived in a state of fear, with the feeling that the next attack would happen at any moment, and this time there might be no survivors at all.

The figures came closer, and now amid the claws and teeth and horrible yellow eyes Marcus could make out facial features and physiques, could recognize individuals. His father was among them, his badge pinned to a shredded shirt, his jaw hanging open, a bit of bloody gristle dangling from his teeth. Stella Olemaun was there, too, clicking her razor claws together like tiny castanets. Eben Olemaun came from behind her. He was carrying a syringe—maybe the same one he had used to plunge tainted blood into his own veins, on that dark day's night in 2001.

Marcus tried to run, wanted to run, but he couldn't make his legs work, and then Eben grabbed him by the wrist, turned his arm so the fleshy underside faced up, and jabbed the needle into it.

The former sheriff released the syringe then, but not Marcus's arm. He leaned in close, a foul stench issuing from his mouth, like he'd been eating diseased rodents left out in the sun for days. "What's it going to be, kid?" he hissed. His tongue lapped his teeth and his gaze ticked from Marcus's eyes down to the hypodermic, and Marcus understood what he meant.

You will *become one of us,* this creature was saying. *The only question is how. Do you push the plunger and change yourself? Or do I bite you?*

What's it going to be, kid?

Marcus tried to wrench his arm free, but he couldn't

break Eben's grip. They were all around him now, close on every side, their claws and fangs clacking. Marcus wanted to argue but could only force out a strangled, blubbering cry, and then tears rolled from his eyes like blood from a cut.

Eben's grip on his wrist hurt, the vampire's claws digging into the tender skin there, and he leaned still closer and his ghastly tongue, long and almost prehensile, darted forward and tasted the salt of Marcus's tears. "What's the matter, kid?" he asked, his voice as rough as pumice. "Afraid of needles?"

Marcus sat up in bed, screaming, screaming, the sheets cold and wet above and beneath him, his limbs trembling, and even though he knew he was screaming and his dad was at work and wouldn't hear him, he couldn't make himself stop until his throat was raw and the pungent stink of his own urine snapped at his nostrils.

He couldn't take much more of this.

He was not particularly self-aware, but he knew himself well enough to know that. Night after night, week after week.

He climbed out of bed, rolled off his soaked pajamas, wadded them up in the soiled bedding. He'd have to carry it all to the laundry room and start the wash before Dad came home, then bathe, change pajamas, make the bed, and try to get back to sleep. It was becoming horribly routine.

He hadn't wet his bed since he was five.

Until now.

Until Barrow.

Something had to give.

Stella Olemaun had lost her appreciation for music.

She had never had any special musical talent, but she had enjoyed listening to it. As a teenager she had always had a radio or a CD going, usually whoever the latest pop star was. In her adult years, that habit had slipped away—sometimes the radio was on, as background to her daily routines or when driving, but tuned to talk radio as often as to music. She only truly realized that her ear for music was gone entirely when she tried to sing "Twinkle, Twinkle, Little Star" to baby Dane, one restless night, and discovered that even that simple tune escaped her.

It was as if music was inextricably tied to humanity, and having given that up—or having it snatched from her by her husband, Eben—meant abdicating her ability to enjoy or create it.

She and Dane were staying in the little cabin outside Barrow, constructed with wood shipped in from the vast pine forests of southern Alaska. The only heat came from a woodstove, but she didn't require much heat. Dane—the result of an unwanted union between a young human named Ananu Reid and infamous vampire Bork Dela—seemed to have at least some of his father's natural resistance to cold, so while she burned the occasional log she didn't make nearly the fuss about it that she would have for an entirely human infant.

Instead of singing to little Dane—a noise that hurt her own ears, like pulling nails from sheet metal—she simply rocked him and cooed motherly nonsense until he drifted off.

After setting him gently in his crib, she found herself wondering if she would feel the same about art as she did about music. She had even less of a history with art—in Barrow, Alaska, a person didn't get much exposure to the great works, and she hadn't spent much time in the world's capital cities browsing through museums. She still loved going outside just after sunset, when the red light of alpenglow hung on the horizon, the stars showed their first evening glimmer, and darkness had not yet swallowed her beloved Arctic landscape.

She thought that counted as aesthetic appreciation, of nature if not art, and wondered if it too would fade as her postlife period grew proportionately longer.

After Bork Dela's assault on Ananu down in Georgia, Dane—the original Dane, Stella's once-only lover and the vampire the baby had been named for—had found the young woman and spirited her away from an Operation Red-Blooded assault team. With the help of a human named AJ Roddy and Ferrando Merrin, an old vampire friend of Dane's, they had kept her safe through her miraculously brief pregnancy, but she had become increasingly weak, and had died giving birth. In a whirlwind of circumstance, she and Andy Gray had agreed to take baby Dane back to Barrow, where he could be protected from the forces on both sides who might want to do him harm.

Little Dane was the first of a vampire-human union known to have survived, and the voices of reason wanted him to be allowed to grow up unmolested by vampires or the agents of Operation Red-Blooded. Barrow and its environs, having survived two major vampire invasions and learned how to defend itself, seemed like the safest place for him, and Stella and Eben his ideal caretakers.

By the time Stella and the baby made it back to Barrow, however, Eben had already taken off for Norway, along with the adult Dane. It had been weeks, and they hadn't returned. Both had taken cell phones with them, and had been in regular contact with Andy and Stella on their way to Georgia, and with young Marcus Kitka in Barrow, until they had closed in on the object of their search.

All they had known was that Bork Dela had boasted of "something big" going on. By studying hundreds of disappearances, Andy and Marcus had been able to narrow that down to a sawmill in Norway. Following that slim lead, Eben and Dane had gone there, and the last time they had checked in with Marcus by phone, had seemed close to discovering what they were looking for.

Then they had fallen off the earth, as far as anybody knew. Rumors of some sort of disaster had filtered back from Norway, via the *nosferatu* grapevine, but they were vague and never mentioned Eben or Dane by name. Meanwhile, Stella soldiered on, taking care of Dane, mostly keeping to herself in the cabin outside town.

She wished Eben would come home, though. Or at least answer his goddamn phone.

She had effectively adopted a baby without consulting him—and not just any baby, but a miracle one, potentially the first of a new breed that would finally bridge the gap between vampire and human. "It would be nice," she whispered from the baby's doorway, "if you could meet your daddy and the man whose name you wear."

Baby Dane cooed in his sleep. But he didn't answer, and neither did anyone else. Stella checked his blankets, then wandered alone outside, where night had fallen and stars glittered in a black sky like chips of ice.

NOW

3

THE ROAD TO Los Angeles had been a long one, and there had been times Eben Olemaun doubted his marriage would survive it.

He still wasn't entirely sure that it had.

Otherwise why would he be sitting in a twenty-four-hour coffeehouse, sipping from a white ceramic mug a liquid he had once craved but which now seemed pale, flavorless, and did little to increase his energy and nothing to sustain his life?

He had today's *Los Angeles Times* spread out on the big table. There were a couple of other occupied booths, one filled by a quartet of punks still high from a show at one of the clubs on Sunset, another by a couple of detectives from the LAPD's Robbery-Homicide division. The waitress, a single mother on the far side of forty with an air of desperation about her, flirted shamelessly with the cops and ignored the punks until they banged their mugs on the table and chanted "Refill! Re-fill! Re-fill!" in unison.

She was probably glad Eben was drinking slowly and minding his own business.

He and Stella had argued. Again. Nothing new

there. They had been the most loving, supportive couple ever, when they were both human. Before . . . before the first attack. They were the kind of couple that made single people ill and other couples nervous.

Since then, they had seen and done too much.

Eben had been dead for a year and a half before Stella brought him back. He thanked her by biting her, turning her. There had been a second attack. There had been her book *30 Days of Night,* the fallout from that, her time as a vampire hunter, which collided, now and again, with her new afterlife as a vampire.

Then there was Norway.

Would he ever be able to shake the memory of that?

He and Dane had managed to find a little heaven on Earth for vampires, a multistory combination of diner, slaughterhouse, and social club. People had been snatched from their homes and stored there, fed, bred, and bled . . . livestock on the hoof. They had infiltrated the place and eventually destroyed it. But the smells—of so many vampires compressed into a small area, of the human pens full of blood and shit and filthy, diseased flesh, of pipes that ran day and night with blood—those he couldn't drive from his memory.

The carnage of the battle, during which he and Dane must have destroyed fifty vampires, and during which Dane had met his own end—that still haunted him when he slept. And then again when he woke up.

Even though he had experienced it for himself, there

were still moments when Eben couldn't quite believe the horror that the vampire overlord Enok had created, and had called good.

He had since taken his time getting back to Barrow and to Stella.

He didn't want to rush back, to arrive with his mind still full of the slaughter, his pores reeking of it. He spent weeks walking in the wilderness, alone, living as best he could off the blood of animals. He let the snowfall scour whatever passed for his soul. He let himself go hungry until his stomach twisted itself in knots and threatened to rebel, and then he killed a deer or a rabbit or a fox, whatever he could find, and he drank deep, then vomited it up again. Those times, he had to start over, drinking slowly, taking careful sips, when his stomach wanted gulps.

After a couple of weeks he took a person, a woman who made the mistake of going outside her house one night to smoke a cigarette and look at the stars.

Her blood tasted sweet and fine.

Taking her life, after what he had seen at Enok's paradise on Earth, sickened Eben, but after he fed he felt better than he had in weeks. He had become a vampire, a being who needed human blood, that was all there was to it.

It wasn't a negotiation, it was survival.

When he had finally got back to the cabin they occupied, on the snow-swept tundra outside Barrow—and before everything started falling apart—Stella shrieked and ran to him, throwing her arms around him and drawing him close. He loved the feel of her, and the smell, and the sounds of her laughter and sobs. He ran his fingers through her fine red hair, then let his hands slip down her back to cup her excellent ass, pulling her against him. Their lips met and crushed together. When he drew his head back, there were tears in her eyes.

Then she smiled, that wry half-smile she had, and said, "I guess you missed me."

"I guess I did," he admitted.

"And I guess cell phone service went down world-wide, because obviously you couldn't fucking call!"

"Sorry," he said, aware that that didn't begin to cover it. "It was a bad time."

"Where's Dane? Is he back, too? Is he here?"

Eben didn't answer. He didn't need to. She read the truth on his face.

"Oh, Eben . . . fuck no, no! What . . ." Her face darkened over. She had stopped herself from asking it, but he knew where the question had been going. *What did you do to him?* She had never quite believed that Eben had forgiven her or Dane for the affair they'd had while Eben was dead. He wasn't sure he ever had, but it was a little late to worry about it now.

"He fought Enok. He won. But he took a lot of punishment in the process, and he didn't survive." As with telling a lie, sometimes when telling difficult truths it was best to keep things simple. *Just the facts, ma'am.*

"Enok?"

"Yeah . . . look, Stella, we're going to have to get into this later. It's a long story. Real long. I need to . . . I just don't have the energy to get into it all right now."

"That's probably just as well," she said, "because if he's up from his nap, there's someone you need to meet inside."

"Nap?"

"Well, he is just a baby. . . ."

Introducing Eben to baby Dane allowed him to put off the full explanation then, but not for long. That night, they sat at a pine table outside in the cold, watching the wind whip snow into funnels and flurries. A rare fire in their woodstove scented the air. He told her everything, from landing in Norway to discovering the sawmill with many layers of vampiric madness beneath it. He told her about finding Lilith there, Enok's prisoner, kept alive so vampires could feed on her flesh and blood. He told her about Enok's dream of a world where vampires ruled, where humans were bred as food and kept the way humans keep cattle, where vampires could hunt at will. He told her of Enok's power, his telepathy, his influence over untold legions of *nosferatu*.

Enok. He had been one of the oldest of vampires, the one who had turned Vicente, who had turned Lilith. Practically as ancient as God, and among vampires, as feared and worshipped. The idea that Eben had been in his presence terrified her, and she held on to his leg while he talked about it, her fingers digging deep.

Telling her these things frightened him all over again. By the end of the tale, he was shivering, and not from the cold. Stella put her arms around him. "Shh," she said. "It'll be okay, Eben. You're home now."

Somehow he had failed to convey the true horror he had experienced. "Okay? It'll be okay? How? This isn't something we can fix, you and me. We can protect Barrow, for now, but this is bigger than that. If there's war, and Enok's disciples win? How do we protect Barrow if the whole planet is against us? What's the point?"

"You don't think anyone can really pull that off."

"I don't know. I would have said no, until I saw what they managed to create in Norway. Enok wasn't alone. There are many who feel the same way. Maybe most of them. Of us, I mean."

They were quiet for a while. There was still one more thing he hadn't told her about. When he couldn't think of a good way, he just said it. "When Dane was dying, he bit me."

She released him, gazed at him with concern written on her features. "*Bit* you."

"That's right. He said it would help." Eben stood, paced around in circles, as if he could outrun the memory. "He was right. It made me stronger, faster. I don't think I would have survived without it. I mean, stuff was falling down, timbers, pipes, the whole infrastructure of this incredible complex was falling apart, and things smashed down on me that should have crushed me. I just plowed through it all and kept going. And it's still with me, too. It's how I survived out there for so long with nothing to eat, just existing in the wilderness. There was something about that bite, after being turned—I mean . . . it's like it enhances the effects of vampirism, somehow."

"Dane said he had been bitten twice, too. It's one of those things that's sort of mythical or legendary."

"So you already knew all about this?" He shoved his hands into his pockets.

"Not knew. It's hard to explain. Until you mentioned it, I hadn't thought about it in a long time, since the time Dane talked about it. I don't know how it's possible, but somehow when you did, maybe it jogged a memory that's been there all along?"

Eben saw no point in trying to go any further, not right then.

In the days that followed, they decided they needed to get away from Barrow for a while. Or Eben decided it, and convinced Stella. Barrow was the most secure town in the world. It could take care of itself. He needed to be someplace different, to experience a change of scenery, some new people. Someplace that hummed with human activity, even if he could never be part of it. The isolation of Barrow, the northern clime, the snow-blanketed plains, reminded him too much of Norway . . . and Enok.

She suggested Los Angeles, since she was comfortable there, knew her way around. And there were safe houses there for their kind—including Dane's old apartment, which they found with the help of the vampire community.

For a week, maybe two, it seemed like the change had done them both good. But even there, with the streets and avenues constantly abuzz with people, the sounds of traffic, horns honking and sirens wailing, Eben couldn't let go of the fear gripping him like some debilitating illness, and although Stella tried to understand, she couldn't.

He tried to devote his attention to the infant Dane. He and Stella had once talked about having kids someday, but they'd always put it off. Now she would never get pregnant—Ananu aside, pregnancy within the vampire community was so uncommon as to be considered virtually impossible—but they had a miraculous child to raise . . . and he had to admit he was just as curious as Stella to see how Dane might turn out.

He and Stella fought, though, with increasing fury.

Surrounded by millions of people, they felt isolated from the world, trapped with just each other and the constant demands of the infant. Eben took to leaving her and the baby alone for hours at a time. Then days. Each time, he went back to her, happy to see her, still as desperately in love as he had been when they first married.

But each time, the arguments returned, the silences between them grew longer and more full of anger, and he left again.

Tonight's argument had been the usual one. She poked at him for being morose. He countered that if the vampires who were cut from the same cloth as Enok weren't stopped, there would be little reason to smile. Vampires had to stay in the shadows. They were naturally inferior beings, for all their strength. They could be killed by the sun, and there was no stopping the sun from coming around once each day—in most places, anyway. For the survival of the species, they had to return to their former status, as nightmares, as stories.

"You're wrong," she said. Stella was inclined to make grand statements. "There is a middle ground, and Dane fought and died for it. I will, too. We *can* coexist with the world. Regular people have something we need, but we can offer them something, too. We have time, lifetimes, for humans, that could be devoted to study, to creative pursuits, if we didn't have to spend it hiding and hunting. We can work at night, without lights. Our blood can conquer humanity's worst diseases. There's no reason there can't be something for everyone in this."

"Yes there is," Eben said. "There's the fact that they'll never go for it. They'll destroy us. And of course the vampires will react as they always have, and the battle will be on again. Your 'middle ground' is fantasyland, that's all."

"It's the only way of ensuring long-term survival."

He slammed a mug down on the dining room table. Blood splashed out onto the oak surface. "Then we're fucked!"

From another room, little Dane started to cry. Eben tried to love the baby as much as Stella did, but, goddammit, did it have to be named after *him*? The guy Stella slept with? It was bad enough that Dane came up in every argument. Dane this, Dane that. To hear her tell it, he could've been perfect. Thanks a lot, honey.

But when he said that, she turned on him, eyes blazing. "You . . . *bastard*! You selfish prick! I never wanted him, because I loved *you*! Because I wanted to bring you back from the dead, and be with *you*! You remember all that?"

"Yes, Stella, it's just—naming the kid after him—"

"Now that he's gone, I'm especially glad I did. It gives him a kind of legacy. And it's perfect. He preached coexistence. The baby could be key to that . . . and the other Dane would have loved it."

"The other Dane loved you."

"Maybe he did. But can you just stop? Eben, he was just a friend—"

"Yeah, some friend."

"He was a *friend* I let go to Norway with you, a friend who didn't come back. Go figure."

Little Dane was screaming now, and Eben was about

to do the same thing. Instead, he stormed out of the apartment. Stella didn't try to stop him. ("Sure, just go, tough guy. Walk away again.")

Hours later, after walking through the southern-California night, he ended up in a coffeehouse, listening to a waitress tell a pair of detectives about her latest trip to Victoria's Secret.

He was calmer now. He wanted to go back to Stella. But if he did, he would probably find her asleep in bed, cuddling baby Dane—in the bed that she and grown-up Dane had no doubt fucked in—and he would lose it again.

Better to find someplace else to hole up for the day, then hit the road. Maybe Stella and the baby could do without him for a little while.

He had other things on his mind, anyway, things that had been tugging at him since Norway. God knew he and Stella could use some time apart.

One thing about being undead—your sense of urgency changed. With all the time in the world ahead of you, a day or a week or a month didn't really make a hell of a lot of difference.

4

DAN BRADSTREET hated meetings.

They were the bane of bureaucracies, the opposite of constructive. They took people who should have been doing their jobs away from those jobs and put them in a modern version of hell—a stifling box of a conference room with glass or wood-paneled walls, sometimes even with those ridiculous inspirational posters tacked to them. Worse still were the seemingly inevitable PowerPoint presentations, when some numbnuts would read aloud the same words that appeared on the screen next to arrows and charts and graphs.

What Dan wanted to be doing was emptying a large-caliber weapon into some bloodsucker's brain.

He wanted to drag one kicking and screaming from the shadows into a shaft of sunlight and smell that peculiar smoked-meat aroma when it fried. He wanted to lop one's head off with a scythe and watch its body jerk around frantically trying to find it before it finally dropped.

Instead, here he was, stewing in the worst kind of meeting—a government one—in the worst kind of conference room. Federal conference rooms were, in general, bland and senses-dulling . . . but the ones at top-secret installations, where the black-bag budgets went into hardware instead of decor, were even worse. The walls were concrete block, painted *Exorcist*-puke green, like *that* was a calming color. They sat on cheap plastic rolling chairs. The table was steel with a transparently phony wood-grain veneer. During the days in which people had been allowed to smoke indoors, cigarettes left burning on the table's edges only melted odd little furrows into it. There was nothing on the walls, no windows, only one wooden door that had to remain closed while the meeting was in progress.

Worst of all, he had called the meeting, he was running it, and he had completely lost the thread of the conversation.

But at least there were no laptops in the room, and hence, no goddamn PowerPoint.

". . . blowing up the *Icarus* and the *Armstrong*," Clarence Bettesford was saying. Clarence headed up Operation Red-Blooded's Life Sciences unit, an ironic way of saying he was ultimately responsible for all of the nation's scientific understanding of the living dead. He looked like a chemist should, Dan thought, scrawny, with an unruly shock of white hair, thick glasses, at home in a white lab coat with a pocket protector in his poly-cotton shirt pocket. But he was a brilliant man, wickedly funny when he wanted to be, and he had an unequaled success rate at bedding young female federal employees—a statistic he attributed to "a schlong the size of an Apollo rocket."

"That was a last resort," Ops Chief Belinda Snyder cut in. "Nobody wanted to do it, but you saw the footage."

Dan had seen it too—*Icarus*'s mission commander, Cobb, had been turned, but his transformation hadn't taken full effect until the shuttle mission was under way. He'd finished off his own crew, then had turned some of the crew of the *Armstrong,* a shuttle sent to find out what had become of *Icarus*. Together they had made short work of the remainder of the *Armstrong*'s crew. Most of it had been caught on tape by one of the omnipresent cameras aboard space shuttles.

"That's ancient history," Dan said. He pressed his palms flat against the table, trying to will the blood to circulate through his brain faster, to wake him up. He hoped cutting the space shuttle talk short would steer the conversation in a new direction, so he could follow it. "Do we have to rehash it again? I want to talk about what's going on now."

"That's what I was trying to do," Clarence said. "What we learned from that, about the virus's gestation period—"

"Is nothing we haven't seen, anecdotally anyway," Marvin Dotts interrupted. He was a number cruncher, a former CPA, a statistician. He had been making a decent living as a political pollster before Dan brought him into the fold. Dan was especially pleased with that recruitment—not only was he great at amassing and interpreting data, but he'd been working for Democrats, and doing it too well. Dan's true, abiding hatred was for vampires, but if they hadn't existed, he would have been perfectly happy despising Democrats.

Marina Tanaka-Dunn sat between Marvin Dotts and Gentry Chambers. Chambers was boring, a hardware guy who made sure Red-Blooded had all the tech toys they needed to blow away the bloodsuckers, but thought everyone should cater to his whims because he kept the gear coming. But Marina—she was something special. Her father had been a brilliant Japanese scientist-turned-industrialist. Her mother was the American journalist sent by *Vanity Fair* to do a profile on the guy. Except he had charmed her to the point that she stayed in Kyoto, called in her resignation, and married him. Only then did she realize he was also tied in to the Yakuza and through them to other criminal organizations throughout Asia. At that point, she didn't care.

Marina was educated in all the best places—Switzerland, Cambridge, grad school at Harvard. As an undergrad, she had briefly been married to a classics professor, but he died in a skiing accident. Her degrees were in international law and astrophysics—Dan thought she had picked them because of the intellectual challenges they offered, not because she was especially interested in either field.

The only thing that seemed to interest her was killing things. Her title was Western Region Field Supervisor, which officially put her in charge of all field agents west of Denver, but everyone in the room knew her true specialty.

Marina was so good-looking it hurt to see her in a stuffy conference room with the rest of them. She had straight black lustrous Japanese hair, a slight uptilting of her eyes that made her look like she understood a joke you didn't, a full-lipped mouth with just the faintest overbite. Men, Dan believed, had wet dreams after a single glimpse of that mouth. Her body held up its end of the bargain, too, with high, firm breasts that strained the man's cotton shirt she wore, untucked, like a lover's shirt she had thrown on after sex to answer the door, narrow hips with just enough curve to them, and long powerful legs, currently sheathed, between the short leather skirt and the black leather boots gripping her ankles, in black fishnet stockings. She leaned back in her chair with her legs stretched out to the side of the table, and she looked more like a porn star than a federal employee.

Marina had tried to hold civilian jobs, but her natural proclivity toward violence had brought her to the attention of the NSA; when they failed to offer enough targets to hold her interest, bringing her over to Red-Blooded had been easy.

"What I want to talk about," Dan said, tearing his gaze away from those fishnets with great difficulty, "is what we're going to do about the fact that the undead story seems to be spreading, no matter what we do to hold it in. It's like a meme, or one of those stupid internet surveys. Today it's in one place, tomorrow it's in fifty, the day after that in a thousand."

"Why is this a problem?" The questioner was Kylie Randall, who handled press and public relations for the operation—meaning she squashed stories right and left. An African-American, she and Marina were the only non-Caucasians in the room. Or not fully Caucasian, in Marina's case. Since the operatives had been recruited from the American intelligence community, and that pool was only just emerging from the nineteenth century where race was concerned, that wasn't surprising. "At some point we're going to need to go—"

"This isn't some point," Dan said. "This is now, and for now we need to keep a lid on it. The immediate problem is that a lot of what's getting out there is misinterpreted, and the undead get romanticized all out of proportion. I mean, Stella Olemaun's book, *30 Days of Night,* came out a long time ago. We thought we'd buried it by getting it labeled fiction, but it's still in print, and it's selling faster than ever. It's come close to cracking the extended *New York Times* bestseller list a couple of times now. Any book that stays around that long, shows legs like that, is going to get more attention as time goes on. It seems this is happening with *30 Days*. You've all heard about Frank Cartwright?"

"Who?" Marina asked. It was the first word she had

said during the meeting. She didn't keep up on the news.

"He ran a book club in suburban New Jersey. They thought it'd be fun to read and discuss the Olemaun woman's book. They even did a little internet research on the side. By the time they were done, they had not only convinced themselves that vampires were real but that one of their neighbors was one of them. He was a loner type, didn't socialize with the rest of the block, so they jumped to conclusions. They killed him six ways from Sunday. A real bloodsucker would've had them for breakfast, but this guy really was just an old man who didn't much like his neighbors. The story was all over the tabloids and cable news. Would've been a lot worse for us if any of the participants had been a real vampire, or had proof of their existence, but still—it's the kind of thing we don't want to see more of. But we will, if word keeps spreading that they're real."

"The Norway affair could have been a real mess too," Marvin Dotts said. "That smoke could be seen from space."

"It's a good thing all our astronauts were killed, then," Dan said. It was a joke, but nobody laughed. Maybe a smirk out of Marina, but it was hard to tell with her. Clarence looked like he might have a small stroke.

"I'm serious," Marvin said. "If the Norwegians had investigated—"

"The Norwegians are richer than they've ever been,

thanks to their offshore oil business. They're fat and happy and not likely to screw with a good thing." Dan was pretty sure his crew—handpicked, thoroughly professional, as discreet as it came—had been the only people who had investigated the Norway site, certainly the only ones who had lived to talk about it. And the stories they told, the reports and memos still being written and consumed . . . Jesus, they chilled *his* blood.

What they brought back? That was even worse.

He didn't like to think about it too much. And thinking about it could be genuinely dangerous, so that was the best approach.

"No, the Norwegians aren't our problem, at least not at the moment," Dan continued. "Our problem is people who saw Nancy Grace or Star Jones blabbing about Frank Cartwright on basic cable and think they know something. Our problem is nons thinking it's sexy or cool to know a real vampire and hanging out with them, helping them." He was thinking of a man named Albert Roddy who had killed himself in custody (on Dan's watch, no less) rather than talk about the vampires he was protecting. "When non-vampires side with them against their own kind, that's a sure sign that things are going to hell, no? We can't let that keep happening. We've got to let the world know there are no vampires, *there are no vampires,* and if there were, they'd be sharks with legs—unfeeling, uncaring eating machines who would rather swallow them whole than have a cup of tea with them. They're not sexy or romantic—idealizing them is like idealizing the Ebola virus."

"Oooh," Belinda said, throwing her arms around herself and shivering melodramatically. "That just fucking creeps me out. Pardon my French. I can't stand the idea of nons and vampires commingling."

"I'm sure we're all on the same page there," Dan said. "The question becomes, what do we do about it? How do we stop it? I've got some other particular interests, too. We missed Weston Beale, but he was just spreading the news; I don't think he had any personal contact with them. There's an old fruit named Ferrando Merrin kicking around—he's a genuine bloodsucker, but he's made friends with more nons than any of us in this room have." He glanced toward Clarence. "With the possible exception of you, Mr. Bettesford. Anyway, I've got his voice on phone calls—if Al Qaeda had known how much I'd like the post-9/11 America, they never would have attacked us. I've got his face on security videos. Plus, I've also got him in contact with former special agent Andrew Gray of the Bureau—you've all seen *that* file."

Nods all around.

"That's one traitorous bastard I'd loooove to get my hands on personally." Dan said. "And Gray's been linked to Stella Olemaun. My God, it's like a communicable disease, this whole thing. Someone doesn't wash their hands and the next thing you know, everyone in school is infected. It's out of control, or as good as. So here's the deal, people, and listen well. I want a lid on it. I mean as of right now. Find Olemaun. Find Gray. Find this Merrin pansy. Use whatever resources you need to. Equipment, money, people, I don't care. Just *find them*."

"When we do . . ." Marina said, swiveling her chair toward Dan. The shadow between her legs receded up under her skirt, and Dan felt his mouth go dry. "When we find them . . . can I kill them?"

"Once I'm done with them," Dan promised. "Except for Andy Gray. That fucker's mine."

Gentry Chambers caught up with Dan outside. Dan was taking long strides toward the helicopter sitting on a pad, long blades spinning lazily overhead, waiting to take him away from the sagebrush expanses of northern Nevada's bleak, empty Great Basin and down to Nellis Air Force Base, outside Las Vegas, where he could catch a flight back to D.C. His mind was on Andy Gray, who had shot him in the hand a couple of years back—it still hurt in cold, damp weather.

"Special Agent Bradstreet!" Gentry called. Dan stopped, turned.

Like everyone else associated with Operation Red-Blooded, Dan remained on the payroll of his previous agency—the Bureau, in his case. One more way of stretching the operation's secret budget. He retained his title, too, in addition to his title as Director of Field Operations for Red-Blooded, and his salary now far exceeded any other special agent's. "I have a chopper waiting, Gentry," he said. "What's up?"

Gentry stopped close beside him, shouting to be heard over the helicopter. "I just wanted to say, Bradstreet. I see the way you look at her. You be careful."

"At who?" Dan asked, although he knew full well who.

"She's a devil," Gentry said, not playing the game. Good for him. Sometimes Dan underestimated the man. "She's trouble. You watch your step around her, that's all I'm saying."

Dan considered himself a God-fearing man, a churchgoer when he was able. But Gentry had a reputation for proselytizing, pushing his beliefs on his coworkers—just one more thing that made him an awkward fit in an operation like Red-Blooded, where all the gears had to mesh seamlessly.

"I'll take it under advisement," Dan promised him. Then he turned away and hurried to the waiting chopper. If Gentry said anything else, Dan couldn't hear it. Not that he would have listened, anyway.

5

HEATHER BLAKESLEE knew it could be dangerous for a woman to be out on the streets at night, particularly in a city far from home. But she lived in the country, outside the western Kansas farm town of Ulysses, and sometimes a woman had to travel a bit to find the kind of fun she was after. Ulysses proudly declared itself the biggest city in six counties, but that wasn't saying a whole lot. The drive to Enid, Oklahoma, took several hours, but at least Enid resembled a real city. It had nightspots, clubs and bars and honkytonks, places where a woman could look for a little action, a little danger.

Anyway, Heather could take care of herself. She had been doing so for the last 107 years, ever since a stranger had ridden up to her Kansas farm late one April night and killed her husband and daughter. Heather had screamed and screamed and dashed for the rifle mounted on the wall above the fireplace. The stranger tipped back his hat and peered at her with dark eyes that carried a hint—or was it a promise?—of madness. "Not you," he said softly, pulling at the hairs of his long black beard. "You're a special one, you are."

He had not remained a stranger for long, of course. His name had been John Kilgallen, and he had stayed with her on the ranch for almost a year, teaching her the ways of the *nosferatu,* before finally moving on.

During the decades that followed, Heather had traveled the world, but she always returned to Kansas. Its prosaic landscapes, seemingly as flat and featureless as a carving board, took time to love but love them she did. She adored the vast stretches of sky overhead, the way the fields greened up in spring, the flocks of birds wheeling overhead (fewer decade by decade). In such a landscape, her husband, Caleb, had often said, a man could cast a long shadow. And so could a woman, if only she could stand in the sun. Heather stayed on the farm, and she went away from home to hunt.

In Enid, she clung to the shadows, and before long she spotted one of those women who should have known that danger lurked in the darkness but apparently didn't. This one stumbled out of a corner bar, a dive with graffiti on its thick stone walls and neon in the windows and a broken sign over the door proclaiming it The In-Spot. *Not during the lifetime of anyone I know,* Heather thought. And she knew some folks with very long lifetimes indeed.

The woman had parked in a fenced lot half a block away. Heather thought driving was a bad idea in her condition, given that she could barely manage to walk. Driving like that was a good way to get killed.

Then again, she wouldn't live long enough for that.

Heather broke from the shadows.

So did someone else, coming from across the street at a silent run, covering ground fast with long steps. A man, in dark clothing, his build sturdy, his hair short. He was heading for the woman too.

That was okay. Heather preferred women—they usually smelled better than men, and she liked the smoothness of their skin when she fed from them—but she could always have the woman now and save the man for later.

She raced forward, vaulted the chain-link fence, and landed on the pavement behind the woman, between her and the man. He skidded to a surprised halt, his mouth falling open, and that's when she saw that he was a vampire, too.

She knew most of the undead in the region, and this was definitely a new face.

"She's mine," Heather said.

The male smiled, letting his tongue loll out of his mouth, licked his lips. "Why don't we share?"

The woman was very drunk, but by resting one hand on the trunk of her Impala she managed to stand and stare at them, wearing a disdainful frown, her other hand against her cocked hip.

"I don't think I know either one of you," she said. "So if you're talking about me, I think I get to have some say in the matter."

Heather didn't even spare her a glance. The woman wasn't going anywhere. "Not really." She returned her attention to the male. "You're not from around here."

"Passing through," the male admitted. "Sometimes these small towns away from the coasts offer interesting menus. Not as much competition, I guess."

"That's true. But locals get priority."

"According to who?"

"That's just the way we've always done it."

The male shrugged. "Maybe someday—soon would be good—we won't have to make these tradeoffs. We'll take what we want, and cultivate enough for all of us."

Now Heather was intrigued. The woman jingled her keys as she tried to insert them into the Impala's door lock. Heather took a couple of quick steps toward her, batted the keys to the ground, and backhanded the woman, who gave a little screech and fell to the pavement, where she started to sob quietly. "Are you a follower of Enokian principles?"

"Isn't everyone?"

"Everyone on the right side of history."

"That's what I meant."

Heather turned her attention back to the woman. "We can share you," she said. "Consider yourself blessed." She drew a claw across the woman's throat, slitting flesh and muscle and her carotid artery. The woman dropped back down, gurgling wordlessly as her blood fountained into the air. Heather cupped her hands and caught some, holding it out to the man. "To Enok, our father," she said.

The male cupped her hands gently in his, leaned into them, and said, "To Enok, our father." He drank from her hands, then captured blood in his and gave it to her.

The ceremony done, Heather went to her knees and pressed her mouth against the woman's torn flesh. The woman's blood tasted bitter, fouled by too much alcohol and salt. When she had drunk deep, she moved and let the male in. They were so close their hips and shoulders touched as they took turns feeding from the woman.

When the blood ceased flowing, both stood. No one else had come near the parking lot. A few cars had passed by on the road, but the parked vehicles protected them from view.

"My name is Charles," the male said, wiping his mouth and chin on his hands, then licking his hands clean. "Charles Raney."

"Heather Blakeslee," she said.

"Are there other followers of the Enokian principles in the area?"

"There might be," Heather said. She had to hedge. Enok's beliefs remained controversial, and no one could be admitted to the inner circle without a thorough vetting. Anyway, she had other business in Oklahoma, and couldn't spend all night talking to this man, no matter how pleasant that might be.

"I'd love to meet them."

"That might be arranged. You have references?"

"I can put you in touch with some people."

"In that case . . . come to Ulysses, Kansas, in two nights, at midnight." She gave him the names of two streets in the small downtown area. "I'll make some inquiries on my own, and when you come, bring me your list. You might be interested in some things we're doing—if you check out."

"I'm sure I'll check out, Heather," Charles said. "I look forward to seeing you. Two nights."

"Two nights."

He was already making his way through the vehicles, back to the parking lot's entrance. "And thanks for sharing!"

My pleasure, Heather thought. *You just might make a good addition to our little group, Charles Raney.*

Eben Olemaun hurried out of Heather Blakeslee's sight, wiping his mouth on the back of his hand. Contact made. About time, too—through other connections, he had identified her as a follower of Enok, and believed that she was a member of a small group of like thinkers. She had more or less confirmed that for him. He knew such groups were out there, since Norway.

It was important to shut them down wherever he

could, to limit the influence of Enok's beliefs and teachings on the vampire community.

He figured he should phone Stella, check in, let her know he was safe. He assumed she was—so far it seemed that there was no threat she couldn't handle—and he wondered how the baby was doing.

But he hadn't been able to bring himself to make the call.

She would disapprove of what he was doing—not the reasons for it necessarily, but the solo nature of it, the idea that he had taken it upon himself to decide the fates of others. He didn't mind making that decision—he'd taken out plenty of vampires in his time, and he'd keep doing so as long as he remained upright. But he knew Stella wouldn't see things the same way.

Rather than fight with her, he kept very busy by researching the various Enokian groups and making plans to take them out, one by one.

Starting with Heather's. Now he had two nights to kill before he'd see her again.

When he did, he had to be ready for whatever came up.

Eugenia Parsons was sitting in the straight-backed padded wicker chair in her room at Daffodil House when she heard the sound behind her. It sounded like a little girl either laughing or weeping, but she couldn't tell which. Either way, there shouldn't have been anyone in the room with her at all. Much less a little girl in a senior citizens' home in the middle of the night. Eugenia's spine stiffened as she bent forward and turned her head to see what might have made the noise.

She saw two beds in the corner, one along each wall. Both had bedding in disarray, and there were lumps on each that could have been a very small child hiding from her. She knew something was wrong, though, because her room had only one bed, and it wasn't in the corner. The noise repeated itself, and this time the bedding on both beds shifted a little, as if the girls under the covers were wriggling, trying to remain still but not quite succeeding.

Eugenia was dreaming. That was the only reasonable explanation. She was dreaming, but she had to wake up before the girls came out from under the covers. She had been plagued by nightmares these last few weeks, and she knew that if she saw the girls, they wouldn't be girls at all, but some sort of monsters in girl forms. She knew she was dreaming and tried to snap herself awake, to close her eyes and open them again to see the room as it should be, bathed in darkness, under the blankets herself.

But the blankets were moving, lifting and drawing back, and the little girls who were not girls at all were beginning to emerge, and when they did they would lunge toward her from both directions and—

Eugenia woke up shivering, clutching at the bedding like a shield. The room was dark and just warm enough, not too hot, and smelled like the sandalwood sachet she'd received as a gift from her sister. She was a Christmas baby, born on the twenty-second of December, so all her life she had received combined Christmas and birthday gifts, even from her own sister.

This year she had reached eighty-eight a mere three days before Christmas. She felt like she could make ninety easy. Maybe one hundred, if she played her cards right and didn't slip and fall on an iced-over sidewalk—and the staff at Daffodil House were good about keeping the walkways salted and scraped, but the rest of the city of Woodward, Oklahoma, wasn't always so cautious—and then that nice Willard Scott would say her name on TV. Or he would if he happened to be the guest weatherman on the *Today Show*. She didn't care much for that Al Roker, who laughed too easily at other people and never honored the elderly like Willard Scott had for all those years.

To reach ninety, much less a hundred, she would have to get better about sleeping, she thought. For most of her life she'd slept like a baby. No guilty conscience to keep her awake, no children to fret over, no worries about money. Cleve had been good about that, had always earned plenty for the both of them, and his company had provided a pension to keep them going after he'd retired. After Cleve's death in 1996, his life insurance policy had kicked in. Between that and her medical insurance and the pension, she had kept the house in Woodward going as long as she could. When she could no longer negotiate the stairs up to the front door or the interior ones to her bedroom, and when it became apparent that a fall might trap her a dozen feet or more from a telephone, she gave in to necessity and made arrangements to move to Daffodil House. Her friend Callie Barbour already lived there, and liked it. Callie had even met a widower who liked her, and claimed her sex life hadn't been so full since 1962.

Moving to Daffodil House, then, hadn't been a hardship for Eugenia. More of a transition, from one phase of her life to another. She understood this would be the last one—she wouldn't be moving out of Daffodil House under her own power, and her next change of address would direct her mail six feet underground. But she had plenty of time left before she had to worry about that, and she was determined to get as much as she could out of the place while she was able. She took advantage of trips into Enid or Oklahoma City or Tulsa for shopping, museums, and theater. Sometimes buses would take them all the way to Dallas or Kansas City, or out to an Indian casino. At Daffodil House there were card tournaments, board games, a fabulous pool with water calisthenics, a book club, shuffleboard, crafts, baking and cooking opportunities, as well as superb food prepared by the staff under the direction of the dietician. She had friends and companions. She could watch TV in her own private room or out in a common room. She had the run of the place, day and most of the evening.

Doors to the common rooms were locked at eleven, but room-to-room visiting was still allowed provided it was quiet and discreet. This, she soon learned, was when Callie Barbour and Wendell Hickling went at it, in Callie's words, like jackrabbits in spring.

But when she had trouble sleeping, which was often these days with the nightmares coming out of nowhere and waking her up, she was largely on her own. There were orderlies she could summon, or drop in on, but they didn't want to hear from her and would just encourage her to lie down and close her eyes. "If that worked, I wouldn't be talking to you," she would say. She didn't want to be argumentative, though—they really did do their best to take care of the residents.

After this particular nightmare, Eugenia had turned the TV in her room on for a while, but found only crude movies and home shopping channels selling things she didn't need and had no room for. She had switched it off and tried to read a Victoria Holt paperback she had borrowed from the lending library off her wing's common area. She found it hard to concentrate on the words, though. They were tiny black worms writhing around on the page, and she couldn't make them mean anything. She felt oddly edgy, anxious. She went to the window to look out, wondering if perhaps a full moon had set her off, like it sometimes did, but she couldn't see the moon through a thick mass of clouds.

The longer she sat in her chair holding a book she couldn't read (a blanket over her legs—the Daffodil

House staff turned the heat down at night and refused to let residents keep space heaters in their rooms), the more ill at ease she became. Her gaze kept drifting to the window that looked out toward the high wall around the facility—one of the reasons she felt so safe there, day and night—but because the lights were on in her room all she could really see was her own reflection, floating on the darkness like a seated, cold ghost ignoring a backwards book.

She was just thinking about how quiet the house was when she heard a noise outside. She glanced at her wall clock with its extra-large numbers. It was after one in the morning. No wonder the place was so still. But what, then, had the noise outside been? An orderly going out for a smoke? That happened sometimes. She didn't want the orderly to look back at the house and see her sitting there reading, or not reading. She stood up, put the blanket on her bed, put the book on top of the blanket, and used the bedside remote to shut off the lights in her room.

Then she crossed to the window to see who was outside.

At first she didn't see anyone. That was because she was looking at the ground inside the wall. When she looked up, toward the top of the wall, then she saw someone. Two people, in fact. One was a woman who looked to be in her thirties or forties, the other a younger man, heavy-set and thickly bearded. She didn't like the looks of either of them, and certainly didn't like the fact that they were skulking around on the Daffodil House walls, illuminated by the building's security lights.

How did they get up there, anyway? she wondered. The wall had to be twelve feet high. The road outside was a fairly major thoroughfare, and someone would notice ladders leaned up against the wall, even in the dead of night. A truck rumbled by, its headlights gleaming through ice-encrusted tree branches, but the people on the wall paid it no mind.

The longer she stared at them, the more she wondered if she was still asleep, trapped in another nightmare. At first glance she had identified them as people, but now that she looked more closely, she wasn't at all sure of that. They were shaped like people, but there was a bizarre light in their eyes and their jaws were distended, their mouths filled with what appeared to be dozens of needle-sharp teeth. They held onto the top of the wall with gnarled hands ending in long yellowed claws. The woman (*or "woman,"* Eugenia thought) let her jaw drop open as she studied Daffodil House's façade and a tongue that seemed to be the length of a standard necktie flopped out of it, scraped across her chin, and disappeared back inside past all those teeth.

The fear that had gripped her during her sleep had returned, but magnified a hundredfold because she was convinced that she was awake and watching monsters at least as frightening as any she could have dreamed.

If in fact she was dreaming, then her dreams had taken on terrifying new reality, which might mean that she was losing her mind. And if she was awake, there were two other options—either she hallucinated the things on the wall, which would mean that she really was cracking up, or she was genuinely seeing them, which meant that the world she had occupied for almost ninety years was not at all the place she had believed it to be.

None of the scenarios were good news.

As she watched from her darkened room, the man (his mouth gapped open just enough, behind his thick black beard, to show row after row of wet glistening teeth) scanned Daffodil House's front wall, turning his head at a slow, steady pace, until finally his gaze came to a rest locked dead on hers. She tensed, wanting to duck away but knowing it was too late. The light of recognition shone in those eyes; he had seen her and didn't care if she knew it. As they stared each other down he brought out his dismayingly long tongue and lapped his lips a couple of times.

Eugenia did what she should have done in the first place. Every room had a panic button by the bed, and she abandoned the window (hoping they couldn't cover the forty yards or so from wall to window in a single leap) and rushed to her bedside, snatching the button up and pressing it over and over. Down at the orderly station an alarm should be ringing, lights going off, something to indicate a resident in need. She tried to gather her thoughts, so that when they came she could be coherent, but felt tears springing to her eyes and every muscle in her body beginning to quiver.

By the time two male orderlies banged in through her door, all she could do was point at the window.

6

THE GULF COAST, since Katrina had sucker-punched it and Rita had completed the ravaging, had become a marvelous place to hide if one had a few resources and a little bit of skill. Ferrando Merrin had been on the move for weeks; a few days in Gulfport, a week in Beaumont, back to New Orleans for a couple of days, or New Iberia, then over to Biloxi. Most people didn't know their neighbors anymore, or their neighbors had moved to Chicago or Phoenix or Bangor, or they were the only people left on their street, living in a FEMA trailer while kudzu swallowed the rest of the block. In that setting, no one paid much attention to a new arrival once they realized he wasn't bringing a government check.

He hadn't settled anywhere because settling down just wasn't safe. He didn't know much about what was going on, but he knew that for certain. He had thought he was safe in rural Georgia with Ananu—now dead, the poor thing. He had grown quite fond of her during their short time together. And Dane, his dear friend, who hadn't been heard from since he'd gone somewhere in Scandinavia. But the authorities had found AJ, even after Merrin had set him up with a new identity that should have been unshakable.

Merrin and Ananu had been staying in AJ's house. They had been compromised from that moment, if not before, and they scattered—Andy Gray and Stella Olemaun taking Ananu's baby with them, Merrin left to dispose of Ananu's body and then disappear.

He wanted to light somewhere—he was a homebody, after all, someone who was most comfortable when he was rooted—but until he knew it was safe, he didn't dare.

The trouble was, he couldn't find anyone who might be able to tell him how safe he was. Periodically, he tried Dane's cell phone or his number in Los Angeles, calling from pay phones or cells he picked up at liquor stores with the minutes preloaded. Merrin tried some of his other acquaintances, as well, but no one had heard from Dane. Everyone he spoke with was buzzing with the same fears—that something bad had happened and something worse was on the way.

In Beaumont, standing near the feet of a giant Alfred E. Neuman statue someone had adapted from a plaster muffler giant, Merrin dialed Dane's number on a cell phone he had bought from a convenience store clerk with more gold in his mouth than teeth. He'd had to sustain the illusion of humanity while completing the transaction—keeping his blood close to the surface to warm his skin and give it the pinkish cast of life, keeping his fangs and long probing tongue withdrawn.

When the line clicked, his heart jumped. "Dane!" he said, not waiting for his friend to answer.

A moment's silence met his outburst. Then, "Ferrando?" A woman's voice, not Dane's. He thought he knew it.

"Yes . . . who's this? Stella?"

"That's right."

"You're with Dane?"

"I'm at his place . . . it's a long story."

"I've paid for plenty of minutes."

She took a deep breath. "Dane's gone, Ferrando. He and Eben got into some trouble in Norway. Eben made it out. Dane didn't. I'm . . . I'm so sorry."

"Oh," Merrin said, just to make a noise. His mind was whirling. "Oh. Oh my."

"I know. I know you were close, Ferrando."

"Yes. Close. We were. Of course, our kind . . . we shouldn't make deep attachments, Stella. They so rarely end well."

"So it seems." She sounded as if she wanted to continue in that vein, but then stopped herself. "So if you were calling to talk to him . . ."

"Well, I was hoping to, since I haven't heard from him in so long. But honestly, I had an ulterior motive, too. I'm glad to hear your voice, I must say. I was wondering if you and Andy Gray had made it safely home with the child. . . ."

"Baby Dane is fine," she said. He could hear the smile when she said his name. "And so is Andy Gray, I think. I'm here in L.A. and he's back in Barrow, or at least he was when I left town."

"So then, I must ask: have you heard anything . . . about me?"

"You? I'm not really sure. They were close to us, there in Georgia. I expect closer than we imagined. If you've left—"

"I haven't left a trail, if that's what you mean. At least, I don't think so. And this is a secure line. I'm quite skilled at flying under the radar."

"I'm sure you are, Ferrando. I know Dane trusted you with his life. That means a lot to me. It's just— understand something, things are different Changing."

"What do you mean?"

"The pressures on all of us are coming from too many directions at once. Eben and Dane confirmed the worst about those who want open war with humanity. Then there are those who want to retreat into the shadows again, and those of us who think there's a path toward some kind of coexistence . . . and I can't help thinking that we're all headed toward some kind of showdown. It's going to be really ugly. Plus there are still the humans out there to contend with, the ones who want to hunt us—ones like I used to be? It's all very complicated now, and we've got to keep our senses sharp if we're going to make it. That's all I'm saying."

It was more than enough. Merrin had never suffered the illusion that the lot of the *nosferatu* was anything but precarious. But for Dane, *Dane*, to be killed? And the great Stella Olemaun to be so worried? Well, things *had* devolved. Significantly. The days when a vampire could keep a low profile and exist in the shadows, feeding when necessary without raising a fuss, seemed to be rapidly disappearing.

"Ferrando? I need to go now."

"That's fine. You take care, Stella. And thank you."

He clicked off and looked about for a sidewalk trash can to toss the phone into. A few cars passed by as he walked. When their headlights swept over him, he felt like they were searchlights belonging to hunters seeking their unliving prey. He turned his head away from the street and kept walking.

"Busy week," Helena Bair said. She was driving the Hummer today. Forrest Tilden sat in the passenger seat with a Styrofoam coffee cup in his hand, the plastic lid peeled back, steam escaping through the opening.

"They always are lately," he said. "Busier and busier."

"It's Bradstreet," she said. "Since he took over as director of field ops, everything's clicking faster than it used to. He's upped the pace of operations, upped the budget, increased pressure on the supervisors. It's almost as if it's . . . I don't know, *personal* for him?"

"Yeah." Forrest didn't care what the reason was. He just liked the action, hated being bored.

They had left the Dallas field office the previous morning, heading south on Highway 45 to Houston. Traffic had been terrible in Houston, but they'd taken a room at a motel on the edge of town and sat it out. This morning they had left early, cutting toward the Gulf Coast. More palm trees, more sand, more water everywhere. It was like a different world than Dallas. Really, Red-Blooded needed a Houston field office in addition to the Dallas one—they were spread too thin, the distances were too great, for just the one branch. Texas was a giant state, never mind including Oklahoma, and it seemed to attract more than its share of bloodsuckers. But everybody's budget was strained these days, so he didn't expect anything to change.

They were going to a lot of trouble to respond to a tip anyway—or a tip combined with some telecom surveillance that may or may not have had any real meaning: multiple incomplete calls to a suspect number. The discovery that very morning of the partially drained body of a homeless man seemed to confirm that there was some sort of vampiric activity in the area. If they found that the tip had merit, more field operatives would be sent out from Dallas and probably New Orleans.

They rolled up to the Coast Inn on North Eleventh Street shortly after one. The air was crisp and sunny, just cool enough to be comfortable out of the car with a blazer concealing his holster. Forrest shielded his eyes to scan the motel, on a fairly busy street, and the area around it. Helena walked toward the door of room number nine, where the tipster had claimed their suspicious person was staying. She glanced back toward Forrest and he held up one hand in a *hold on* gesture. She puffed out a breath and stalked back toward him.

"What?"

"We're not supposed to engage the subject," he reminded her. "We're just supposed to determine if he's a vamp."

"Which we could do by kicking his door in and opening the curtains. If he fries in the sunlight, he's one of them."

"That would be engaging him," Forrest said.

"So what? We wait till night and see if he comes out in a black cape and tuxedo?"

Forrest appreciated Helena's intellect, but sometimes her directness manifested itself as a lack of subtlety. "We wait," he said. "We surveil. We find out if he's really one or if he's just a guy. Then we call for backup."

"It's hours until dark."

He looked at the sky. Almost cloudless, as blue as swimming pools seen from an airplane. This time of year, in the long post-Christmas stretch of winter, it would be dark by five or five-thirty. Four hours and change. There was a Denny's a block away where they could kill some time, sipping joe and watching from the window. It wouldn't be as bad as some stakeouts he'd been on.

"Let's go." He nodded toward the coffeehouse. "I could use a cup or two."

"It's a chain place. I hate those. Can't we find an independent?"

"You see one with a view of this motel, let me know," Forrest said. "I'll be in there."

An hour later, Forrest had read the paper front to back, then watched the motel while Helena took a turn with it. A few people had come and gone, but the occupant of room nine had not been one of them. The drawn curtains hadn't so much as wiggled. Helena read faster than he did, and after about twenty minutes she folded the paper and laid it on the bench seat. "That's always such a joy," she said. "The news is so good for the soul. Murders, rapes, war, poverty, environmental degradation, hunger, rampant greed, and commercialism. Why are we doing this, again?"

"Doing what?"

She looked around. The restaurant was almost empty, and the nearest other party was several tables away. "Tracking down and eradicating vampires with extreme prejudice. I just read page after page of horror—none of it, as far as I could tell, caused by the undead. Greedy fuckers running giant corporations, check. Politicians, check. Economic forces beyond the control of simple human beings, check. Lust, thuggishness, and general assholery, check. Vampires . . . not so much."

She stared at him like she expected an answer. He shrugged. She wrinkled her nose. "That's all you got?"

"I guess . . . it's like Everest, you know?" he said. "Because they're there? We can't do much about politicians and assholes and corporations. We can't end a war. But we can take out some vamps . . . and if we do, then some people—maybe a lot of them, over the course of time—won't be murdered. Maybe it's a small thing. But it *is* something, so if we can do it, we should. We have to."

"You don't think we'd do the world just as much good if we exploded a dirty bomb in Bentonville, Arkansas?"

Forrest tasted his coffee, flagged a waitress. "It's cold," he said. She took the cup away to fetch a fresh one. "You're a funny woman, Helena," he said when the waitress was gone. "Remind me again how you ended up in the intelligence game?"

"Thanks a lot. I was recruited. The Bureau recruiter said I'd be working to keep the country safe. He lied, or I misheard him. End of story."

"So, you don't think you're keeping people safe?"

"Short-term maybe, sure. Safe from bloodsuckers so they can get their blood sucked the slow, legal way, by rising gas prices and inadequate health insurance, too much processed sugar and high fructose corn syrup, substandard nursing homes, bankrupt Medicare. And if they survive all that, some megaweather catastrophe will just kill 'em by the thousands. That about the size of it?"

The waitress returned with his cup, steam rising from the brown surface of the liquid. Forrest sipped it, then spooned in some sugar. White sugar. Helena shook her head sadly.

7

He had stayed in Beaumont long enough. Too long.

Ferrando Merrin liked the Gulf Coast, but maybe it was time to move inland again. Not north yet—one of his most-well-known residences was in Michigan, but if they were looking for him specifically, they might have that one staked out. Anyway, he enjoyed the South, and it covered a lot of turf, much of it rural, remote. He could hide out in the hills of Kentucky, the swamps of Florida, the lowlands of South Carolina. As long as there was electricity and a roof to keep out the weather, he'd be fine.

His needs were few. Blood, shelter, power, and peace.

Merrin was a social creature, but he knew too well the hazards of getting close to others. What had happened with Dane was a good, if painful, reminder. Over the course of decades, they had become fast friends, and now . . . Dane's death had left a hole in his heart that wouldn't be easily filled. Vampires were supposed to leave frank emotion behind with the rest of their humanity, but Merrin believed that was a choice, a conscious decision some made as a defensive measure. It wasn't innate to the species, just . . . easier. Letting go of emotional attachments made survival by murder an acceptable option. For Merrin, it was a more difficult choice, one he gave in to as needed but never without regret for the life he was snuffing short. Vampires were monsters, by definition. But monsterhood didn't require action taken without thinking or feeling—it only required the decision that one's own survival had paramount importance.

It was ironic that the humans, capable of such horror themselves, had difficulty understanding that.

Now, forces other than blood-starvation might be putting Merrin's survival in jeopardy. He believed he was safe, but acting on that belief would be a good way of ensuring the opposite result. So he had traded in his old car for a used pickup truck, paid for with cash and bought with a fake ID, and gassed it up. He was in the motel room packing his patched red cloth suitcases. He had said quiet good-byes to his few friends in town the night before. Then, on his way back to the motel, he had made a kill.

The man had been homeless, mentally disturbed in some way that gave him a sideways, shuffling gait and eyes that gleamed with madness. Dried food and damp spittle mingled in his wiry beard.

Merrin had dragged him into an alley where deep shadows promised a degree of privacy, and slit his filth-caked throat with a razor. Precious blood splashed against brick and concrete before Merrin could swallow his distaste and press his mouth against the wound.

After feeding, he took a collapsible five-gallon plastic bottle and a funnel from under his coat and filled the jug with as much blood as he could coax from the dying man's veins. Its heat warmed the plastic sides as the container expanded.

Finally, he had capped the bottle, licked the funnel clean and shoved it back into the big pocket he'd sewn into his coat, and carried the heavy bottle back to the new truck. It would come in handy on the road.

He looked out through the curtain and saw that darkness had settled over the city. Time to get on the move. He checked more carefully through the window, then opened the door and carried a suitcase to the pickup's bed. He placed it up against the cab's back wall and went back for the next. When suitcases were in place, he secured them with a cargo net. One more trip into the room, for the jug of blood and his briefcase containing the things he wanted in the cab with him, and he would leave Beaumont behind. He would drive without a plan, without a map, stopping when he felt secure or dawn was closing in.

He returned to the room one last time after the cab was loaded, put twenty dollars on the dresser for the cleaning staff, and switched off the lights. The open road called to him.

It was time to roll.

"He's on the move!"

After spending as much time as they dared in Denny's,

Forrest and Helena had returned to their Hummer, parked most of a block away from the motel. From here, they could see the entire parking lot and all the doors facing onto it. Helena had taken a shift watching while Forrest leaned the driver's seat back for a quick nap. Now she shook his leg, jolting him awake. "Forrest, we gotta go!"

"He's what?"

"He's loading suitcases into a truck. He's leaving town. We've got to intercept him."

Forrest felt like a blanket was wrapped around his brain. He tried to push through it, giving it almost physical effort. He raised his seat back and looked at the motel parking lot. Sure enough, the door to room 9 was open, and a tall, lean man was putting something into the cab of an old gray pickup.

"So much for not engaging," Forrest said. "Either we stop him now or we risk losing him altogether."

Helena was already double-checking an Ithaca 12-gauge. "I'm locked and loaded."

"Could get messy if we start blasting with shotguns."

"You see a way around it?"

They had high-intensity TRU-UV lights in the vehicle that they could use to spear bloodsuckers, their beams approximating rays of direct sunlight. For close-up work they had a couple of Ryobi chain saws. Staking the heart was a myth—it could slow them down, but to finish them off completely required severing their heads, killing their brains, or exposing them to sunlight. The shotguns were meant to get their attention, and at the right range they could destroy the brain or blast the head into the next town.

But that *Do Not Engage* order was stamped on Forrest's brain. "Hold up," he said. "Let's call it in and see what HQ says."

Helena sighed. She was ready to rumble and hated to be hauled back from the edge. But Forrest already had his cell phone out, punching the buttons with unsteady fingers. A minute later it was answered, and he explained the situation to the dispatcher on the other end. The message was relayed to a superior—he guessed probably Marina Tanaka-Dunn, but it could have been Dan Bradstreet or someone else at the executive level.

The response came back within minutes. He listened, indicated his assent, and ended the call. "Do not engage," he said. "Try to make sure he's a bloodsucker, and find out which direction he's headed. Apparently he might be someone important, so they want him alive if possible."

"Make sure? They have any suggestions for how to do that without alarming him?"

"I think it's okay to alarm him as long as he doesn't make us," Forrest pointed out. They were still most of a block away, and cars raced up and down North Street all the time.

Helena got his drift. She was a fine marksman with

pistol or rifle. She lowered her window, drew her service Beretta 9mm, and leaned way out so her left arm, resting against the door, could steady her right. When there were cars moving in both directions, their lights flaring in other drivers' faces, engine roar masking the sound of the shot, she fired.

Forrest watched through binoculars. The man from room 9 was shutting his room door, having turned off the lights inside. His shirt puffed out in front, just beneath his right collarbone, then he staggered back a couple of steps. The round passed through his body and slammed into the stucco motel wall, spraying dust into the circle of light from the lamp mounted above the door. The man's face froze into a shocked expression, mouth almost a perfect O, and he clapped a hand over his chest where he had been shot. He leaned against the wall for a few seconds, then shook his head, ducked behind the cab of his truck, and looked for whoever had shot him.

"Guess that answers that," Forrest said. He had hunched down in the Hummer's front seat, with Helena beside him, eyes at dashboard level. "A human would've gone down."

"At least for a few minutes," Helena said. "So we assume he's undead, and stick with him?"

"That's the idea. When he's out of town, we'll call in what highway he's taking, and they'll try to flank him."

"Flanking. I like flanking."

"Whatever works," Forrest said. The guy—the bloodsucker—started the gray pickup. Forrest twisted the Hummer's key and the engine growled to life. The truck pulled out of the motel lot suddenly, causing oncoming cars to brake and squeal, horns to honk. The driver cut across the lane, prompting more honking. Forrest pulled into the lane, gunning the engine, trying to keep the pickup in sight.

Within ten minutes they knew he was on Interstate 10, headed for Louisiana. Helena called it in while Forrest drove. He scootched his ass into the seat, ready for a long night behind the wheel.

He only wished his nap had been a little longer.

Merrin could smell the richness of the soil on either side of the interstate, the sharp tang of the pines, the dank swampy understory, the saltwater bite. Port Arthur slipped past, the Sabine River, Calcasieu Lake, the Intracoastal Waterway. Headlights lit the road's surface but the fringes were pitch black, the highway a pale ribbon bisecting the infinite void.

The anxiety was eating away at him.

As he drove, he was again second-guessing—fiftieth-guessing might have been more apt—his decision to remain in the South. He was comfortable there, but sometimes comfort equaled danger. The safe house outside Wells, Michigan, near the shores of the Great Lake, was perfectly good and probably safe. He had another in Fort Dodge, Iowa. And he had friends and acquaintances spread across the country. The question was, could he call upon them for aid without putting them at risk?

That, ultimately, was the wearisome part about an endless existence of undeath. And probably, he mused, what drove those who wanted to force a confrontation with the living world. Always wondering when one would be caught outside in the sun, or spotted and destroyed by the vast majority, the mortals. Looking over your shoulder, listening for the scuff of feet behind doors, the click-clack of a cocking weapon, the whistle of a slashing blade. Without warning, someone had shot him just tonight—a single small-caliber bullet, and it had passed through without causing significant damage. Had it been a random act, a bullet fired from a moving car in a drive-by shooting, perhaps a gang initiation? Or was it a warning? He couldn't tell. But he pressed harder on the accelerator pedal.

Iowa, he decided. His place there was a small cottage on a quiet street. The trees would be bare this time of year, with snow covering the tiny patch of lawn. The air would have a deadened feel to it; sounds would be muted, but aromas would linger. Yes, Iowa. He'd peel off the 10 at Interstate 55, in Hammond, and head north through Jackson, Memphis, and St. Louis. A few days spent in roadside motels, a few nights on the highway, and he would be there.

He would be safe.

* * *

A horrible wreck on the interstate.

A flipped-over SUV. A Toyota sedan with its driver's side caved in, passenger doors sprung, hood crunched open with black smoke billowing from it. Ambulances, fire trucks, and state troopers' vehicles surrounded it, their lights strobing red and blue and white like a patriot's acid flashback. Headlights and floods from the patrol cars made the scene—bodies on the ground, one draped, one being worked over by EMTs—almost daytime bright. Traffic slowed to a crawl as a pair of flashlight-wielding sheriff's deputies waved vehicles through the tangle one by one.

It was all staged. A setup.

Forrest Tilden held one of the flashlights, Helena Bair the other, having helicoptered out to the site after making the informed assumption that their quarry would stay on the interstate for a while. The flashlights were TRU-UV. They made sure to play the light across some bit of exposed flesh on every driver and passenger who went through the blockade. Some flinched, but just because the light was bright in their eyes after all the night driving.

They'd been at it for almost forty minutes before they found him.

A man, alone, still driving that ugly gray pickup. Slender, he had neatly combed gray hair and a refined manner. His winter jacket had a black-edged hole below the collarbone. Forrest didn't even need the light, at that point—he was certain, and he caught Helena's gaze and raised an eyebrow, nodding once, to make sure she knew it too.

But Forrest had the light, so he used it. When he shone it on the man's face, the man jerked away from it with a choked scream. Forrest leaned into the open window. Vivaldi played on the car stereo. Forrest sniffed; he preferred George Strait, Toby Keith, Hank Junior. "Pull over," he snarled. He kept the light trained on the dashboard, just off the man's skin, a warning. "This is TRU-UV. I can fry you in seconds."

The man—the *bloodsucker*—glared at him. Helena was already climbing in through the passenger door, her own TRU-UV flashlight clutched in her hand. The vamp looked like he'd like to tear her head off, but the threat of the lights kept him in line. Forrest walked alongside the car as the vamp drifted to the gravel shoulder. A van waited there, motor idling, driver and another guard inside. Its rear compartment was equipped with dozens of TRU-UV lights that could flood it at the flick of a switch. The walls were made of three inches of steel plate, held together with more rivets than a 747. A sound system could enable communication between the back and the cab, at the driver's discretion.

When he stopped the car and handed over the key, the vamp looked defeated. He had not yet spoken; the only sound he'd made had been the throaty shriek when the light first burned his face. He dropped the key into Forrest's open left hand, and Forrest closed his fist over it with a reassuring finality.

He'd get a commendation for this one—he and Helena, of course. The target had to be fairly high profile, or Red-Blooded wouldn't have mustered all these resources so fast. From just the pair of them sitting outside his motel to a vast, elaborately staged accident shutting down a major interstate, over the course of a few hours.

"See that van? You're getting in the back, bloodsucker. We'll take you someplace nice and safe. You're wanted for questioning, that's all."

The vampire glared at him. "Questioning? Surely you don't believe that. And you don't think that I do. Please, let's show some respect for one another's intellects."

"It's just something we say, sir," Helena said. She had slid from the passenger seat and come around the car, grabbing the vamp's left arm as he emerged. "We all understand what's happening here."

"I'm sure we do," the vampire said. "But thank you for being honest about it."

"Please, sir, just get in the back of the van. There's a bench seat in there. It's not comfortable, but if you strap in you won't slide around."

"And should I refuse?"

"You could maybe kill me. *Maybe*. But not both of us. And not all the other agents around us, who are armed and watching closely."

Forrest saw the vampire raise his head, turning it a little, scanning the area. The traffic control continued. On the road, EMTs hoisted a draped body onto a stretcher and wheeled it to the back of their ambulance. But everywhere, people in uniform and out stared at them, watching the drama unfold. Fists clutched TRU-UV flashlights, shotguns, automatic pistols. The vampire must have understood that a wrong move, a sudden break, would bring an instant and lethal response.

"All right," he said finally. Forrest opened the rear door and Helena led him to the step up. The bloodsucker climbed in and took his place on the bench seat. He buckled in.

"Don't try anything back here," Forrest warned. "The driver can microwave you in about two seconds."

"I understand that," the vamp said. Forrest was surprised he had given in so easily. The odds were stacked against him, but still, Forrest expected every bloodsucker to fight to the death rather than surrender. This one's quiet acquiescence aroused his suspicions. Forrest remained alert for the slightest move as he and Helena swung the door closed and secured the various latches and locks. When that was done, he went around to the front.

"You're loaded," he said.

The driver nodded. He looked sleepy. Forrest hoped he was awake enough to deliver his cargo to Dallas or New Orleans or wherever it was headed.

But as the van shifted into gear and started down the interstate, as the ambulance drivers and firefighters and uniformed cops worked quickly to restore the flow of traffic, as the whole scene was torn down with the brisk efficiency of a practiced film crew, Forrest felt a sense of unreality overtake him.

What had he just been a part of? Some sort of charade, in which he was only the smallest of players. He didn't know who the captive was, where he was going, what his import might be. He didn't even know who had given the order to follow and detain rather than eliminating him on the spot. When it came down to it, he knew no more about this vampire than he did about who had killed young Weston Beale. And that was essentially nothing at all.

A big machine had kicked into operation, and Forrest was only a single cog in a single gear, somewhere in its depths. The vampire was more important than he was.

Suddenly he felt very weary indeed.

8

Heather knew the streets of Ulysses would be quiet at midnight. Once in a while someone who'd had a few too many beers might be out buzzing up and down them in a pickup truck, maybe with a couple of friends whooping and hollering, but for the most part people around there went to bed early. Farm hours, up with the sun and down not far behind it.

Spotting Charles Raney wouldn't be a problem, and they'd be unlikely to be observed by anyone else. She had thrown out his name to a few in the community, and one of them claimed to know of him, if not to know him personally. His reputation was secure, though. He'd been a longtime follower of Enok's, even an occasional visitor to Enok's Norwegian haven, although not at the end. She didn't have a picture of him, but the physical description her contact gave seemed to match the man she'd met in a parking lot in Enid two nights earlier.

She drove into town from her farm on its outskirts and parked outside The Movies on North Main, the city's indoor movie theater, at about 11:45. The last feature had ended at 10:30 and the staff would have all gone home by now. She looked up at the vertical sign; its triangular *O* had always seemed to make it read THE MAVIES. Leaving the truck by the curb, she walked the couple of blocks to the designated intersection, scanning the windows to make sure no one was up late and watching the streets. Street lamps shone down on her but she didn't see any people.

Near the intersection of South Court and West Central she found Charles Raney waiting for her, standing in the shadows of a recessed doorway.

"Hello, Heather," he said as he emerged onto the sidewalk.

"It's nice to see you, Charles. I hoped you would make it."

"Wouldn't have missed it."

She didn't stop walking, and he fell into step beside her. "Do you hunt here?" he asked.

"No, not so close to home."

"You said there were other followers of Enok around. Are they all from Ulysses?"

"We're the county seat of Grant County," she said. "So people from all around come here for all sorts of things. Likewise, the members of our little group come from all around."

"So you've checked me out."

"Or I wouldn't have acknowledged the existence of our group. Yes. You said you'd bring me some more names, though."

"References." He handed her a sheet of paper, folded into quarters.

"I'll call these people too," she said.

"They'll vouch for me."

"I hope so."

"Why are we walking, Heather?"

"I don't like taking chances. That's why I didn't invite you to my place. Here we're just two people taking a late-night stroll around a sleeping town. If anybody wanted to listen to us, they'd have to be walking with us, and I think we'd notice that."

He let his gaze drift over the empty street. "Yeah, I guess we would. Do you . . ." he hesitated, like he wasn't sure how to phrase his question. "Do you have any connections with the others out there?"

"Some," Heather answered. She wasn't sure what he was driving at, and didn't know how much she wanted to give away until she had checked his additional references. She hadn't existed this long without learning caution.

"That's part of what I like about it," Charles said, without bothering to define "it." "The loose affiliation lets us feel associated with something bigger, but still allows us to determine our own futures."

"That's true," she said. That much seemed safe enough. The truth was that she did have fairly constant contact with a bigger group, and sometimes took direction from them. Their recent raid in Norman,

Oklahoma, had been just one example. A human had been posting potentially dangerous information on his website—threatening to name names. There would come a time, and soon, when the *nosferatu* didn't have to hide their identities, but could stand proudly and claim their birthrights. Until then, however, some teenage computer nerd couldn't be allowed to expose them. Carter Knightsbridge had been a little carried away, risking daylight, taking the kid's head with him, but Heather had to admit that was the kind of detail that could have a chilling effect on other humans who might think about crossing them.

They had been directed to act, and they had acted.

There was a bigger action on the way, too, but that one was self-directed, the result of a motion and a vote within their own group. She would clear it with the bigger group, but they wouldn't have veto power, or ask for it. It was the kind of thing that no one could ignore or step away from—her little group's plan to make a statement much larger than anyone expected of them.

She hoped Charles would be part of that bigger action. She'd seen him move, and he was fast, strong, and efficient. They could always use someone like him on their side.

Besides, he was no matinee idol but he wasn't hard on the eyes, either.

She wouldn't mind seeing him in action once again,

before she checked his references and brought him into the group. "You hungry?" she asked.

"Pretty much always. Got something in mind?"

"Little town called Holcomb, outside Garden City. Not too far away. We can easily make it there and back before sunrise."

Charles stopped walking, rubbed his chin with his right hand. "I've heard of it."

"*In Cold Blood*," she said.

"Sorry?"

"The Truman Capote book and movie. He wrote about a family murdered there."

"That's right. Guess it's a place with a grim history."

"That's why I figured they wouldn't miss another person or two," she said.

Ferrando Merrin had been taken to New Orleans.

They didn't let him see out of the van, of course, and it had reached its final destination inside an enclosed building, not quite a garage. The smells of exhaust and leaked oil were thick in the stuffy, humid space, but they couldn't completely overwhelm the aromas of New Orleans, post-Katrina, a fecund mixture of burgeoning plant life, old sewage, coffee and booze and piss.

When they opened the door, Merrin was surrounded by men and women in Kevlar vests and helmets. Riot gear. They carried electric prods and TRU-UV floodlights and shotguns, for the most part, although a pair of them had flamethrower tanks strapped to their backs. Behind them were concrete block walls, and the floor was poured concrete. The ceiling was the same, with exposed ductwork and conduits for wiring. They were taking no chances. Part of him wanted to give them what they no doubt expected—a monstrous display of rage and power. He could easily tear into them, spill blood, rend flesh.

But they would take him down in a heartbeat. They had the numbers on their side, and technology. And history.

Better, then, to see what they had in mind. Despite the low level of fear churning away inside him, they hadn't destroyed him outright, which meant something. He didn't know what yet. He doubted that he'd ever be allowed to leave this place, but if he was, and if he learned anything, it might help others of his kind.

Merrin looked to his left, where a figure watched from a shadowed doorway. As if summoned by his glance, the figure stepped into the light. He was tall and broad-shouldered, blandly handsome, with short brown hair, wearing a suit of almost the same color. The top button of the suit's jacket was buttoned over a striped tie. His shirt was white. He looked like he was going to dinner at the boss's house, or to a meeting of middle managers at a large corporate office.

"Welcome," the man said. "I'm Dan Bradstreet. And you are . . . ?"

There was no advantage to lying. "Ferrando Merrin."

"You've been trying to get in touch with . . . Dane, is it?" Merrin didn't reply. "You reached someone at his number, but it wasn't him. It was Stella Olemaun, right?"

"If you already have all the answers, why have you brought me here?"

Dan Bradstreet smiled. It was a bland smile, to match his looks and, apparently, his personality. He showed no teeth, and the smile didn't reach his eyes, which were cool, appraising. "I know a lot. More than you'd like to think about, Mr. Merrin. I don't know everything, though. That's where you come in."

"I don't know that I'm inclined to help you."

"You will be."

"Do you think so?"

"I do, yes. I'm pretty certain."

"And why is that?"

"Let's just say I have my reasons."

Merrin didn't respond. The man knew who Stella was. He probably had a tap on Dane's phone in Los Angeles. Maybe even people surrounding Dane's apartment. How long had that been going on? If Stella was still there, she could be in danger.

As long as Merrin was a captive of whoever these people were—likely the agents of "Operation Red-Blooded," he had to guess, that's what Andy Gray had called it—he couldn't warn her.

Again he gave brief consideration to trying to escape,

but came up against the same set of facts he had before. They had too many people, too much equipment. The best he could accomplish by trying to get away would be a quick destruction. But they *had* been decent to him, so far—decent considering they represented an end to his freedom. Causing trouble might change that, might quickly turn their behavior toward him violent. He had a high threshold for pain, but that didn't mean he couldn't be hurt. If there was a way to avoid pain—and no possibility of success anyway—then he should just go along, learn what he could, look for a better chance.

Ultimately survival would be most beneficial, particularly if he could spot an opening and slip their bonds at some future time.

"Very well," he said finally. "Since I don't imagine we all want to spend our days here in this garage or whatever it is, why don't you take me wherever you intend to put me?"

Dan Bradstreet nodded agreeably. "Let's do that. I'll just point out that you can't get away. The elevator and hallways and rooms we'll be in are all equipped with instant-on TRU-UV lights. If you should resist at any point, you'll be ashes within seconds. We're armed, too, and there are, I expect, a good number of itchy trigger fingers around us right now. Your kind tends to make our kind . . . nervous. We squash spiders, we shoot snakes, we trap rats. It's instinctive. I wouldn't take any chances if I were you. No sudden movements, go where you're told. They didn't cuff you up front, and I won't do it now if I have your word you won't try anything stupid. Okay? Are we in agreement?"

"You have my word." Merrin could smell the blood in the man's veins, rich and life-giving. He could almost hear it rushing through thick arteries and narrow capillaries. He imagined it splashing red and hot on the concrete floor, imagined the taste as it washed over his teeth and across his tongue and down his throat. But to move against Bradstreet would bring the others down on him. It wasn't worth it.

"All right." Bradstreet turned his back to Merrin and went back into the shadowed doorway. Inside the shadows, he punched a button, and an UP arrow glowed green. Doors slid open, an illuminated elevator car with steel walls. "In here."

Merrin followed him in. Some of the soldiers or cops or agents followed him. The car was large, but smaller than the space outside it, and others stayed behind. There were enough, though, and he could see the murderous lightbulbs just waiting to be switched on. Head down, he stood where Bradstreet indicated. The doors shut with a hiss. The elevator moved.

Merrin's freedom was at an end.

He was trapped, penned in, restricted. He thought he knew what convicts felt like. And animals in zoos.

It was a horrible sensation.

9

Dan Bradstreet had to struggle to keep his jubilation in check.

He had Ferrando Merrin, and he knew Merrin had been in Georgia with Stella Olemaun and that fucking Andy Gray. He knew Stella was in Los Angeles, and he would have an address soon. He'd heard of this Dane character over the past few years via Red-Blooded intel—maybe he'd get his hands on Dane as well? Score the hat trick? Either way, as clever and innovative as the bloodsuckers were when it came to hiding, there was only so much rerouting and cross-circuiting someone could do—sooner or later a landline phone had to connect to a trunk line, and Stella had foolishly talked to Merrin over a landline. Big mistake.

There seemed to be only a handful of bloodsuckers that Dan could gauge were the important ones, movers and shakers of the vampire community—and the pro-vamp human community, in the case of Stella Olemaun. She had started off as a hunter, but somewhere along the way her allegiances had shifted. There were even rumors online that she had become a vampire, had joined the bloodsuckers herself.

That seemed like an extreme move for someone like her, someone whose husband had been turned, whose life had been essentially destroyed by vamps, and who had become a virulent anti-vampire crusader.

That was part of what he wanted to find out from Merrin—what exactly had happened to Stella Olemaun? Were the rumors true? And what about her husband, Barrow's former sheriff? He was *definitely* a bloodsucker, according to Dan's intelligence. So where was he?

He sat at the Café du Monde, bundled against winter's chill in a gray wool topcoat, and warmed his hand on one of their heavy white mugs of café au lait. The chicory had a warm, earthy bite to it. The sun was just coming up, and the city was awakening with it. Across the street, by Jackson Square, the first horse-drawn carriage clopped up, getting ready for the day's tourist trade. Hustlers and grifters and con artists had drifted away from the park, but another set would show up soon; it was a shift change, not an abandonment. A merchant from one of the shops on Rue St. Ann swept the sidewalk in front of her place with a broom.

Humans could watch the sun rise. Bloodsuckers couldn't. It was just one advantage, among many, that the human race had. He could sit in the sunlight and enjoy some beignets and a cup of coffee. He didn't have to murder anyone to eat, or try to subsist on animal blood, knowing it was hopeless. He could have a fast food burger for lunch and a perfect steak for dinner and not have to worry about sneaking around for it. He could earn a steady paycheck, buy a house, have a family. Yes, he would die one day, hopefully of natural causes at a ripe old age, but he intended to have had a full life before that.

Most vampires, he was sure, didn't become that intentionally. But if Dan had to give up the things that humans did—and for what? Strength? Eternal undeath?—he'd commit whatever passed for suicide in the bloodsucker crowd.

Some days it all seemed so complicated, the things that he knew. The knowledge of how things really played once the sun went down could make people's heads explode out there in the unsuspecting "real world." But wasn't that what he was always told as he moved up in the Bureau? Always expect the unexpected?

Dan Bradstreet had been one of those all-American kids with a dozen avenues open to him, a dozen possible futures, each more golden than the last. He'd played football at USC, a wide receiver with fast legs and strong hands and a knack for knowing where the ball would come from. In the off-season, he had a show on the campus radio station. It was a time when his fellow students were listening to new-wavy "hair" bands or heavy metal, but Dan loved movie soundtracks, from musicals, dramas, comedies, animated features—whatever had a good, stirring score—and he played selections from those for two hours every Thursday night. He'd earned good grades, though not exceptional ones, in most of his classes. He could have gone for an MBA and wound up on Wall Street or running a bank or a company somewhere.

But the only thing that had really captured his attention had been criminology. He had decided early on that he wanted to spend his life catching bad guys, and the rest of it, the football, the radio, girls, liquor—those were all distractions, things he did because he could, not because he loved them.

The day after graduation Dan unplugged his phone. He spent his mornings surfing, his afternoons lying on the beach or working out at the gym, his evenings drinking in beachfront bars or grilling steaks and downing beers on the balcony of his Santa Monica apartment. He didn't turn on the TV or listen to music that whole time. Instead, he thought. He made lists in his head, pros and cons. He tried to plot career paths.

The following Monday, he plugged the phone back in and called his parents, then his little brother, and he told them he was applying to the FBI. Then he went into the Los Angeles field office and did just that. His grades were good enough to get him considered, and the first guy who interviewed him was a USC alum. He breezed through the interviews, and he headed for the academy two weeks after that.

He had thought the Bureau would be his life. Someday he'd find a woman, get married, raise some kids, but not right away, not until he felt comfortable in his career.

The path had not run as straight as he had expected, though.

He was recruited for Operation Red-Blooded, and he discovered that he couldn't turn down the opportunity. Being told that vampires really existed shook him to his core; being told that he could do something about them was like having a lightbulb in his brain switched on after decades of darkness.

It had been the right decision for him. He'd moved rapidly up through the ranks. He was good at his job, and he loved it. Finding a woman was no longer a priority. A family would only give him people to worry about. They'd slow him down. They'd want him home for holidays, weekends.

Vampires didn't celebrate holidays. So Dan didn't either.

He kept vampire hours, and he loved what he did.

Speaking of which . . . he had let Ferrando Merrin stew for almost twenty hours, in a cell with few comforts and no company. Time to start working on him. Dan left a tip on the wrought-iron table, under his saucer so it wouldn't blow away, and headed for his car.

"I know there are attack plans under way. I know the vampires are looking to strike somewhere besides Barrow for a change. So what's the plan? What's the target?"

Merrin simply shrugged.

"That's not good enough."

"If I knew, perhaps I would tell you. If I thought it might save lives. But I don't."

"You saying you guys don't talk to each other?"

"I'm saying there are some who I talk to and some I don't. Vampires aren't a homogenous lot, any more than people are. Do you talk to the president every day? Or ever? Does he know you even exist? Do the leaders of France and Russia know you?"

Merrin was in chains now, manacles around his wrists and ankles, both sets chained to one another and connected to a D-ring sunk into the smooth cement floor. The interrogation took place in a small room, maybe twelve by twelve or thereabouts. He sat in a steel chair. Dan Bradstreet stood, one foot propped on an identical chair. There was a single steel door and a video camera in the corner. Otherwise, like everyplace else in this facility, the walls were blank concrete, painted white or pale green. The building looked like it could withstand a nuclear explosion.

Or a vampire attack, which is probably closer to the point.

He thought Bradstreet was bluffing. If he knew of a vampire attack in the works, it wasn't anything Merrin had heard about. That kind of thing, organized and premeditated, usually made the grapevine, as the agent believed it did. Oh no, Bradstreet was fishing, trying to convince Merrin that he knew so much there was no point in trying to keep secrets.

Merrin had no intention of sharing what secrets he

did know. He felt vampires and humans could possibly learn to live in peace. But that would require a commitment and compromise on both sides, and Dan Bradstreet wasn't a man who could be negotiated with.

"Maybe not homogenous, but there is a power structure," Dan said. "Who's calling the shots now? Who runs the show?"

Merrin shook his head slowly. He didn't bother to pretend humanity, but let Dan see the vampire he really was. "Who 'runs the show'? Obviously you're laboring under some misconceptions. You think we elect a president? Or crown a king? Most of us can't even agree on what day it is, much less pick a 'leader' of any kind. When it comes to sheepishly following authority, I'm proud to say that humans are much better sheep than we are."

"That's not what I hear."

"Then you hear incorrectly. Or you just don't have the background to understand what you're hearing."

"You'd be surprised."

"Perhaps."

Bradstreet took his foot off the chair, scooting it noisily on the cement floor as he did. "You'd do yourself a favor if you were a little more forthcoming, *Ferrando*."

"I've always had that problem. I do favors for others—for those who are deserving—but leave my own needs for last. A martyr complex, I believe they call it."

"The thing about martyrs is they always die in the end."

"Not always."

"Often enough. And if there's nobody there to witness their tragic end, then the whole martyr bit isn't worth much. Kind of a waste, you ask me."

"I suppose then we'll have to agree to disagree."

Bradstreet came around to where Merrin sat, trussed up and immobilized. He put a hand on Merrin's shoulder and squeezed, fingers digging into the skin hard enough to leave bruises in a human. "I don't like disagreement," he said in a hoarse whisper. "I like cooperation."

"Then you might as well let me go."

"Not gonna happen."

"There's nothing more I can tell you, and nothing you can do to me except destroy me. You can't threaten me. You can't hurt me."

"Really? I'd like to think we can get very creative here."

"Let me venture a guess. Waterboarding, is it? I understand your kind is very fond of it. Or *holy* waterboarding, perhaps? Now *that's* getting creative . . . albeit in a misguided ineffective way, but bravo, Agent Bradstreet. Commendable. But I'm not frightened, if that's what you had in mind."

"You've really got a death wish, don't you?"

"I'm afraid it's a little too late for that, as you can see."

Bradstreet paused. The man was clearly growing flustered.

"You have to feed sometime. Doesn't it hurt if you're deprived of blood?"

"For a while, perhaps."

"A while might be all the time I need."

"Well, I do hope you're a patient man, because I might just surprise you."

"Oh, I have all the time in the world," Bradstreet said.

"Somehow I doubt that."

Bradstreet released his shoulder and circled around him, close enough to brush up against him. The blood in his veins was pungent. Merrin kept himself from snapping at him when he came near.

"Well, we'll just have to see, won't we?" Bradstreet said.

Merrin supposed that was true. Watch . . . and wait. See who blinked first.

10

THE EXPERTS INSISTED that torture didn't work, that information extracted through the threat or infliction of physical pain was false as often as it was true. Maybe more. People being tortured were desperate to make it end, and would say whatever they thought the questioner wanted to hear.

Maybe so. But experts had once denied that honeybees could fly. Experts had claimed that people couldn't safely ride in trains, because to hurtle through space at such speeds would knock them flat on their backs.

Experts were wrong about a lot of things.

And although Dan had never worked for the CIA, he had read some of their unclassified documents, including the *Kubark Counterintelligence Interrogation* handbook, a manual that laid out detailed torture scenarios. They had tortured for decades, sometimes fruitlessly but sometimes with very positive results. They put people into stress situations, wired up their genitals or fingertips or scalps to batteries, beat them, starved them, froze them. The idea was to strip away the personality, the individual they had been, and to arrive at the point all people had when they would be willing to do or say anything to their captors.

It could take time, depending on the subject. Months of isolation and "extreme interrogation." And it still didn't always work. But it wasn't the nonstarter the experts claimed.

Anyway, those experts were talking about people. Vampires had given up the right to be called people, or treated like them.

Ferrando Merrin thought he could hold out. He was wrong, and he would find that out quickly enough.

Dan didn't want to spend forever working the vamp, getting into his good graces, making him think they were friends. Hell no. That was what the experts suggested as an alternative. It had proven successful in thousands of interrogations over the years, and Dan had used the technique often. Not this time. The situation was too dynamic—he wasn't sure what was percolating in the bloodsucker underworld, but something was up and he didn't want to be taken by surprise when it happened.

So torture it was. It had been almost forty hours now since Merrin had fed. They'd had a couple of brief sessions. Both times Merrin had refused to answer his questions—had scoffed at the idea that he ever would.

Well, playtime was over.

He'd had Merrin sitting in the interrogation room, shackled to the ring in the floor, for the last three and a half hours. He wore a loose gray T-shirt and loose cotton pants. Barefoot. Waterboarding was pointless, temperature manipulation wouldn't work, and there was, Dan believed, no way to shame a monster who killed to survive.

But that didn't mean he didn't have options.

He nodded to the two agents watching the video monitor. At the slightest hint of trouble they would flood the room with artificial sunlight, and that would be the end of the bloodsucker. And the end of the interrogation, so Dan hoped that didn't happen.

He went into the room. This time there was a table set up inside, with a black drape over it covering the items he had laid out there earlier. He didn't greet Merrin, and the bloodsucker didn't acknowledge him. Instead, Dan went straight to the table and carefully removed the draping, folding it neatly and setting it on the empty chair.

He didn't speak until he had a knife in his hands, with a long, narrow, very sharp blade. "Changed your mind, Fernando?"

"It's Ferrando."

"Whatever."

"Please, at least show some degree of respect."

"Don't count on it." He approached the vampire, showing him the blade.

"I'm disappointed in you," Merrin said.

"I'm heartbroken."

"Really, I expected better from you. You're clearly an

intelligent man with some education, an accomplished fellow. To see you stooping so low . . ."

Dan didn't wait for the vamp to finish. He took the knife and pressed it against the flesh of Merrin's left upper arm, just beneath the T-shirt sleeve. Merrin tried to flinch away but couldn't go far. Dan kept pushing against it until he felt the resistance of bone, then he twisted it ninety degrees to the right and yanked it free.

Merrin made a hissing noise, trying to escape the blade. Figuring he had little to lose—it wasn't like he could accidentally kill the guy—Dan jabbed it in again, this time in the side of Merrin's neck. Blood leaked from both wounds. This time Merrin hissed louder and snapped at Dan's hand.

Dan kept at it, silently probing with the knife. Merrin jerked away from it but couldn't avoid the blade. Dan opened up wound after wound. The vamp was a mosaic of pale bluish skin and red tracings of blood.

As he worked, Dan asked questions in low, almost whispered tones. "Who's calling the shots in the vampire world? . . . Where is your headquarters, or capital, or whatever you want to call it? . . . When's the next big action scheduled? . . . Who's responsible for the increasing number of websites and blogs about vampires? . . . Where the fuck is Andrew Gray? . . . What do you know about Stella Olemaun?"

Merrin's answers were invariably unsatisfactory.

Which led to another jab with the knife, another

twist, another pocket of flesh opened up. Dan's wrist was starting to ache from forcing the knife in and turning it over and over again. Finally, he allowed himself a break, leaving the vamp in the interrogation room while he went to swallow some ibuprofen and close his eyes for twenty minutes.

The bloodsucker wasn't going anywhere.

Merrin had hoped the agent would lose patience, or realize that causing him pain wasn't going to make him talk.

He didn't enjoy the pain, but he could survive it.

Most of his responses were true—the questions Bradstreet wanted answered, Merrin simply didn't know about. Some of them—a headquarters for vampires?—were just laughable. Utterly preposterous. Bradstreet had started out trying to convince Merrin that he knew a lot about the *nosferatu,* but as the line of questioning continued, the truth was apparent that the special agent was nearly as ignorant as most humans. Maybe he knew bits and pieces, but he hadn't put it together into the cohesive whole he thought he had—partly because he still believed there *was* a cohesive whole. They weren't bees, for heaven's sake. Even if Merrin had explained about the vast and growing divisions between vampires, Bradstreet probably wouldn't believe him.

So Merrin took the pain, teeth clenched, and tried to imagine himself in other, more pleasant, places.

Music had always soothed his nerves, so he tried to recall some of the favorite live performances he had seen over the years. In his mind, he sat in a smoky cabaret in Paris, around 1897, listening to Erik Satie perform his early compositions. He watched Jerry Lee Lewis blow the doors off a tin-roofed backwoods Louisiana beer joint in 1961, after his ill-considered marriage to his thirteen-year-old cousin became public and his big concert hall gigs had vanished. He spent a warm July evening grooving to Miles Davis at the Montreux Jazz Festival in 1973.

Merrin had been to every major art museum around the world—the Louvre, the Hermitage, El Prado, the Met, and all the rest, and had the pleasure of meeting Pablo Picasso, Jasper Johns, Andy Warhol, Ansel Adams, and scores of others. He had tried to make the most of his long life, rather than spending it skulking around dark alleys and shadowed dens like so many of his brethren. Many vampires found that their appreciation for the creative accomplishments of humans dulled over time, but not Ferrando Merrin.

Every now and then, Dan Bradstreet's vicious probing dragged him back from those happier places. He never stayed long, though. Merrin answered, or refused to answer, Bradstreet's questions, then sent his mind sailing back through the mountains and valleys of memory.

When the door opened again, Merrin saw that Bradstreet had brought a flashlight with him. He was really getting sick of those flashlights. He wondered if

Operation Red-Blooded had developed them in their own labs, since he had never seen them until he started running into their agents.

He couldn't help wishing he still had never seen them.

"Are you ready to cooperate, Fernando?" Bradstreet said, deliberately mispronouncing his name again.

Merrin bit back his anger at the agent's childish games. "I thought I had been."

"You answer what you want, and yet somehow you never really tell me anything that's helpful."

"Maybe you're asking the wrong questions."

"And if I was asking questions that might put your kind on the endangered species list, you'd answer them?"

"Well, I imagine that would depend on how you define 'my kind.'"

"Bloodsuckers. Who should all be staked outside in the desert at sunrise."

"At least you're not shy about making your prejudices known."

"Apparently you still want to dance. I, on the other hand, want results. And I want them now, or things will get very ugly in here very quickly."

Merrin looked down at the clothing hanging from him in bloody shreds, at the dozens of small, seeping holes in his skin. "Uglier than this?"

Bradstreet clicked on the flashlight. "Oh, much uglier, my friend." He played the light quickly across

Merrin's left arm. The damaged flesh there sizzled and smoked, a smell like burnt rubber reaching his nose. He jerked away from the light. If the chair hadn't been bolted down he'd have knocked it over; as it was, he nearly slid out of it, but the chains held him awkwardly in place. As he tried to straighten up, Bradstreet let the light's beam slide across his left leg. Where the knife had torn his pants, the light scalded. The pain made his joints seize up, his every muscle tense, but he couldn't escape it. He tried his trick of leaving it all behind in his mind, but this was sheer *agony,* so much more than what the knife had caused. Pain consumed him, stole all his attention.

"Where's Andrew Gray hiding?"

Merrin looked at him, his eyes now wide and pleading, his mouth frothing a little.

He still didn't answer.

Bradstreet swung the light's beam across his neck. Merrin screamed and, having started, couldn't stop. It had all become too much. He screamed and screamed, twisting and writhing in the chains, wrenching at the chair, and something that must have been adrenaline filled him, powered him, because suddenly he was on his feet, the bolts that had held the chair fast sheared off, the chains rattling but loose because he had snapped some of the links, and he spun so the chains lashed out at the now-terrified agent. One caught the bastard on his bland, handsome forehead and cut a gouge in the smooth flesh there. Bradstreet dropped his flashlight, which bounced once, landed on its side, and rolled toward Merrin. Merrin caught it with one foot and kicked it across the room. When Bradstreet turned to follow its path, Merrin was on him, chains looping around his throat, pulling tight, and—

The room was bathed in TRU-UV light, flooded with it from dozens of hidden bulbs.

Dan felt pressure on his back one second, a chain cutting off his air, and the next he felt only heat. The chain clattered to the floor, and Ferrando Merrin's final, deafening scream died out as he blazed, a human-shaped ambulatory bonfire one moment, a scattering of hot ashes the next.

"Damn it!" Dan shouted. He knew whoever had switched on the lights could hear him over the monitor. *"You stupid assholes!* I needed him! *We* needed him! What the fuck did you do?"

No answer came. Dan wiped the blood from his aching forehead with his sleeve as he looked at the ashes that had been the vampire. He understood the reaction—he had only hoped it wouldn't have come to that. It was entirely possible that, in another minute, the vampire would have killed him. Dan had definitely lost the upper hand, had pushed the bloodsucker too far, until agony and fear gave him the strength to break his bonds.

But . . . all that time and effort, lost. Days. Tens of thousands of dollars. And for what?

The ashes said it all. For nothing. Merrin had given them absolutely nothing.

Dan attempted to will the anger to drain from him, before he did to whoever was on the other side of those lights the same thing he had been doing to the vampire.

All for nothing . . .

Marina Tanaka-Dunn sat close enough to Dan to make him nervous. She shouldn't even have been in New Orleans, which was outside her turf as western field supervisor. But she had insisted that Merrin's capture had a western connection, because Merrin's phone call to the L.A. apartment had been instrumental in pinning down his location. And he'd been picked up in Texas—east Texas, but still officially her territory.

After Merrin's destruction under the lights, Dan had stormed into the office set aside for him when he was visiting and had thrown himself down on the couch with the shades drawn. He'd had high hopes for Merrin, because his intelligence had shown that Merrin was close to others . . . maybe even to whoever Dane was, part of whatever had gone down in Savannah a few months before. He wasn't clear on the details of that, but it had caused a buzz in the vampire community, and there was still a ripple skimming across its surface.

It had been a while since he'd heard any news of this Dane, but there was a separate buzz building about that—apparently that vamp had been mixed up in something significant. Trouble seemed to follow whomever Dane was around, and Dan had no doubt he'd found more.

Dane's importance was magnified by the fact that he was close to Stella Olemaun. She—vampire hunter possibly turned vampire? still no answers, *goddammit*—had become a major player in the community, with a following that crossed the lines between the undead and vamp-fans of the still-living persuasion.

She was the real prize he had his eyes on, and he would work every lead until he got her.

While he sat in the dark with his eyes closed, Marina came in, shut the office door, and squeezed in next to him on the short leather couch. She smelled like she had just come from an orgy, but he thought that was simply a regular fragrance she wore. On the other hand, if anyone could find a midday orgy in New Orleans, it would be her, so that option was certainly possible.

"Sorry it went down that way, Dan," she said. He felt her hand rubbing his thigh, then her fingers digging into the flesh there through his suit pants. He opened his eyes and glanced her way. Maybe she had just come from an orgy after all. She wore a leather bustier that lifted her breasts almost to her collarbone, and her tight black pants might have been her own skin. Her boots ended in heels at least four inches long. Her coal-black hair was tied in a ponytail that came over her shoulder and nestled in her cleavage. "I know that wasn't what you had in mind."

"Not even close." He moved away from her on the couch, putting some air between their legs, but she shoved over beside him.

"If there's anything I can do to make it better . . ."

"You can bring in Stella Olemaun, how about that," he said. "That would help a lot."

"I was thinking something more immediate." She put her hand back on his thigh.

"Marina, this is a place of business. I'm your boss. How do you imagine it's appropriate to even talk like that? You think I'm going to do something like that here in a borrowed office?"

"So what?" she said. "We both have needs. I'm sure you need to take your mind off of things right now."

"Well, I don't think so."

She squirmed on the couch, rubbing her crotch against the leather. "I'm not blind. I see the way you look at me, Dan. It doesn't have to mean anything."

"It wouldn't," he said. "And because it doesn't, what's the point?"

She squeezed her arms together, almost popping her breasts out of the bustier. "The point is I'm hot for you, too, Dan. Come on, what do you say?"

"Marina. If you keep talking like that I'm going to have to write you up. So just stop."

She pouted dramatically and sat back against the corner of the couch, arms folded beneath the prominent globes of her chest. "Okay, whatever," she said. "I just wanted you to know that I'm available, if you change your mind."

"Thanks, but that's not likely to happen."

She watched him from beneath hooded eyes, still playing the role of the put-upon victim. "Fine. Whatever. So . . . how bad is it, then? Losing Merrin?"

He was relieved to get back to business, if only to ignore the aching in his crotch. "It's bad. We've spent a lot of time and money trying to find him, ever since that mess in Savannah. I'm not going to say it's any kind of tragedy—the problem is we hoped to use him to get to Stella Olemaun. Hopefully Andy Gray. Or at the very least to learn what Stella's mixed up in. Now we're just back to—well, I won't say square one, because we know Stella was in L.A. recently, so that's something."

"We're pretty sure she's still in L.A."

"Then you should be there, too."

"My people will get her, don't worry about that."

"I always worry, Marina, until they're in custody. And even then things don't always go right, obviously. But if you want to know the truth, I'm feeling pretty good about things overall. Yes, I'm pissed that we lost Merrin. But we're getting a much better sense of the forces operating in the bloodsucker world than we used to have, thanks to some other high-value targets we've picked up lately. We know there's trouble between different factions of it . . . and I think there are ways we can use that internecine warfare to our advantage. I'd like to think we're closing in—I always feel like Hitler when I say this, except we're not talking about people here—on a final solution to this problem. You and I could both be out of a job soon, Marina. And I mean really soon—months, instead of years, maybe."

She smiled, opening her eyes wider and pressing her hands against the leather couch. "Then you can fuck me, right?"

Dan sighed, eyes rolling. *Quite the professional, aren't we?* he thought. "Then," he replied, "we can talk about it."

II

THE TRIAL HAD gone on so long, held in the glare of the national media spotlight, that by the time Frank Cartwright arrived in the maximum-security block of the New Jersey State Prison, many of the prisoners had seen him on TV and knew his name. He was, in some ways, a celebrity. He knew Geraldo Rivera and Nancy Grace and Larry King. Women had written him love letters, sent him their nude photos, offered to marry him. His face had appeared at supermarket checkout stands from coast to coast, sharing space with Angelina and Brad, Britney and Paris and O.J.

They had all been part of it, of course: Sadie and Dave, Doug, Bill and Lisa. They were all doing time at various prisons around the country. But Frank had been labeled the "ringleader," and he was the one the media focused on. The book club had met at his house in Sally Hill that night—the night they discussed Stella Olemaun's book *30 Days of Night*—and Frank was the one who had done some independent online research, finding websites that claimed the book was true and offered supporting evidence. Frank was the one who had pointed out that his neighbor Oswald kept to himself, and only seemed to come out at night. The others all knew Oswald, knew who he was, anyway, and they readily agreed.

Oswald *had* to be a vampire, they all said.

Maybe they had just worked themselves into a frenzy, but there were no doubters, no objections raised. Finally, it had been Frank's gardening tools they had used to destroy him.

At trial, of course, a different set of interpretations won the day. Oswald worked nights as a janitor at a manufacturing plant, and he slept days. He'd always been a bit of a loner. He had a low IQ and a speech impediment that made him shy about introducing himself to people. If he'd bothered to explain any of this to Frank and the others when they showed up with garden implements, he would be alive today and Frank wouldn't be in the Capital Sentence unit of NJSP. His attorney had wanted Frank to accept an insanity defense, which would have been supported by the numerous confessions he had made in which he had explained that they only killed Oswald because they believed he was a vampire. Frank insisted on a self-defense plea, since he had considered Oswald an imminent threat. The jury had not agreed.

His attorney assured him that he had hit the jackpot when New Jersey had abolished the death penalty shortly after his sentencing. The sentence was automatically changed to life without parole. There were still appeals to be made, and he might spend the rest of his life behind the prison's fences, but that life could easily be as long as it would have been out of prison.

The days were pretty much all the same. That was one of the ways they got to you, Frank decided. The unvarying routine was as much a punishment as the lack of freedom. At six-thirty in the morning, they were awakened. They had breakfast alone in their cells, instead of going to the mess hall with the general population. Since today was Thursday, it wasn't Frank's turn for outside recreation—that happened every other day. At 8:30, he and Joey Pavallone were let out of their cells and allowed to play cards, do a puzzle, read a magazine. Joey cheated at cards but always wanted to play, usually some game Frank barely knew like whist or casino or crazy eights, so Frank hated recreation module with him. Joey had locked four people inside a ramshackle garage and set it on fire. When they tried to break out through the burning boards, he had shot them. Some choice—bullets or burning. He, unlike Frank, really deserved to be in here, and Frank didn't like to piss him off.

Lunch at eleven. Shower in the early afternoon. TV. A book. Maybe, on very rare occasions, a visit from one of his nephews, or a phone call. Dinner at four. Lockdown at nine, everyone back in their individual cells. Being in gen-pop might be better, if only because

Frank—unlike Oswald—was a social guy, and would enjoy some company, as long as people didn't try to get friendly in ways Frank didn't appreciate.

It was 9:40 now, and Frank was kicked back on his cot reading a John Grisham novel. He'd never been much of a legal thriller fan before, but during his time on trial and appeal, he had found himself drawn to them.

"Hey, Buffy!" Joey had started that, and Thomas Lee, who had strangled eleven women with their own pantyhose, had taken it up next. Now more of his fellow CSU inmates called him that than used his real name. Ignoring it was pointless.

"Yeah?" He put a finger on the page he was reading and closed the book.

"Do silver bullets work on vampires?" That was Calvin Jefferson, murderer of two of his own wives and all three of his children. "Or is that just the Wolf Man? Tommy and me, we been tryin' to remember."

Frank sighed. Tomorrow he'd get outside, jog, maybe play some hoops. Work off some of his pent-up energy. "I believe that's werewolves."

"I worn my St. Christopher medal since I was twelve," Joey called. "That must be why I never had no vampire trouble."

"I think it's all that garlic you eat," Calvin replied.

"That garlic thing, Buffy, that's bullshit, right?" Joey asked.

"Garlic. Yeah, that's bullshit."

The unit broke out in raucous laughter. Like vampires were a source of amusement, nothing but the subject of low-budget movies and trash novels. So maybe Oswald hadn't really been one. Frank couldn't feel too guilty about that, because what if he had been? That book and the websites he had read were utterly convincing. Vampires existed. The guys on the unit didn't think so. The judicial system sure as hell didn't think so. But Frank was convinced. For a while, during the trial, he had been afraid he had made too much of a fuss about them, afraid they'd come after him. At least here, where the lights never went out completely and there were always armed guards and tall fences and locked doors, he finally felt safe.

He realized he could barely keep his eyes open. He slid a bookmark into his book and set it on the floor next to the cot. He pissed into the seatless steel toilet, brushed his teeth at the little steel basin, and climbed into his cot, pulling a thin blanket and stiff sheet over him.

Within a few minutes, with the laughter of the other guys on the unit still ringing in his ears, he had drifted off to sleep.

At first he thought he was dreaming.

A voice whispered his name, right in his ear.

"Frank. Frank Cartwright."

After he heard it a few times, he stirred, realized he was awake. But how could someone be so close to him?

A guard? Fully awake now, he started to jerk his head to the side, but it was held in place by something like a steel vise.

Only that vise had fingers. And hot, sour breath. "Huh?" Frank managed before the fingers clamped over his mouth.

"Frank. Did you think we didn't notice you? Or that we've already forgotten about you? Some of us would like to remain hidden, Frank. Safe in the shadows. The stuff of legends, of stories told in tremulous voices around campfires. When we come out, it'll be on *our* terms."

Not a guard, then, unless this was a truly elaborate prank. Frank didn't recognize the voice, either. Whoever it was spoke in a low, sibilant whisper, a male voice with just a trace of a European accent of some kind. Frank tried to smack it away, to tear those hands from his head, but he couldn't.

"You pulled back the curtain, Frank. We can't have that, not yet. Don't look at the man behind the curtain, because you might not like what you see. And you . . . you tried to get everyone to look. You'll just keep trying, too, won't you? Appeals. Interviews. I heard someone was talking about commissioning a true-crime book about your little book club. The author would be interviewing all of you, getting your side of things. I'm sorry, Frank. You must understand that can't be allowed."

The voice seemed to be getting closer to his ear. The

hairs around Frank's ears vibrated from the speaker's breath. Then he felt something, sharp as broken glass, slicing his neck from the ear toward the front.

Frank whimpered as the blood started to spill, and the speaker stopped talking because he began lapping it up with a long, coarse tongue.

Frank thought for a moment that it would be a problem for him that tomorrow was Friday, because Friday was the day the men in the CSU had to clean out their cells, mop the floors, change the sheets, and scrub the sinks and toilets, and he had just soiled his sheets and cot. But then he realized that was a stupid thing to worry about, and then he ceased worrying, and thinking, altogether.

Marina Tanaka-Dunn didn't always use sex to get what she wanted. Often she used violence. Sometimes she used sex, which was mostly a tool and a hobby, to get violence, which was an utter passion.

Sometimes, when it was more effective, she used more prosaic means of persuasion. To get the address of the apartment in Los Angeles that the vampire Ferrando Merrin had called, for instance, she had tried sex and fear but had wound up settling on patriotism. The guy who could trace the path through all the re-routing Dane had arranged through his own contacts in the phone company was happily married and not interested in her physically. He loved his job and he was secure there. But he was a true-blue American, and when Marina let it slip that Islamo-fascist terrorists might be plotting against his country, he became willing to set aside his initial reluctance and do the job.

Marina had to sit with him while he did it. He tapped on a computer keyboard. On a big screen across the room, diagrams of the Los Angeles County phone system switched from one region to another with a speed that made Marina's eyes hurt. A glowing spot let Alden Tennerov keep track of his progress, even if Marina couldn't follow it.

All the while, he mumbled to himself. It took twenty minutes before Marina understood that she wasn't expected to be able to understand him; until then she had kept asking him to repeat himself, which he did, but most of what he said remained meaningless to her.

"This guy's good," Alden Tennerov said after he'd been working for almost an hour.

Marina didn't answer.

"I said 'this guy's good.'"

"I'm sorry, were you talking to me?"

"Yes, I was."

"Well, I'm sure he didn't do it himself."

"Whoever did it, I mean. It's not untraceable. Nothing's untraceable. But if you just followed the signal to where it would ordinarily lead, you'd wind up at a pay phone in Watts. From there it jumps to an office in downtown L.A.—an office that's been vacant, without telephone service, since 2002. Then it randomly skips over to any of four different locations spread across the San Fernando Valley."

"I understand your professional appreciation," Marina said. "But can you pin down the ultimate location?"

"I'm getting there, Miss Tanaka," he said. He may have been a genius with telephone systems but he couldn't remember her full name for ten minutes.

Fortunately she had agents doing old-fashioned legwork. They had pictures of Stella Olemaun, which were easily come by since she had been, for a couple of hours at least, a media celebrity. That had been a few years ago, and no one knew what she might have done to her hair, her weight, her style of dress, but they'd mocked up a few different versions of her as she might look now. There were also photos of the mysterious Dane for good measure, although they weren't as good, just operations photos from Georgia enhanced as well as they could be.

Armed with those photos, they scoured the streets around where they thought Dane's place might have been, based on questionable intelligence and the first apparent location of the phone they had tapped, in Watts. Marina was beginning to believe that this Dane had never lived in Watts, maybe never even set foot there, and that her agents were stirring things up for no reason. If she was Dane she would have lived downtown, or in West Hollywood, or maybe back in the canyons. Someplace where a handsome white guy could come and go at night without calling attention to himself.

"Here you go, Miss Tanaka," Alden said a little while later. He gestured toward the screen, which had stopped changing. Now the glowing point bounced around within a set of lines.

"What am I looking at?"

Alden got up from his chair and crossed the room. "This line is Pico," he said, pointing to the upper one. "The one down here is Venice. These two verticals are Second Ave and St. Andrews."

"Why is the dot bouncing between them?"

"His last stunt. I'm guessing he's got the wires so crossed up at the switching station down there that this is as close as I can get from here. Someone's going to have to go in physically and straighten it all out."

"Well, can't you do that?"

"Oh, no. I'm strictly an indoors guy. I wouldn't know what to do with physical wires."

"Can you recommend someone?"

"You'll have to go to the station and find someone familiar with that equipment."

Marina looked at the map projected on the screen and silently cursed. He was talking about blocks and blocks containing probably hundreds of apartments and condos.

Legwork it was, then. She thanked Alden for his efforts and left the building, out into bright afternoon sunshine.

At least he had narrowed down the search grid. If Stella Olemaun was still there—and because she still used the phone occasionally, Marina believed she was—they would find her.

Today, tomorrow, the next day, they would run her skanky traitorous ass to ground.

12

"YOU SAY they had lots of teeth?"

"Oh, yes," Eugenia Parsons replied. "It seemed like . . . I don't know . . . far more than anyone I've ever seen."

"And they were sharp?"

"Have you ever been to Florida?"

The agent—Tilden, he'd said his name was—nodded. "Miami, Fort Lauderdale. Daytona once, when I was in college."

"My husband used to take me to Miami and the Keys every five years or so. For my birthday, he said, although we didn't leave until after Christmas. There was a restaurant we went to down there called The Reef, and on the walls the owner had hung dozens of shark jaws. You know, wide open with all those teeth showing?"

"So it was like one of those jaws?" the female agent asked. Helena something, Eugenia remembered.

"No. Like all of those, put together."

Eugenia was frankly astonished that anyone had come to investigate her claims. The orderlies hadn't seen anyone when they had looked out the window that night, but the Daffodil Hill security force had apparently found something—footprints in the snow, scuff marks on the wall, she didn't know what—that convinced them that she wasn't hallucinating. They had called the Woodward police, and the police had brought in the FBI. That surprised her even more, because she wouldn't have believed the FBI would have any interest in a couple of people (*not people, but something*) peeking in at a bunch of senior citizens. Of course she followed the news and understood that terrorists could be anywhere, but not only did these not look like any terrorists she had ever imagined, but she couldn't guess what interest terrorists would have in Daffodil House. If they were going to strike in Oklahoma, she believed it would be in Oklahoma City, like that awful bombing several years before, or perhaps Tulsa, and they would choose a more significant target than a retirement home.

These agents were asking all kinds of questions, though, and seemed to take her seriously. From her window she had already seen them inspecting the wall, perched on a tall ladder, and the ground on both sides of the wall.

"Did they say anything to you?" the man named Tilden asked her. "Or could you hear anything they might have said to each other?"

"I don't know if they spoke at all," Eugenia said. "They were pretty far away there, on the wall, and I had my window closed of course. I really couldn't say if there was any talking going on."

"Right," Helena said. "But they didn't communicate with you in any other way?"

"The male one held his eyes on me for a minute or so, before I got too scared and went to call the orderlies. That was the only way I knew that they knew I was watching them."

"Probably just as well," Agent Tilden said under his breath. Helena shot him a sharp glance and he swallowed whatever else he might have said.

The two agents looked at each other for a few more seconds, then Agent Tilden went to her window and looked out toward the wall for the third time. He looked back at Helena and shrugged. She returned the gesture. "Thank you for your time, Mrs. Parsons," Helena said. "If we have any further questions we might come back, but we're done for now."

"That's fine," Eugenia said. She hadn't had company stay this long in months, and wouldn't have minded if they'd wanted to sit and chat for a while. But they had more important things to do, and many-toothed terrorists to chase, so she understood their urgency. Agent Tilden nodded to her and showed something that might have been a smile as he backed out of her room.

When they were gone, the room seemed larger than usual, and emptier. She still didn't understand why they had come, but for a few minutes, at least, she had felt part of something very important indeed.

* * *

It wasn't that Heather didn't like Oklahoma. It was just that going into the next state for major hunting trips and operations seemed safer than staying in Kansas. If the feds got involved, they could cross state lines all they wanted, but local cops would be stymied by the border. At least that's what she hoped.

The Norman mission had been dictated by Suzanna Clarendon, her main contact at a larger cell. For the winter, Suzanna and most of her cell were staying in Rattenberg, Austria, a town nestled so deeply between tall mountains that the sun never reached its streets all winter long.

As far as Heather knew, Carter still had the Beale kid's head rotting in his house in Satanta, although she hoped not because that was the kind of security lapse that could get them all destroyed.

But vampires went their own way most of the time, set their own rules, and even when they had formed into small revolutionary cells, no one could dictate everything to them.

This night, she and Griff Oliphant were driving back into Oklahoma, for the final reconnaissance trip before their own mission.

She had taken to calling it D-Day.

The *D* stood for Daffodil House, an assisted living center/retirement home down in Woodward. They had made two previous visits, most recently the night she met Charles Raney. The place had security, but nothing that would pose a problem to a whole group of motivated *nosferatu*. A high concrete block wall surrounded it—the beauty was that it wouldn't keep them out, but it would keep the home's residents in when the blood started to run.

Their main purpose this time was to identify the best routes into and, especially, out of Daffodil House's neighborhood. The biggest potential hazard they would face would be residents calling the police. A few cops they'd be able to handle, but if there were enough calls to prompt a major response—if Woodward had enough cops to mount a major response—then escape could be a problem.

But Heather also wanted one more look at the structure itself. The grounds covered a couple of acres of land, all of it behind the high walls, and she needed to be sure she knew exactly where all the gates were so she could post watchers to them. She figured they would want to spend about an hour inside, feasting on the blood of the almost two hundred residents.

Her hope was that they could prevent any calls for help from getting out, and no one would come in until morning, at which time the drained corpses of the elderly and special-needs patients would announce to the world carnage on a scale never imagined in the state of Oklahoma. It would be the vampiric equivalent of the American Revolution's "shot heard 'round the world." And like that shot, it would spur others into action. When they could stop hiding and move into the spotlight—figuratively speaking—when their actions could no longer be ignored or denied by the masses, then those same masses would huddle in terror, their worst nightmares shown to be reality. It would be the birth of a new world, built in the shape of Enok's dreams.

Realistically, though, she recognized that even if they could take out the phone lines, some of the residents and staff would have cell phones, even computers with wireless access. They wouldn't be able to completely shut down communication, and would have to rely on terror to keep the residents from reaching out.

In the event that failed, though, she wanted to know how the authorities would arrive, so they could leave by a different route. She had plotted out the locations of the nearest police stations and figured out what routes they would probably take, so tonight their plan, after the last look at the walls and gates, was to drive those same routes, checking the terrain, how many stoplights and signs the police might need to negotiate, and to identify any other potential obstacles.

They drove in on the route they expected to take. Daffodil House was on Woodward's northeast side. They'd be coming in from Kansas on a highway with a veritable math book's worth of identifying numbers: 3, 270, 412. The Daffodil House property was past Fort Supply and just inside Woodward's city limits. The countryside there was flat, bleak, and colorless on a late winter's night, snow-covered plains with sparse trees.

The acreage itself had some rolling hills, covered in

grass during the rest of the year. A few tufts poked up through the snow. Tree limbs were rimed in ice. Daffodil House consisted of a compound of four main buildings and a handful of smaller outbuildings, storage sheds and the like. The outer wall and the buildings were painted a cheery daffodil yellow, with blue trim and accents. Paved walkways cut across the grounds, allowing residents to roam about at will. At night, low path lights illuminated the walkways, while floods mounted high on the buildings washed the grounds with light. Additional floodlights were mounted at spots along the wall, some facing into the grounds and some out, illuminating the wall itself and the sidewalk in front of it. Behind the grounds were more fields. Escape might be possible that way, but it would be out into open country, and they would leave tracks in the snow. She would rather have a straight, unobstructed trip back out the many-numbered highway and into Kansas.

She and Griff met in Liberal, Kansas, and he drove the rest of the way into Woodward. He was a burly man with thick black hair and a heavy beard and a raw sense of humor. If he found something funny he laughed long and loud. When he'd been turned in 1978, he was thirty-seven years old, and he still dressed like the redneck he'd been then. Tonight he wore a plaid flannel shirt over a thermal undershirt, blue jeans, and work boots, all covered by a canvas barn coat.

He parked in front of Daffodil House, about a

hundred yards from the main gate. That gate was attended most of the time by a single security guard. When no one was on duty it was simply locked up tight, and anyone wishing to drive onto the grounds would have to buzz an attendant inside, who could see the visitor via a closed-circuit video surveillance system.

This late, the guard was gone. The street was quiet, with just a handful of cars, pickups, and SUVs parked on the other side, where a convenience store and gas station stood in front of a housing development occupied largely by Daffodil Hill staff.

"I want a look at that gate," Heather said. "I want to see how hard it'll be to take out the camera."

"Knock yourself out," Griff said with a wide grin.

"You're not coming?"

"Oh, fine." He got out of his truck and started toward the gate.

"Go time," Helena Bair said.

Forrest Tilden grumbled. It was cold out there. He had a full-length cloth coat, as did Helena, but even with that and fur-lined leather gloves on his hands, the chill would bite at his nose and cheeks and make his eyes water.

She was right, though. A couple of people, a man and a woman, had pulled up in an old pickup truck and started walking toward Daffodil House's main gate. Anyone with genuine business would have driven straight up to the gate and buzzed for admittance, while the lateness of the hour and the cold in the air argued against the merely curious.

He popped open the Hummer's door and started across the street, his footsteps clicking in time with Helena's. They both carried TRU-UV flashlights, and their guns were in hip holsters so they could be easily drawn through their open coats.

They'd gone only a few steps when the woman heard them and looked over. She spoke a couple of words to the guy, who glanced their way. He hesitated for only a fraction of a second, falling slightly off his pace, but then caught himself and continued on, the woman beside him. They walked casually, as if they hadn't a care in the world between them.

Forrest and Helena adjusted their angle of approach slightly and moved to cut them off before they reached the main gate.

"Excuse me," Forrest called when he was still ten yards back. Even if they rabbited, at this range the UV beam would pin them like bugs in an entomology display. Forrest's fingertips tingled inside his gloves, the first sign of nerves. You never really knew if a confrontation was coming until it happened, but he was starting to feel like this would become one.

"Yeah?" the male asked. He stopped and turned toward them. You could have laid a yardstick across his shoulders. With his hair and beard in his face, all Forrest could make out of his face was a pair of dark eyes burning back at him.

Forrest drew back his coat to show the FBI badge. "We'd just like to talk to you for a minute."

"It's late and I'm cold," the guy said. "You got any interest in chatting, dear?"

"None at all," the woman said.

Forrest kept closing the distance, Helena right beside him. The people looked human, although he knew it was possible for a bloodsucker to make itself appear that way for short periods of time. He had a bad feeling about them, but nothing to back it up yet.

"Just for a minute."

"Sorry, Jack," the man said. He turned and started back for his truck. The woman with him did the same. Helena and Forrest moved right to cut them off, flashlights clicking on.

"Okay, okay," the woman said, stopping. "What about? We're just here visiting my mom, but we're from out of town so if you're looking for directions . . ."

"It's nothing like that," Helena said.

She and Forrest kept closing the gap. Five yards now . . . Four. . . . The people stayed put, glaring at the agents. They still looked as human as Forrest and Helena. "I thought that old lady was crazy," Forrest whispered to his partner. "Guess I was right."

At two yards, the people still stood there wearing vaguely impatient expressions. Forrest began to relax, that tingling in his fingertips fading away. These were people, that's all—they somewhat fit the description the old woman had given them, but how hard was it to find a bearded guy accompanied by a woman? He wanted to find out what they were doing here at this hour, but he didn't expect either of them to leap to the top of the twelve-foot wall. All that was left now was to play the UV lights over them and see if they burned.

At five feet away, he was bringing the light up to train its beam on the guy's face when the woman lunged.

Only *woman* was no longer an operative term.

She had dropped her human disguise, and came at him with claws out and fangs gnashing and a terrible tongue lolling from her open maw.

He swung the light toward her, but too late. She was already on him, slapping it out of his hand and grabbing his coat with her other hand, tugging him close to her. Forrest let out a yelp, hoping Helena could interfere, but the male of the pair had already charged her. Forrest punched the female with both hands, trying unsuccessfully to knock her off or at least get some leverage so he could pry her loose or throw her. She barreled him down on the cold pavement, one of her clawed hands holding his head back, exposing his throat, while the other pressed down on his right arm. Her strength and body weight did the rest, keeping him so contained that he couldn't buck her off, couldn't reach the gun at his hip. The TRU-UV flashlight had rolled out of reach.

She smelled like a mass grave Forrest had seen early

in his law enforcement career—eight teenage girls buried in a farmer's field in Wisconsin over a three-month period, the most recent only a week before they had found it and dug it up. There had been a special area marked off for cops to puke in, so they didn't contaminate the crime scene, and Forrest had spent plenty of time there. He felt like doing it again now, with the memory burning in his mind and the stink of the vampire tearing at his nostrils.

He could hear Helena fighting against her attacker, the bursts of ragged breath as she struggled, but he couldn't turn his head to see how she was doing. Then he felt fangs ripping at his throat, and suction, like someone giving him the hickey of a lifetime. He writhed and kicked, but to no effect. With each passing instant he grew both weaker and colder, and he knew that his job's greatest occupational hazard had finally caught up to him.

When they were done, Heather wiped her mouth and chin with her hands. "Not bad," she said. "I've had better, but there's still something precious about an unexpected snack."

Griff was just regaining his feet, pushing off the female agent's prone form. "Yeah," he said. "But we should get these bodies out of here. Don't want to tip anybody off."

"We can stick 'em in the back of your truck and dump them in a field somewhere," Heather suggested.

"I wonder if the operation is already blown. These were federal agents. Were they here looking for us?"

"You think they were looking for vampires? Or just here because we were spotted checking the place out?"

"I don't know," Heather said. "We'll have to put it to a vote by the group."

"Makes sense." Griff licked his lips. "Never eaten a fed before. She was tasty."

"I'm sure she was. But they threw our schedule off, and we have a lot of ground to cover. Let's get to it."

Griff stretched, working his broad shoulders, then squatted down to pick up the woman he'd drained.

So much planning, and now so easy for it all to go straight to hell. Dammit.

13

IS THIS HOW *a marriage shatters?* Stella wondered. *Not with a bang* or *a whimper, but with abandonment? Disappearance?*

Eben didn't answer his cell phone, and she couldn't find anyone who knew where he had gone. Not that she tried too hard—he was the one who had left, so he was the one who should be calling.

Eben had never been an emotional guy. A lot of women seemed to want a man who wore his heart on his sleeve, as the saying went, but Stella had been drawn to him precisely because he didn't. It wasn't that he didn't feel anything, it was more a matter of being able to control what he put on display. She thought that control came from strength, from a deep reservoir of self-confidence. He was a man who was comfortable enough with himself to hold some of himself back.

Since coming back from Norway, though, he had changed.

When he managed to sleep, nightmares haunted him, leaving him shuddering and whimpering. Sometimes she caught him crying silently when he thought she wouldn't see. He flew into unexpected rages. She had disagreed with him about a very fundamental issue, but they had disagreed before. The difference was that now he let those disagreements become personal, in a way he never had before.

For her part, she believed she had given up a lot to keep the peace. He had wanted to get away from Barrow. Fine. She loved it there, more than anyplace else on Earth, but she agreed for his sake. She suggested maybe Los Angeles, fully expecting him to veto that idea, but he hadn't. Leaving Barrow had been heartbreaking, especially once she realized that Eben intended for their departure to be permanent. "We'll visit," he said. "Sometimes." She practically had to tear herself away from watching over all the people she had known for so long.

But Eben wanted it, so she went along.

In Los Angeles, the arguments got worse, more heated, and his disappearances became more frequent. He was worried that vampires would go from predator to scourge, and he wouldn't be able to stop it—as if it was his responsibility to save the world in the first place. That was why he had become a cop, though—to protect the innocent—and he just took that impulse to a larger scale now.

At the same time, Stella's focus narrowed. The baby had become the most important thing to her. She had once met a vampire baby named Michael, and responded to him in an unexpectedly maternal way. That had certainly been a surprise. But when little Dane's human mother died, Dane became *hers*, for all intents and purposes, and that ol' mommy mojo really kicked into high gear.

She was an accomplished woman who had helped sheriff a remote Alaska town, fought vampires, gone nationwide with a book about them, then in one of life's little hardy-har-har ironic twists had become a vampire herself. And now there was nothing she liked more than watching the baby grab his toes or coo and smile when he saw her. She loved the way he smelled, even at his least fragrant. She loved bathing him. She didn't even mind changing diapers or getting up at all hours to feed him his particular favorite mixture of milk and blood.

He was a joy. He was also a symbol, the living incarnation of what she and his namesake, Dane, believed could be achieved if vampires and humans would stop killing each other long enough to talk and think, a far cry from how she used to be. Who knew—maybe they were all just being naïve.

She didn't love him as a symbol, though, but as a flesh-and-blood child. Emphasis on the *blood,* given his parentage.

He had been asleep, and should have stayed that way for several hours, but the phone had awakened him. She hated to answer the phone in this strange place, but she also felt that as a safe house it had to be somewhat secure. She hoped it was Eben, but also thought it could be Ferrando Merrin calling back—he had called a few days before, looking for Dane, and she'd had to break the awful news to him.

But this time . . . a wrong number.

She was immediately suspicious . . . then again maybe it was nothing . . . but by the time she hung up, she heard Dane squealing in the crib. She got him out to feed him. He seemed to know his normal sleep routine had been interrupted, and he needed to get back to it. He was already starting to get cranky, fussing, and she couldn't seem to calm him down.

She picked him up and held him close, a small, round ball. "Dane, baby, it's okay, it's time to get some more sleep. Some more sweet dreams. Later on you'll be glad you did, okay, sweetie?"

He just gurgled and sniffed.

She kissed him on the cheeks, kissed him on the forehead, kissed him on the nose, and put him down in the crib. Tucked his softest blanket around him. It was white, with pictures of Disney babies on it—baby Thumper and Bambi, baby Tigger and Pooh, baby Mickey and Minnie and Donald. The nursery smelled like talcum powder and that sweet, indefinable baby scent. Dane squirmed a little, but his eyes were already drooping, closing.

"Good night, dear Dane," she whispered. She turned off the overhead light but left the door open. There was a baby monitor in the room and she kept the receiver clipped to her belt when he was there alone, but she always feared it would malfunction at a crucial moment, so wanted to be able to hear him with her own ears.

She could use some rest, too. A drink, and then a nap. She wished Eben was there to sleep beside, and a wave of sorrow washed over her, slumping her shoulders. She started for the kitchen.

The front door—triple-locked, knob, dead bolt, and security chain—blew off its hinges with a crash, pivoted on one corner, and slammed to the floor.

Stella caught a glimpse of a beefy man in riot gear holding a small steel battering ram. He stepped aside and others swarmed in past him, carrying guns and lights. Stella shrieked in surprise, not fear. The racket of automatic gunfire shattering the living room's big window—and everything behind it, *thock*ing into the stucco walls—cut off her scream. Now little Dane was sounding off, that piercing terrified baby wailing, and booted men thundered in and powerful UV lights scorched her flesh, and she was paralyzed in the middle of all the commotion and noise and dust.

The baby! She grabbed at one of the men, caught the strap of his helmet, and threw him to the floor. A burst of automatic gunfire zipped past her, one of the slugs burning her side. She kept going, tumbling another man aside, but then there were hands on her, dozens of them, it seemed, gun barrels mashed up against her skull, UV lights blazing in through the shattered window and more of them, handheld, all around her.

"That's far enough, lady," one said.

"But . . ." She stopped, as if maybe they wouldn't

notice the baby's keening behind the partially open door.

"Get the kid," someone said.

"No!" Stella shrieked.

"I've got him!" A couple of the armored men shoved past her, through the nursery door, knocking it wide.

"Leave him alone!" she screeched, struggling to break free from the combined grasp of many hands.

The first man to the crib scooped Dane up. "Got him," he called. The man held Dane against his chest, head up.

Near his neck.

It must have been instinct. Stella had certainly never seen the baby do anything like it before. He had tried to suckle at her breasts, of course, before he learned there was nothing there for him, and waited for a bottle. But when the armored man held the tiny infant close to his neck, Dane's head jerked forward, mouth opening. Teeth Stella had thought were still well below his gums must have broken through, because suddenly the man screamed and yanked Dane away from his neck, and blood spurted from the wounds there. Dane's mouth and cheeks and chin were dripping with blood, and the baby was smiling.

Another man rushed forward and roughly grabbed the baby from the first one's hands, as the injured man dropped to his knees and clapped a hand over his neck. Blood squirted between his fingers.

"Give him to me!" Stella pleaded. Once again, she

tried to go to Dane, but gun barrels and strong hands held her back. The man holding Dane looked like he might just hand her son over anyway—he held Dane at arm's length, like the baby was a bomb that could go off at any second.

Instead, though, he spun around and quickly headed away from Stella, back into the nursery. "No!" Stella cried. She did break away then, shoving aside the weapons, twisting free of the groping hands, and she got into the nursery just in time to see the man grab its frilly yellow curtains with his left hand and yank them from the wall, rod and all.

Bright light flooded through the window, as white as the purest sunlight, and the man held Dane up to it.

And Dane screamed and wailed and kicked and squirmed and burst into flames.

The world went black.

Stella could smell roasting flesh and hair, could hear the voices of the men who had invaded her safe place, could see them moving about like malevolent shadows, could see the fiery ball that had been her precious baby Dane, watched as the man dropped it, shaking his hands to cool them, and Dane rolled on the floor, still shrieking, still flaming; her senses all worked, but everything seemed to come from the other side of a dark curtain, some shade of black mixed with red, and only the flames were bright, the crisp crackle and snap of them sharp in her ears.

Stella went insane.

She whirled around on the men behind her, the ones who had poked and jabbed her with their guns, who had prevented her from reaching her baby, using her fear for her own unlife to keep her from saving a child utterly unique on this earth. She grabbed a gun barrel even as it spat flame, the barrel scorchingly hot against her hand, the bullets searing as they stitched up her chest and shoulder. She yanked forward on it and the gunman took an inadvertent step toward her. She twisted the weapon from his hands and kept it moving, swinging around, until its butt drove into his cheek. Bone smashed beneath the gun's stock, the man's left eyeball burst from its socket, pulped bones and brain matter filled his helmet, useless against a blow from beneath it. He fell.

She felt the impact of more bullets, but only distantly. She could no longer hear the gunfire over her own agonized wails. She spun the weapon around and squeezed the trigger, firing without carefully aiming but making sure the bullets went where the armor wasn't, into unprotected faces and necks, into the gaps between thigh and groin armor, into hands. Men shrieked and fell, fired back, ran for their lives. She kept shooting until the hammer fell on an empty chamber, magazine empty, and she dropped that weapon and picked up another one that a dead man had dropped. She fired that one until it was empty too, then picked up another and repeated the process. Acrid smoke blunted the stink of blood and death.

By now nothing lived in Dane's apartment. Stella remained on her feet, ambulatory, sentient, but hardly alive. The men who had invaded her peace were either dead or fled. The walls were dust—she could see into the next-door neighbor's place, and for all she knew, the woman who lived there alone with four cats was dead too. She didn't care.

Another thought wormed its way to the surface of Stella's consciousness.

Those men would have had reinforcements. Someone outside had fired through the windows, beamed the UV lights in. An assault this well planned would have contingency plans, too. More of them would be on the way.

Stella had seconds, not minutes, to come up with a plan.

She and Eben had always kept bags packed with whatever they would need to make a quick getaway. A change of clothes, some cash, some toiletries, fake ID and credit cards, a quart of blood in shatterproof plastic. There was a third bag, for baby Dane, behind the couch in the living room. She left Dane's and Eben's and snatched up her own, looped it over her left shoulder, strap cutting between her breasts. She grabbed another gun. Time to go.

On the way out the door, she saw one of the men writhing on the ground, not dead after all. She raised the muzzle of the gun at him, then stopped herself. This one might be more useful alive.

At least, for the next few minutes.

He tried to scrabble away from her, but his hands slipped on the blood-slick floor and she grabbed the back of his collar, hoisting him easily in one hand. Out the front of the apartment, she knew, more men with guns and lights and murderous intent waited. There were no doors out the back of Dane's place. But the neighbor's apartment had a door that opened onto a little concrete-floored patio and barbecue area in back, separated from an alley by an eight-foot adobe wall. Chances were, the agents were back there too, but maybe not, because they wouldn't expect her to be able to walk through walls.

In that case, they shouldn't have shot the shit out of this one.

Hauling her prisoner, she kicked down what was left of the wall separating the two apartments. Two cats scattered, meowing angrily. As Stella had expected, the neighbor woman was sprawled on the floor with blood running from holes in her right temple, cheek, and chest.

The injured guy in Stella's grip started to protest but Stella shook him, hard, then lowered him so he hung suspended over the old woman's lifeless, wrinkled face. "You want to end up like that?" Stella asked. He quieted again. Stella continued through the apartment, shooing away a white-and-black tabby trying to circle around her feet. At the back door, she paused, looked outside. No uniforms, no lights. She opened the door, shifted her grip on her captive so her arm wrapped around his throat—the better to snap his neck if she needed to—and stepped outside.

She had a minute, she figured, at the most. Two if she was really lucky, but so far this hadn't been her lucky day.

She hoped the poor bastard under her arm could talk fast, because she had a hell of a lot of questions.

14

MAYBE STELLA had finally snapped.

She was running through the dirt roads of Barrow, the ground frozen solid, the sky as black as her soul, the smells of the unburied dead stalking her like a herd of wolves after a weakened elk. There were vampires around every corner, peering out through every window. She had lost track of Eben, her gun was out of bullets, and it would be weeks before the sun came up.

She was running through a forest without trails. The canopy overhead blocked most of the sunlight; only veils of it trickled down, brushing her face like moss as she raced by. Birds darted out of her path, snakes reared back, unseen creatures rustled the underbrush. But crashing through the trees behind her came something huge, something powerful beyond all reason or measure.

She was running on a cold, windy beach, the waves snatching at her ankles, bare feet pounding the sand with every step. Gulls wheeled overhead, squawking disapproval. But the sea was icy and viscous, and when wavelets lapped at her legs they grabbed at her, holding on until she kicked free of them. Some force in the water, of the water, wanted her, and the sea, eternal and patient, would keep trying until it had her.

She was running . . .

she

was

running

through the streets of Los Angeles on a night in late winter when a wind whipped between the canyons of steel and glass brushing pavement with bits of newspaper and food wrappers and plastic from the ends of cigarette packs and the worn shoes of homeless people scraped the streets raw while their shopping carts rattled on sidewalks invisible to the blind people, the straight people, those in suits and skirts and leather coats with collars turned up against the wind, ears inured to the sirens and the wails of the lost, eyes blind to the broken and pathetic souls with their withered hands and newspaper-stuffed shoes and unshaven faces and broomstraw hair and

Stella ran through them without being noticed, her strength propelling her faster than they could have imagined, her grief adding to her speed and agility. She crossed streets without looking, dodging BMWs and Jags, Escalades and VWs, sidestepping pedestrians and lampposts.

She ran from the agents of Operation Red-Blooded, who had been moving into the alley and the apartment at the same time she was leaving it, and she ran from the sound of baby Dane's dying screams, and she ran from the ghosts of Dane and Gus Lambert and William Ikos and Taylor and Judith Ali and everyone else who had died since this had all begun, everyone she hadn't been able to help, including Eben and Stella Olemaun, who of all people she should have saved but didn't.

She ran up Crenshaw and down Olympic, she cut west on Eighth and north on Windsor and east on Wilshire, trying to lose herself in the crowds, and outside the Wiltern she barreled through a pack of punks, knocking one down, and someone flicked a lit cigarette at her but she just kept running.

At first they had shot at her and she'd felt bolts of searing pain as their bullets struck and their lights burned, but she had left their range quickly. Sirens squealed and tires screeched as they tried to give chase, but she ran through apartment complexes and vaulted fences and cut across lawns and before long they were hopelessly behind her, but she just kept running.

She had no destination, no one to run to, no Eben and no little Dane, Barrow was out of reach and so was sanity.

She just kept running.

15

WHEN ANDY GRAY had named his base of operations in the Barrow house the War Room, it had been kind of a joke. He hadn't envisioned anything like a real war in those days. Intelligence gathering, sure. The same basic thing he had done for the FBI—learn what you can about the suspect, work sources, dig for the dirt.

What he had found himself immersed in, however, felt more like a true war every day. He had never anticipated that he would be at the center of things.

He didn't dream that the War Room would be a control hub for a worldwide network of operatives—if that wasn't too grand a word for his people, some of whom were in their teens, or in their eighties, and whose contribution was an occasional blog post about reported vampire activity. He was working up a new post for that network when his young associate spoke up.

"Dude, you got an e-mail," Marcus Kitka said.

"From who?"

"Cylon_Warrior3." Marcus snickered. "That's Bradley, right?"

Andy nodded. The man only identified himself as Cylon_Warrior3, but Andy had researched him, as he did all his contacts, and found that his name was Bradley Bird. He lived with his sister in Green Bay, Wisconsin, sorted mail at his local post office for a living, and when he wasn't working, he watched TV or surfed the net or wrote his blog, which was primarily about what he watched on TV. His sister, Rose, had a clerical job at the U of Wis. Neither had ever been married or had a serious relationship, as far as Andy could tell.

Mostly, when he watched TV, it was science fiction, fantasy, or horror shows, or documentary programming about those topics. He had enduring fascinations with space travel, real-life occult experiences, haunted houses, and, of course, vampires. Which was what had brought him to Andy's attention.

"What's old Bradley got to say?" Andy asked.

"Usual kinda thing. I'll put it on your screen."

Andy waited until it appeared there. Marcus knew more about computers than most people did about anything at all. A moment later, the message showed up. "Chief. Something you should know about. Three bodies have turned up in northern Wis in the past two weeks, on Chequamegon National Forest land. The authorities aren't saying much, but the way they're describing the crimes makes me think maybe they were drained. You think we're looking at another Barrow 2001 in the making?"

"You're right," Andy said. "Bradley has a tendency to overdramatize things."

"You don't think the Chequawhateverthefuck National Forest has to worry about an impending vampire invasion?"

"I'm pretty sure it doesn't."

Andy didn't want to dampen the enthusiasm of a guy who had so little in life about which to be enthusiastic. Bradley had provided a link to an article in a local newspaper, so Andy clicked through, scanned it. Nothing about the piece suggested bloodsuckers to him. He composed a brief reply in his head, telling Bradley—sorry, Cylon_Warrior3—to keep his eyes open and report any new developments. As he started to type it, though, his cell phone rang—the one phone that he always answered, no matter what. He swiveled away from the keyboard, flipped open the phone.

"Gray."

"Andy, it's . . . it's me." Stella? She sounded like she was crying, frantic.

"Stella? What is it?"

"They fucking killed Dane, Andy."

"Yeah, in Norway, I know."

"No, the baby . . . little Dane . . . the motherfuckers *fried him*!"

"The baby?" Andy hoped he had misheard, because any other explanation was too horrible to comprehend. Marcus was looking at him, curiosity burning on his face, and Andy swiveled away. He didn't want an audience at that moment.

"Yes, dammit, the baby."

God. And she had been there? If anything could be worse . . . "Stella, I . . ."

"Listen, Andy. You're the guy who knows everything, right? Here's what I need *right now*. I need to know if you have—or if you don't have it, get it—the location of Operation Red-Blooded. Because that's who fucking did it. I need to know where their headquarters is, who their top dogs are, because I'm going in there and tearing it all down. Top to bottom. When I get done with them, they'll have to sweep the ashes up with a broom and dustpan."

"Whoa, whoa, whoa. Stella. Hang on a second. I don't know if you understand what you're taking on."

"I understand just fucking fine who they are, Andy. A bunch of government goons. So old-fashioned they didn't even have any women in the hit squad that came to the apartment. Your tribe, right?"

"Some of their agents came from the Bureau, yeah." Andy didn't have any love for Dan Bradstreet, the Bureau drone he was damn certain was part of Red-Blooded. He had shot Bradstreet in the hand once, and should have just bought himself some peace of mind and aimed for the heart or head.

"Then what's the problem? You still have enough connections to find out what rock they're under."

Not really. He didn't know, offhand, but he could find out. That wasn't the issue. The thing was, from what he understood about Operation Red-Blooded, while he disagreed with some of their tactics, he was in fundamental agreement with their overall mission. They wanted to eliminate the threat of vampires, once and for all. Much to his own surprise and frustration, Andy had become friendly with some vampires, but even so he wanted the same thing Red-Blooded did. He wanted to expose them, to shine the light of day on the bloodsuckers, then sit back and watch as they were destroyed one by one by one.

He had always suspected that he'd have to betray some of his so-called friends one of these days.

People could never *ever* be safe as long as vampires remained, and any of the ones he met who thought they could were completely delusional. Not that life guaranteed safety anyway—but the threat of vampires was one that most people didn't factor into their plans. As he had learned, the hard way, that was a dangerous oversight. He agreed in principle with Dane's philosophy, that the two species could somehow peaceably coexist—but only in the same way he agreed in principle that rattlesnakes should be kept from extinction. In practice, if one got into his house, he would kill it without hesitation.

"Andy?"

"I'm still here."

"I thought I'd lost you."

He couldn't stall her any longer. At least, not on the phone. "I think I can get that for you, Stella, but it might take some time."

"Don't you keep me waiting, Andy. I want blood."

"Yeah, I can tell."

"Don't fucking waste my time, Andy. I mean it."

He had traveled cross-country with her, early in their acquaintanceship, and had been frightened most of the time. But never more than he was right now, even though she was thousands of miles away. "I'll get back to you as soon as I have something, Stella."

"You do that. And Andy?"

"Yeah?"

"If you ever hear from Eben, tell him to call me."

16

THE FIELDS around Ulysses, Kansas, were covered in snow that had fallen a week ago. It had turned black along the sides of the roads where the snowplows had curled it off the pavement. Stiff grass and brush poked up through it in spots, but for the most part it was as flat as the fields themselves, not quite white anymore, but taking on a gray cast under cloudy gray skies. Snow reflected the nearly full moon with a silvery glow, fooling the eye into thinking the night was brighter than it really was, but color had vanished from the landscape and a sameness fell over everything except impenetrable shadows.

Heather's farm was six miles from Ulysses's small downtown. Beyond her farmhouse, a barn and a grain silo, snow-frosted fields stretched back to a thin line of trees in the distance. The house's windows were shuttered against winter winds, and no lights could be seen from the road. A gate across the driveway was closed. Except for the several cars and trucks parked haphazardly around the house, no one passing by— not that anyone would have reason to pass by on such a bitterly cold night—would have guessed that more than a dozen people had gathered inside to plot revolution.

Well, not revolution, exactly. And not people either.

But that was how they saw themselves. A secret band of resistance fighters. Revolutionaries about to make war on the Man. Fourteen holy warriors ready to be martyred for their cause.

The cadre of revolutionaries was boisterous, arguing and laughing and drinking from the mugs of blood she had set out on the oak dining room table.

"Can we get this meeting started?" she asked. They were in her house, after all, and although the others had never formalized it in any way she had always considered herself the group's leader. Maybe trying to make something like that official was asking too much—it was hard enough for humans, and if anything vampires tended more toward self-determination and individualism than humans did. "We have a lot of ground to cover tonight."

The others settled into their seats in her cozy living room, some on a low-slung couch with huge cushions, others on ladder-back dining room chairs, on the floor (one carpet overlaying another, providing some additional softness there). Charles Raney took one of the chairs. Heather thought it was a diplomatic move—not depriving someone else of a comfortable seat, but keeping himself visible to the others since they would want to check him out.

"That we sure do," Bill Wilson remarked. He was skinny and looked like he'd been turned in his early seventies. He had thick black tufts of hair sticking out from ears Dumbo would have envied, and a nose the size of a Cadillac. Heather didn't think she'd ever seen such a frail-looking *nosferatu*. On the other hand, she had seen Bill tear through two state troopers once, when they'd been caught with a kill out on a quiet country lane, and he had dispatched them like a vampire half his age. Or a third. So you couldn't always judge on looks.

"So let's get to it," Carter Knightsbridge said. He sat on the floor in front of the couch, his back resting against the legs of Millie Kendall, with whom he would no doubt spend a wild weekend or two after their operation succeeded.

"First order of business," Heather said, "is Charles Raney here." Heather had also taken one of the ladder-back chairs, but she looked like she was custom made to fit them, tall and thin and with absolutely erect posture, standing or sitting. Her hair was brown and short, her face lined from sun and hard work in the elements. She cupped a mug of blood in her hands, warmed in her microwave to ninety-nine degrees, the way she liked it. "I've done some checking on him, and he's come through with flying colors."

"What kind of research?" Griff Oliphant asked.

She was proud to have brought a fresh face into their little group, especially one who had checked out so well. "Some friends of mine have vouched for him. Glowingly, in fact. And he and I took a ride up to Holcomb the other night. Some ghastly tourist wanted to see the house Capote wrote about. We were literally standing on a street corner and this fool asked us, 'Where's the death house?' Can you believe it? Well, Charles volunteered to show him. We drove out of town, and he followed, even though it was too dark to have seen anything, and too cold for the idiot to have left his car. After a while, Charles stopped and the man stopped behind us, and when Charles got out the man was squirming, practically orgasmic, saying, 'Is that it? Is that it?' Charles simply opened the man's car door and tore into him. He shared some with me, and I have to say, for an idiot he was downright tasty. I have no doubt of Charles's credentials."

She turned toward Charles, who looked mildly embarrassed by her praise. "Thanks, Heather," he said. He turned his gaze toward the floor. "I appreciate you all letting me be part of this. Maybe it's a small group, but you—we—are sending a big message. We won't be kept behind the curtains, and we won't let an inferior species dictate the terms of our survival."

"Hear, hear," someone said. A few of the others clapped their hands.

"Welcome to the group," said Carter.

"Thanks," Charles said. "I'll try to learn everybody's name, too—just don't test me tonight."

"No problem," Carter said.

"I think we're all on the same page," Heather said. "Charles has been to Norway, to Enok's." For Charles's benefit, she pointed toward Deeanna Leigh. "Deeanna there was in Norway last year."

Deeanna grinned. Heather had noticed she craved the spotlight, which bothered her a little, but Deeanna was also the only other one in the group who had met Enok, so she was entitled to share her story. "I was devastated about the news from there," she said. "I had a great time, and I think Enok and I had a real connection. But even though he's gone, his ideas aren't. Great philosophy lasts through the ages—Enok was as great a philosopher as Plato or Socrates or any of those guys."

"Exactly," Heather said. "There are just a handful of us here, but all around the world there are other groups like ours, determined to put Enok's goals into action."

"Speaking of action," Bill said, "why don't we just get to it? I'm tired of talking."

"We all are, Bill," Heather said. "We're getting close."

"I can hardly wait to get started," Charles said. She had filled him in on the plan on their way back from Holcomb.

"Same goes for all of us," Carter added. Carter could almost taste the blood.

"The trucks are gassed up and ready," Heather said. "There's just one thing—when Griff and I were there the other night we were challenged by a couple of federal agents. We know someone saw us once when we were casing the place—that's what they call it, right? Casing? Anyway, we drained them and dumped their bodies, but what we don't know is if they were staking out Daffodil House because they know we're interested in it, or if they only thought they were preventing a robbery or something. They had FBI badges, but inside their Hummer they had ID from just about every federal agency except the FDA."

"Sounds like Operation Red-Blooded to me," Charles said.

Heather turned toward him. "Like *what*?"

"It's a government agency investigating vampires," Charles replied. "That's what I've been told, anyway. I'm not sure if it's real or imaginary, just a paranoid fantasy. But from the rumors I've heard, that's how they work."

"Well, I don't know anything about that." Dammit. She wished Charles had told her about it earlier—although it wouldn't necessarily have come up in conversation. She didn't like to be caught unaware of something that potentially important in front of the group. "But we've known from the start that this could be a dangerous operation. Revolution always is. The question before us, then, is do we go ahead, or not?"

"I say we do," Griff said. "They may have been feds but they were easy to take out. If there are more of 'em, it'll just help make up for all the wrinkly old necks we'll be munchin' on."

"I think it's an exciting new twist," Millie Kendall said. "Not that it wasn't going to be fun anyway, but this could make it more so."

"We're not doing it because it's *fun*," Bill said. "We're doing it because it's important."

"All right," Heather said loudly. Sometimes she wished for a gavel and a podium. "Is there anyone who wants to back out because of what I've just told you? Now's the time."

For perhaps the first time since they had gathered that evening, the group went absolutely silent.

"Nobody?" Heather asked, feeling a flush of pride.

"Looks like we're all in," Carter said.

"Excellent. Then we should get moving, because we need to spend tomorrow in Liberal in order to make Woodward on time tomorrow night."

A cell phone rang, and conversation ceased. Charles pawed at the pockets of his coat. "It's me," he said. "Sorry, I forgot to shut it off." He found the phone, took it out, and glanced at the screen. "Oh, geez, I gotta take this," he said. His face showed utter chagrin. "I'll take it outside."

He got up from his chair and hurried toward the door. When he was gone, the room erupted in conversation.

"What the hell, Heather?" Millie asked. "He knows the rules, right?"

"He was told," Heather said. "I think he's just a little nervous tonight, and forgot."

"Nervous because he's new? Or because he's some kind of spy?" Griff asked.

"I told you, he checked out," Heather said. She didn't like her judgment questioned by anyone.

"So you said. But come on," Carter said. "We don't know who he's talking to out there. He could be telling someone where we are."

Millie leaned forward, letting her pendulous breasts brush the back of Carter's head. Heather guessed she knew exactly what she was doing to him. "Carter's right," she said. "Someone should keep an eye on him while he's out there."

Griff started to rise, shoulders tensed, but before he even reached the door, Charles returned. "Sorry," he said again. "Family emergency."

What?! "I hope everything is all right," Heather said, attempting to maintain her composure.

"Not really, no. I know it sucks, because you guys have just accepted me into your group . . . but I'm afraid I'm going to have to bow out of tonight's event."

"No way," Griff said. He was already on his feet, so he took a couple of steps toward Charles, his hands balling into fists. "No fucking way. No one walks out at this stage."

"What, you think you can keep me here if I want to leave?" Charles asked him. His tone was a challenge.

Carter rose, pushing off Millie's legs, to back Griff.

Deeanna moved between Charles and the door. Even Heather, worried that this might affect her authority, put down her mug of blood and glared at Charles.

"You agreed that you were in this with us, Charles," she reminded him. "It's only two nights . . . and then you can attend to this . . . emergency."

"But if you cross us, you won't be any good at all to your *family*," Griff said. "Your choice, pal."

Charles took a step back, but he was surrounded.

Heather could hardly believe he thought he would be taken in, allowed to know the plan, and then back out at the last second. And that phone call—most *nosferatu* left the whole concept of family behind, or else expanded it to include their undead brothers and sisters.

All at once, Charles changed, like he had ripped off a mask. His face had been repentant, uncertain, but now he looked like he knew exactly what he was about. He scowled at those around him. Heather couldn't help thinking he looked like he almost felt sorry for them.

"Well, I guess it was bound to happen," Charles finally said. "Because I couldn't live with myself if I let you pathetic weaklings attack a bunch of senior citizens and cripples. Do you even *get* how worthless that makes you sound? You think the world will drop to their knees when they hear about it? Bullshit—they'd bust their guts laughing at you."

"Nobody laughs at us!" Bill shouted.

"Really. You joined up with the wrong crowd if you don't want to be laughed at, Grandpa," Charles shot back. "Or if you wanted to see another sunset."

Griff lunged for him then, but Charles was faster.

He caught Griff's outstretched wrist in his left hand and slammed upward with his right, snapping Griff's elbow. Griff let out a squeal of pain, but Charles wasn't done. He tugged Griff forward and slashed out with his right hand, catching Griff's cheek and pulling. His claws dug beneath the skin. Griff's head turned under the assault, the flesh of his face tearing with a sound like wet paper. Griff screamed and fell back into a couple of the other vampires. The smell of blood was suddenly thick in the room.

Carter and Bill and Deeanna all charged Charles at once. But the vampire was like a whirlwind, here one second and over there the next, moving with a speed that Heather had never seen before. He was strong, too—unbelievably strong even for a vampire. One of his fists hit Carter's chin and lifted Carter off his feet, sailing him backward onto Millie's lap.

Heather saw Bill drop under Charles's assault.

She saw Deeanna's head torn from her shoulders.

She saw Charles slaughtering one after another of her friends.

Then Millie shoved Carter off her lap, back into Charles's field of view. "Kill him, Carter," she said.

Carter never had a chance. Charles's fist broke skin, smashed bone, and continued through to his brain—like a freight train, it was just that hard. He then plowed through the wreckage that had been Carter and stove in Millie's skull with both fists as the woman's screams were abruptly cut off.

Then he turned on Heather, and Heather knew that she had made a very, very big mistake in recruiting Charles Raney.

When they were all down, all destroyed, and he was covered in blood, his hands skinned and aching, his face tender from a few lucky shots, Eben allowed himself to relax.

That had felt good. Well, the last part, anyway, the part where he got to tell them what he really thought of them, and then got to tear them apart. The part where he had spent two weeks pretending to be Charles Raney, who was such an absolute waste of skin that he would plead to be allowed to join an assemblage of vapid sheep—that part had been hard.

But killing them? Oh, that was easy. That was good. He had done it to a couple of cells since leaving Enok's place in Norway. Perhaps this was becoming a macabre kind of hobby.

It had to be tonight, too, before the nursing home attack. Andy Gray's call had hastened it a little, that was all. Pushed up the schedule.

Of course, Stella wouldn't call herself. He didn't know if it was pride or stubbornness, or what. He should be accustomed to it, after all this time.

She needed him. But in a new twist, apparently she needed someone else to tell him so.

Well, there was nothing keeping him in Kansas now. Nothing at all.

Sometimes they fought, but when the love of his life needed him, there was nothing that would stand in his way.

17

DID IT SAY something about Eben that in an emotional crisis his wife had reached out to him through an intermediary? Or did it say something about her?

"You need to talk to Stella," Andy Gray had said.

"What's up?"

"I'm not Dr. Phil," Andy said. "Talk to her."

He had hung up. Eben knew things had turned to shit inside the farmhouse as soon as his phone rang. But then, he had needed to break things up anyway—the phone was a handy excuse.

Now with all the vampires—the followers of Enok—inside destroyed, Eben took a seat (one of the comfortable ones this time) amidst the carnage and called Stella's cell phone.

"Andy Gray says you're looking for me," he said when she answered. "What's going on?"

"I don't know where you are, Eben, but you need to get back to L.A. Like, now."

"What is it?"

There was a long pause, and Eben heard her trying to catch her breath. "Dane's been killed. . . . They *killed him*!" she suddenly shrieked. Then sobbing overtook her and she ended the call.

Which left him with the same conundrum—who did it say most about that the baby, whom they had essentially adopted (okay, really Stella) had died, and she hadn't wanted to call him directly? And why not? Because she was afraid he'd blame her? Because he *would* blame her? Or because she blamed him for taking off instead of staying in L.A. with them in the first place?

Alive or undead, the world was complicated enough without bringing emotions into it. Yet somehow they couldn't be avoided, even when the other traditional trappings of life had been left behind.

Eben had driven the rest of that night, stopping at a roadside motel in New Mexico, then finished the trip the next night, barely making it to a safe house in L.A.'s Coldwater Canyon by sunrise. The house was owned by a vampire who was one of the founders of a powerful Hollywood talent agency. Although the agent had since moved to a beachfront property in Malibu, he kept it available to the others to use when they needed temporary shelter. It was a comfortable place, rustic but high-end, with furnishings that had probably been handcrafted in Mexico by workers who were paid pennies, then sold in Laguna Beach for thousands of dollars. Live oaks shaded the sprawling single-story house, and the air smelled more like a forest than the middle of the city.

He stayed put that day, talking to Stella only briefly by phone to let her know where he was. The sun had dropped an hour before, so he expected her to show up at any time.

Finally he heard the crunch of tires on the gravel driveway. He looked out the front door and saw Stella getting out of an old Mercury Cougar he had never seen before. She had a habit of swapping out wheels almost as often as she did homes, except up in Barrow. One more survival mechanism.

She looked terrible, even for the undead. Her hair was lank, uncombed, and her eyes sunken, raccooned with deep black circles.

He stepped toward her, uncertain. "Stella."

She kept coming, face flat, not smiling. He put his arms out toward her and she looked at them like they were some kind of trap. Then she let out a sob she must have been holding in since she'd arrived, or longer, and fell against him. He closed his arms around her, breathed in her unique essence, and felt her back heaving under his hands.

Fifteen minutes later, they sat at a huge mesquite dining table. Stella had cried until her tears dried up and her throat burned, and there was a box of tissues on the table between them in case she started again. Despite the ferocity she was capable of, she looked as fragile as a baby bird teetering on the edge of its nest.

"I really wish I had been there," Eben said. "Maybe I could have—"

"You couldn't have done shit," Stella interrupted. "You really think there was anything *to* do? Anything I didn't do? There were too many of them, all at once, and they had those lights, those fucking lights blasting through the windows. That's how they got Dane, one of them held him up and tore down the curtains and . . . and it was the most horrible thing I've ever seen in my life."

Eben knew she had a long list of horrible sights seared in her memory, so that was a strong statement.

"Still, we would have been together. I should have been there for you."

"I hated you because you weren't."

"I was afraid of that."

"But I think I'd have hated you more if you were. If you were there and couldn't stop them—I'm not sure I'd ever have forgiven you for that. Just like . . ." Stella's eyes brimmed over again. She snatched up a tissue, held it to her nose. "Just like I don't think I can ever forgive myself."

"Stella, you did everything you could. You just said—"

"I know what I said! Maybe I did do everything I could, but obviously that wasn't enough, because I'm sitting here and Dane isn't."

"Would it have done any good if they'd destroyed you too? Could you have helped him then?"

She wadded up the tissue and threw it on the table. "See, you always try to apply logic to everything. . . .

Fuck logic, Eben. It's got nothing to do with anything. It never did." She scooted her chair back, fast and hard, cutting a gouge in the hardwood floor. "This isn't something you can fix, Eben. It isn't something that *can* be fixed."

He started to say something but she cut him off again, leaning forward with her hands on the back of her chair. The gleam of madness shone in her eyes.

"It's not just Dane, although that's the main thing. It's *all* of it, Eben. It's the never-ending campaign against you, me. All of us. It's the fact that we couldn't just live in peace and have a family like anyone else. We did the right things, we had jobs and friends and we worked hard, and then we became . . . *freaks of nature*. How is that different from someone catching a chronic disease of some kind? But people with Parkinson's aren't hunted down like dogs. Even people carrying terrible genetic diseases don't get their babies slaughtered in front of them. But us, we haven't had a day's peace since 2001, and I'm so fucking tired of it.

"You weren't there! You don't know what it was like. I killed everyone I could, shot them with their own guns. One I let live long enough to question. He admitted they were from Operation Red-Blooded, so that's how I know who's to blame. Then I snapped his spine and left him there to die, and that brought me so much satisfaction—he was in *agony,* and I was *glad*. By the time I hit the street, people had come out of their houses and apartments, crowds were gathering, those soldiers holding them back, and I could see in their eyes that they were hungry for blood, anxious for it, just hoping against hope that they could see one of their neighbors shot to death. They were human, but they were just as vicious as the most horrible vampire we've ever encountered. Maybe worse than that, because we do it to survive—they don't. They're like . . . hunters who kill beautiful animals and then leave the carcasses on the ground, maybe cutting off horns or antlers for trophies, but not eating the meat, not respecting the beast enough to use it. They didn't want to feed, except their own sick souls, psychically feasting on the deaths of others."

She spun the chair around on one leg, straddled it, arms over the back, without losing a beat. "I've already figured out how I'm going to handle it, though. I'm going to take back my life. Our lives, Eben. There's only one thing that'll make these people pay attention."

"Which people, exactly?"

"*All* of them. Whoever. Operation Red-Blooded has been hunting us, they killed Dane, but they don't exist in a vacuum. If they're killing vampires, it's because the public at large wants us dead, or doesn't want to admit that we ever existed. They're a government organization, and we may not like to admit it, but the government is made up of people. And people hate."

"So what's your idea?"

Stella looked at him and blinked a couple of times, as if she had forgotten there was anyone else in the room. Her eyes clouded over and tears welled in them once more. She let her shoulders sag and buried her face in her hands. He watched her weep soundlessly for a few minutes, wishing things had been different, that they had never fallen into the rabbit hole that had led to this. Small-town law enforcement had seemed like a decent occupation, helpful without being exceptionally dangerous.

It hadn't worked out that way.

Now his wife, who had once been a stable, emotionally balanced person, was swinging back and forth between sorrow and excitability faster than he could keep up with. It was like watching a manic-depressive on fast forward.

She said something from behind her hands. He didn't catch it. "Sorry?"

Lowering her hands, she blinked away tears. "I said 'blood.'"

"You want more blood?"

"No! That's my idea. You asked what my idea was. Blood. The only thing that will make people pay attention is blood. Spilled blood. So that's what they're going to get."

"Whose?"

"Those fuckers at Red-Blooded. At least to start with. They killed Dane. That's all there is to it."

"Do you know how to find them?"

"I'm working on that. And when I do, I'm going to start at the top and work my way through the ranks.

I'm going to annihilate every one of those bastards."

"Not you, Stella."

"What?"

"Not just you, I mean. Not alone."

The decision was one of the easiest he'd ever had to make. No hesitation, no second-guessing. He hadn't been there when they had come for Stella, but he'd be damned if he wasn't there for the rest of it. He'd been away, blending in with Enok's followers, picking them off a few at a time. He still thought it was important work, because they could prompt a war between humanity and the *nosferatu* that would decimate both sides while doing nothing to help either.

Now Stella wanted a war, too.

Hers, though, would be more confined. A limited action, a message sent. Not all-out conflict.

If he stayed with her, worked with her, he could manage it. Make sure she was safe, make sure the whole thing was controlled. Together, maybe . . .

Maybe they'd both even survive it.

"What do you mean?" she asked.

"I mean I'm in. I'm with you."

"What if I don't want you in?"

"Doesn't matter. I'm in anyway. You aren't the only one who's a part of this."

For the first time tonight, Stella smiled. A flash of a smile, anyway, a ghost of one. It didn't last long but it was the first one he'd seen from her in a while, and he liked it. "Thanks."

"No problem. They've been asking for a fight. Now they're going to get one. We'll see how they enjoy it."

Stella was about to answer when her phone went off. She looked at the screen, then answered. "Andy?"

She listened for a few moments. "Okay," she said. "Any more?" Apparently Andy's response was negative. "Thanks," she said, hanging up on him.

"What was that, Stella? What's up?"

"News we can use," Stella said. She didn't elaborate.

Another decision came to Eben, just as suddenly and forcefully as the last one. If they were going to go to war against people who knew what they were, who had the equipment and training to fight their kind, they would need some kind of advantage. Both of them. So far, only Eben had it.

"Stella . . ."

"What?"

"Just hold still."

"What?"

He rose, walked around the table, put his hands on her shoulders and lovingly massaged them. "Trust me."

"That feels good," she said.

"This will feel better."

Eben leaned closer, kissed her cheek, her ear, her neck. Then he pressed down harder with his hands, holding her in place, opened his mouth, and bit into the tender flesh on the side of her neck. He tasted his wife's blood, for the first time since he had made her.

As Dane had once done for him, he did for Stella.

She struggled in his grip at first, writhing and squirming in the chair. Then she relaxed, leaned into him, let him drink from her and share his fluids with hers. The bite was hot, erotic, orgasmic. He felt himself growing hard, slid his hands down to cup her breasts. She moaned and pressed her upper arm against his groin.

This would help her, make her stronger, as it had him.

If they were both going to get through this—and they were going to get through it together—it had to be done.

He pulled his mouth from her neck, sought her lips, her tongue, peeling off her shirt, the air suddenly thick with the smell of blood running down her neck, and he reminded himself that it had to be done, it was the only way. . . .

18

FROM HIS CORNER OFFICE at Seventh and D Streets NE, Dan Bradstreet could see the Capitol, the top of the Washington Monument, and a little of the Mall. More than that, when he left his office he could feel the wheels of power grinding around him. You couldn't walk into a restaurant or bar around there without seeing senators and congressional representatives and the lobbyists trying to feed off them, White House staffers, and the thousands of less famous but still important people who made government work. He felt connected to it all, in a way that he never had back in L.A. There he'd been a Bureau drone and eventually a cog in the gears of Operation Red-Blooded, but still far removed.

Here, he was a player.

Even better, he knew something that only a few dozen of the thousands of people around him did. One of the greatest threats humanity faced. And he knew that action was being taken against it.

His corner office was at the center of that effort, and it and the other offices around it were buzzing with activity these days. Ferrando Merrin may not have provided the useful information Dan had hoped for when they'd captured him a few weeks back, but that wasn't the only avenue being worked, not by a long shot.

Karly, his administrative assistant (he still wanted to say "secretary," but he was admittedly a throwback to a different era) brought in his mail. She wore a sharp black suit with white and red pinstripes. Her hair was black with a few magenta streaks, her figure trim, her face composed and lightly made up. Overall, she was far more stylish than Dan. The one thing she couldn't do was go toe-to-toe with a bloodsucker and come out alive.

"Mail, chief," she said as she set the pile on his desk.

"Thanks, Karly." He watched her leave, then turned his attention to the stack. Most of it would be trash—*recycling,* he reminded himself—but every now and then something genuinely interesting worked its way miraculously through the system and wound up in his hands.

This time, it was the fourth envelope down. A square one, made from good-quality cream-colored paper.

There was no return address, just a stamp with a Los Angeles postmark. His name and the office address were written in a careful hand—a feminine hand, he thought—with purple ink.

It looked like a card, but the holidays were behind them and his birthday wasn't until August. A valentine? Only a couple of weeks until Valentine's Day, but he didn't have a girlfriend, didn't really worry much about dating. Some kind of an invitation?

He slit the envelope, which was lined in shiny purple paper that matched the ink. On the front, the card said, *You are invited . . .*

Okay then. Someone was getting married. Not that he would consider attending. He flipped it open and read the rest. A baby shower, it said. In Los Angeles.

What the hell . . . ?

The inside of the card was handwritten, and not in purple ink. He scratched at the writing and some of it came off on his fingernail. He sniffed it.

The invitation was written in blood.

A trap, then. And he knew damn well who had sent it. The only one who would have the balls to issue such a challenge.

Agents had stormed the apartment Stella Olemaun had been staying in, once Marina's team had located it. The few who made it out alive said Olemaun was there, and confirmed Dan's suspicions that she was now one of *them*. Such a waste. Then there was the baby—a vampire baby of all things!—who had attacked one of the agents. The agent had responded by holding the little freak up to the TRU-UV lights and the kid had gone all Human Torch on him, confirming his suspicion.

They had missed Stella. Or rather, Stella had killed enough of them to enable her own escape.

One agent had been found in the back, in a little patio area. He hadn't been instructed to go there, and from the trail of blood leading from Stella's apartment, through a neighboring one, and out the back, it appeared that Stella had taken him there by force.

By the time they'd found him, he had bled out from his wounds. But the fact that Dan was holding this invitation indicated to him that the agent had talked before he died.

So how the hell did Olemaun gather enough information to know where to send him this little call-out in the first place . . . and who to send it to?

Stella hadn't even tried to disguise the fact that she was inviting him into a trap. Which meant she didn't expect him to fall for it.

She didn't care about a surprise attack—she wanted a battle.

Okay then. Dan smiled. Fine. Whatever came next, at least *that* he could provide.

Dan raced up West Sixth in Los Angeles, his boots echoing off the tall buildings. His Motorola crackled at his collar, as reports from agents scattered around the area flew back and forth.

There had been a sighting at Pershing Square, then contact. Two agents down.

Since then, at least a half dozen other bloodsuckers had been reported, but no contact made.

Now someone at the Bonaventure had called in a

police report because two guests had been assaulted in a stairwell, slashed and left bleeding and dying. Could be a coincidence, but Dan wasn't a great believer in coincidences.

The "baby shower" had been scheduled for tonight, at the Museum of Contemporary Art on Grand. Dan had been pretty sure MOCA wasn't in the habit of hosting those. But he knew the location hadn't been chosen randomly.

Stella wanted to engage Operation Red-Blooded in downtown L.A., and Dan was determined that his response would not disappoint.

He had agents in vans, agents on foot, agents in office buildings and hotels, shops, and restaurants, all in place well before the sun went down. They had been ready for anything that came up—that was the plan, at least. Obviously the two in Pershing Square hadn't been sufficiently prepared.

He heard sirens as he ran. The LAPD had agreed to inform his people of anything that might be of interest, but not to keep out of the way. They insisted they had to check out the attack at the Bonaventure. Dan didn't think they'd find anything they were prepared to deal with. His own people had vehicles around, some screeching toward the hotel now, but he had been close enough not to want to bother getting into one.

When he got there, his people were stringing yellow caution tape in the lobby. LAPD officers and hotel security held back a gathering crowd. He walked up to an agent named Catalano, a deceptively slender young woman with a dozen or so marksmanship medals and four vamp kills on her record. She wore a navy blue windbreaker over her Kevlar vest. FBI was emblazoned across the back in big gold letters. "What's the status?" he asked.

"Building is sealed," she said. "If there are bloodsuckers inside there, they ain't getting out."

Dan let his gaze travel up the building's face, its famous futuristic round towers bulging like fat rolls of shiny silver dollars. "There must be a few hundred guests, too, if not more. Any vamps inside could do a lot of damage before we find them."

"That's true," Catalano said.

"So let's find them in a hurry."

The three vampires had started up the staircase, laughing and slapping one another's backs.

This was a real kick—intentionally attracting attention to themselves, getting people to chase them, taking out the occasional government agent at the same time. They dashed through the Bonaventure's lobby, startling the straights milling around there. One of the old men at the front desk actually shouted "Here! Here, you!" at them as they sprinted by.

Then they heard a door open above, and a young couple started down, chatting casually about a play. When they came into view, the vampires saw that they were expensively dressed, nicely coiffed; they were wealthy visitors here to enjoy some of the Los Angeles high life.

When they spotted the vampires, the woman started to scream. The man played brave for about fifteen seconds before he joined her.

The vampires swarmed them, slicing and tearing, taking deep gulps before continuing up.

They ran upstairs until their shoes stopped tracking blood, then slid down the banisters, past the couple, getting out of the stairwell on the second floor. There they rushed to another staircase, and left the building by the exit door at the bottom.

By the time they hit the sidewalk outside, they already heard the alarm being raised, people shouting, calling for the police. The three vampires high-fived and hurried up Figueroa.

This certainly was turning into a fun night. And there were still hours to go before the dawn.

Dan examined the bodies in the stairwell. They were a young couple, maybe newlyweds judging by the shininess of their platinum wedding rings (hers with a cluster of five huge diamonds, his with one small, understated stone not much more than a chip). Affluent, and very dead. The woman had fallen with her head down the stairs, her biggest wound in her neck; as a result, blood had waterfalled all the way to the next landing and pooled there. It was already starting to get tacky at the edges. Three sets of rusty brown footprints led up away from the bodies. He turned to Catalano. "Get a chopper here, stat."

"You think they went to the roof?" she asked.

"If they did, I want eyes on them. Go round up that chopper."

Catalano hurried away.

A couple of things bothered Dan about this. Witnesses at Pershing Square had reported five vampires, not three. And witnesses in the lobby had insisted that these three were all men. Which meant Stella Olemaun was not among them. He wondered just how many bloodsuckers were out tonight, and when the trap he was waiting for would be sprung.

Agents Washington and Obrician had been told to hold down the corner of Fifth and Grand. The big Central Library at their backs, they gripped their FN SCAR-H assault rifles anxiously. Washington's had a 40mm grenade launcher attached. He had grenades and a TRU-UV light slung on his belt, but he really wanted to see the damage his 7.62x51mm rounds would do to a bloodsucker's head at 550 rounds a minute. The hell with wooden stakes and garlic; this thing would just fucking obliterate the bitches.

"Sounds like the whole city is full of 'em tonight," Obrician said. He was a little guy wearing little round glasses. Jittery. Washington didn't like him. He looked like a geek, like a computer guy. Washington knew how to send e-mail and play Halo 3, but that was about it, tech-wise. He didn't even like cell phones.

What he liked was combat. He'd served a couple of tours in Iraq and Afghanistan. When he got home from the last one, he'd been offered two gigs—Blackwater and Operation Red-Blooded. Blackwater would just send him back to Baghdad, although at a much higher pay scale. But Red-Blooded promised action of a type he had never seen before, against enemies who really were striking inside the U.S. For a poor black kid from Sunflower, Mississippi, to be given weapons like these and entrusted with their use was just about as good as life got.

Obrician, though, was a city guy, from New York or New Jersey or someplace like that. Washington thought his name was Russian. He didn't trust the guy to have his back, that was for sure. He always looked like he was thinking about something. That could only be trouble, by and by.

He was right about one thing, though. The city was crawling with bloodsuckers. The radios kept buzzing with reports. Sirens wailed and helicopters stuttered overhead and official vehicles raced around on streets that had been closed to civilian traffic. They were in a war zone, and it was them against the vamps. Just like he'd been promised.

"Did you hear something?" Obrician asked.

Washington hadn't, but he hadn't been listening, either. He realized he had retreated into his own head.

Thinking, when he should have been paying attention. Always trouble. "No, dawg, I didn't hear nothing."

"Well, listen!"

Washington listened. He heard the rasp of the radio, the sounds of the trucks and helicopters and sirens. "What?"

"I'll check," Obrician said. He sounded pissed. "I thought I heard someone around the corner."

Washington thought maybe he should go with Obrician. They were supposed to stick together, watch out for each other. But if he did that then no one would be able to eyeball Grand Avenue. "Okay," he said. "Be quick."

"Roger that," Obrician said. He was always doing that, trying to talk like a soldier when he had never served a day. He disappeared into the darkness around the corner. Washington tapped his right foot, beat a little rhythm on the SCAR's stock with his fingers. Waited.

Obrician didn't come back. *What's he doing?* Washington wondered. *Having a smoke? Taking a leak?*

Grand was clear. Washington ducked around the corner, looking for his partner. "Obrician? The fuck?"

Nobody there. Washington took another couple of steps down Fifth. Maybe Obrician had taken shelter in a doorway or an alley. Shelter from what, Washington had no idea.

On his third step, his right foot kicked something. He looked down just in time to see Obrician's head rolling toward the curb like a lumpy soccer ball.

"Shit," Washington said. He flipped the SCAR into combat position, but there was no one to shoot at. Obrician's body lay sprawled across the sidewalk, arms out as if reaching for his runaway head.

The head teetered for a moment at the edge of the curb, then tipped forward and dropped.

Washington wondered if he should pick it up. Instead, he decided he should call this in, but not touch anything. Whoever did this (*bloodsuckers, had to be them damn vamps*) might still be around. He needed backup, that was what he needed, and in a powerful hurry.

Then he realized that Obrician's SCAR wasn't on his body. That realization was his last thought; reaching for his radio mike was his last act.

19

THE DOOR that led to the roof of the Bonaventure's south tower was kept locked. KEEP OUT—AUTHORIZED PERSONNEL ONLY was stenciled on it in large red letters. Nobody could go through it by accident.

Mason, a hotel security man in a blue blazer, Oxford shirt, and khakis, kept staring at the door like it might start talking to him.

"There's no way it was left open," he said.

"Someone left it open," Dan pointed out. The door was ajar, after all. The evidence didn't lie.

"Yeah. No, I mean by one of us. We wouldn't go away and leave it like this."

"I got that. But someone opened it anyway." He took a closer look. The door had a deadbolt lock, but the steel deadbolt had been snapped in half. "They didn't use a key, though."

"That's good," Mason said.

"Not the way I look at it." Dan didn't bother to add that anyone who could break that steel bolt scared him a lot more than someone who could steal a key. "I think we need to go up."

"Right," Mason said. "Sure." He started to go through the door, to the steep stairway leading to the roof.

Dan caught his shoulder. "Us," he said. "Not you."

Mason looked surprised by this. Then again, he had spent much of the night looking surprised, at least since Dan had arrived. It was almost like he had never expected vampires to take refuge in his hotel. *Some people,* Dan thought, *just have no vision at all.*

Dan beckoned his Red-Blooded compatriots. Nine of them, all in full assault gear except for Dan himself. Marina Tanaka-Dunn tossed him a quick grin from behind her helmet's shield and led the way. Dan brought up the rear, reminding Mason as he went not to follow them.

He didn't have any idea what vampires would want to go on the rooftops for. Unless he had seriously misread the intelligence, that whole idea that they could turn into bats and fly away was a myth. Falling from these heights would be just as final a step for them as it would be for a human—nobody's brain could stand up to being splashed all over the sidewalk.

The agents spilled from the doorway onto the rooftop. It was remarkably bare—a couple of small vents, a helipad, but nothing someone could hide behind.

"Damn," Marina said. "I was so hoping for a firefight."

"Aren't you always?" Dan answered.

"Sometimes I enjoy more low-tech activities," she said.

Was she flirting again? And at a time like this? Dan couldn't be sure. He looked out at the other high-rise buildings around, the Union Bank Building, the World Trade Center, the Bank of America tower, and others. This was the kind of neighborhood you didn't want to be in when the big quake finally hit, because it was too easy to picture these buildings falling like dominos. Overhead, the blades of law enforcement and press helicopters sliced the air, searchlight arrowing down toward them. The wind was strong up here, the choppers adding to it with their downdrafts.

His radio crackled, and he heard his name. He responded. "We've got two men down," agent Fontana said. "Fifth and Grand. Their weapons are missing, and they've both been"—Fontana's voice caught—"beheaded. Jesus Christ! The bastards cut their heads off!"

Dan felt bad for the men down, but he was more interested in the first part. Their weapons were missing? He thought he could see a brief flash of movement, on the roof of the B of A tower, but it was so far away. "Who's got binocs?" he asked, holding a hand out as if someone would hand them right over.

One of the choppers made a pass overhead, its brilliant beam strafing the Bonaventure's roof, and everything clicked into place. "Get those copters out of here, now!"

Agent Innocente immediately barked the command into his radio. At the same moment, though, a dull thump came from the B of A tower. A flash of light.

Grenade launcher.

The helicopter directly overhead erupted into an enormous ball of flame. The concussive wave knocked most of those on the roof flat. Flaming shards dropped on and around them; steel, glass, burning fuel.

Body parts.

Dan kept his balance until a fiery foot smacked him in the forehead. The foot's shoe, or boot, was nowhere to be seen, but the foot plummeted like a bag of quarters.

As he fell, he heard the thump of another grenade being launched, followed by the roar of another chopper exploding. Fire bloomed like a skyrocket. The burning wreckage of this second one missed the Bonaventure but fell toward the street below, where onlookers were massed, mostly civilians kept out of the relative safety of the building by the barriers he had ordered. He imagined he could hear the screams of those down below, but his ears still rang from the first explosion. He gagged on black oily smoke.

"They're on the roof of B of A!" he screamed, forcing himself to hands and knees. "They've got grenade launchers!"

He couldn't tell if anyone heard him. They were all still scrambling themselves, trying to dodge the wreckage that kept crashing down around them, the fires burning here and there across the roof.

Fires. He was slow tonight, half a step behind where

he should be. "Down, everyone!" he shouted. "Flatten!"

Some, like Marina, obeyed without a second's hesitation. Agent Barwick might not have heard, or might have simply lagged in his response time, but he was still half-standing when automatic weapons fire started peppering the roof. A couple of large-caliber rounds punched into him, making him jerk like a hyperactive puppeteer held his strings. Blood and flesh geysered out behind him.

The fires on the roof were like signal beacons for the bloodsuckers with the guns, while reducing the agents' night vision. This was Stella Olemauns's trap, and it was a damn good one after all.

Dan aimed his automatic rifle toward the top of the Bank of America tower and squeezed the trigger. He wasn't sure where the shots had come from, but he knew the grenades had been launched from there. He also had no way to tell if his rounds were reaching the tower, or if they were crashing through windows on the upper floors, endangering more civilians.

Marina threw herself down beside him and lent her own firepower to his, spraying toward the tower. They belly-crawled up to the edge of the roof, where a low ledge gave them some cover, and kept firing. Rounds whizzed above their heads, and Dan heard another agent cry out as she was hit. He turned just in time to see her arms windmilling at the air. She spun on one heel and tumbled over the side, her scream following her down.

Two had been killed by falling debris from the first chopper, two more by the hail of gunfire. That left five on the roof, scattered, everyone shooting at some rooftop or other now, hoping there were actual targets there. This had turned into a clusterfuck of the hugest possible proportions, and Dan had no one but himself to blame.

Well, himself and Stella Olemaun. *Can't forget her.*

A round grazed agent Innocente's shoulder. He would have been fine, but pain and surprise made him lurch up, and the next one took the top third of his skull off.

Down to four.

Of course there were still dozens of agents, not to mention FBI and LAPD, down below, combing through the hotel and out on the street. By now they'd be closing in on the other buildings. Dan's radio wouldn't stop buzzing but he couldn't make anything out over the roar in his head.

"Dan!" Marina shouted.

"What?"

"We should get off this rooftop!"

Absolutely right. They were being picked off like game in a fenced hunting enclosure.

"Go!" he yelled. The others were looking at him, so he waved them toward the doorway. *"Go down!"*

Lead whistled intermittently through the air above their heads. He and Marina dragged themselves across the roof toward the door. Agents Fitch and Conaway did the same from their positions. Marina reached the door first and was about to scoot down the stairs when something came arcing over her head, landing behind her on the rooftop.

"Grenade!" Dan shouted. That was pure instinct talking—the object was clearly too big to be a grenade. And it didn't explode when it landed, just rolled and came to a stop, faceup.

The face belonging to Mason, the security guard.

"They're downstairs!" Dan called.

"Not for long," Marina said. She clipped a TRU-UV light to her weapon's barrel and flicked it on. Dan did the same.

The four of them made it into the relative safety of the stairwell. Behind them, the clatter of bullets slamming into the roof continued. Before they broke out into the hallway, they all looked to Dan, who silently gestured the details of an assault plan. Marina went first, rolling to the far side of the hallway and covering the lower range, while Dan swept out with his weapon aimed high. Fitch aped Marina facing the other way, and Conaway went back-to-back with Dan.

The hallway was empty. Whoever had tossed Mason's head up had already retreated. Mason's body lay in a spreading pool of blood.

"Looks like we're clear," Dan said. "Stay sharp, though." Twenty doors lined the hallway, and the vamps could have been behind any of them, or they might have gone down the stairs. The elevators had all been shut down and secured.

"Door-to-door?" Marina asked. "Or call it a night?"

"Someone call for backup," Dan said. "Once they get here they can go door-to-door. I think we've had enough action for the moment."

Marina tilted up her face shield. "Is there such a thing?"

Dan was about to yell an answer when the hallway went black.

"Crap!" Dan said. "Power's out!" He keyed his mike. "This is Bradstreet. Is the power out throughout the building, or just here on top? Someone come back to me."

His radio crackled a reply. He couldn't hear it, because Fitch's shrieks drowned it out. Dan spun around, his TRU-UV knifing through the darkness. Its beam caught someone's arm, but then that someone dropped behind Fitch—his head twisted sideways, blood spurting through a gash in his neck—and was gone. Conaway's gun spat a short burst, muzzle-flash almost blinding in the darkness. Then it stopped and crashed to the floor, followed closely by his intestines. Marina's UV flashlight showed Conaway clutching feebly at his own guts, trying to hold them in place as his knees buckled and he dropped facedown into his own mess.

Dan sprayed the hallway with lead. Marina did the same in the other direction. Both had TRU-UV lights carving the blackness, but Dan caught only fleeting glimpses, a face, an arm here, a leg there.

Then they were alone again. The hallway had a different feel to it, abandoned. Fitch and Conaway, both dead, didn't count.

"The stairs!" Dan said. He pushed Marina's shoulder, and she broke into a sprint. He followed. They hit the stairs and kept running, three and four at a time, more when a landing came into view. They didn't stop until they had reached the lobby level, out of breath, panting.

All the way down, one thought kept cycling through Dan's head.

Those faces, upstairs. They looked wrong. Different. Changed, somehow.

But take away the changes, turn on the lights, put them in repose.

Do those things, and he would have sworn, just like he had seen in their surveillance photos, that they looked like Eben and Stella Olemaun.

20

Dan Bradstreet despised spending time at the Nevada facility. It was full of scientists, for one thing, and they seemed to speak in a special code designed to make anyone who wasn't one of them feel like an idiot. They didn't even seem to function on the same plane of reality that he did. Their concerns were strange to him, removed from what he considered the real goals of Operation Red-Blooded. They loved having live subjects to test, for instance, while all he wanted was to kill every bloodsucker he could once they had given him whatever information he could extract. Sometimes he worried that they sympathized with the vamps, just as he'd heard about earlier generations of scientists feeling sorry for the monkeys and dogs and rats they experimented on.

Besides, this place was on Marina's turf, so she always knew when he was going to be there, and usually managed to show up. She had made him increasingly uncomfortable over the past few months, to the point that he wondered if he'd have to find a reason to fire her.

He had come here this time because one of those

scientists, a biologist named Darrel Keating, claimed to have uncovered something new and significant about the so-called "vampire cell." Dan had wanted it put in a report and sent to him, but Clarence Bettesford had insisted that Dan should fly out to Nevada and let the whole life sciences team brief him in person. Against his better judgment, Dan had complied.

Then, as it turned out, Dan had not been able to understand the first thing Keating said—the guy could barely speak in English, it seemed—or Bettesford's explanation. The words had sailed over his head, as if everyone was speaking Latin, and he had eventually tuned them all out, sitting there with a blank expression on his face, nodding occasionally, thinking about baseball statistics so he didn't fall asleep.

After it was all over, he asked Marina into his on-site office. He sat behind the desk, leaving a comfortable visitor's chair for her. She came in ten minutes late, bearing a bottle of wine and two wineglasses.

"Are we having some kind of celebration?" he asked.

"Don't you think we should?"

"That's why I told you to come in here," Dan admitted. "I was hoping you could tell me what all this is about."

"All what?"

Is she being deliberately obtuse? he wondered. *Making me spell it out for her?* Maybe she'd been sleeping with Clarence, and the two of them would have a big laugh later on. "You know I'm good at organization, at finding and killing bloodsuckers. But I suck at science. I was hoping you could kind of translate all that gobbledygook for me."

"In *lay* terms?" she asked.

He ignored the bait. "Yes."

"Okay." She held the bottle between her legs and spirited up an opener from somewhere. She was conservatively dressed, for Marina, in a snug black top and jeans. Squeezing the bottle between strong thighs, she worked out the cork. "If they're right—and I don't think Clarence would have called you out here if he wasn't pretty convinced—then yes, we might have something to celebrate. There are still a lot of tests to run, and it's all theoretical until those are completed, but the raw data is—"

"Remember, English."

"Right." She poured two glasses of wine, pushed one of them toward him across the desk, and sat back down with hers. "In English, if they're right, Keating might have found a kind of . . . vaccination against the gene."

"Like a shot?"

"It could probably be delivered any number of ways. A shot, a mist, a liquid, even a pill. Ideally, it could be sprayed from the air over a population and inoculate an entire population at once."

"So it's a *cure*? Why the hell didn't he say so?"

"Not a cure in the sense that it will reverse the effects in those who already have it. It won't kill a vampire, or turn him back into a human—which would also kill him, since the human he had been is already dead. But it would prevent him from being able to spread the plague. He wouldn't be able to turn anyone from the inoculated population."

Dan picked up his wineglass and took a big drink. "I wish Clarence or Keating had put it in those words."

"Well, you know scientists. They like to hedge their bets. Until they're absolutely certain, they don't want to make any grand pronouncements."

"Sure, but this—"

"This is potentially the best news we could ask for. It would mean this whole facility has finally proven its worth. But the possibility remains that further testing will show some flaw in the data, some mistake Dr. Keating made in his studies."

"Now you sound like one of them, Marina. Hedging your bets."

"You know me, Dan. I'm all for celebration. But I like to know that what I'm celebrating is real."

He finished off his glass, picked up the bottle, and refilled it. He was more of a Bud man, when he drank at all, but this stuff was good. "What do you think the odds are?"

"Like I said, Clarence must have thought it was pretty close to a slam dunk or he would've kept a lid on it. I'd say we have maybe . . . a seventy-five percent chance that it'll really work."

"Wow. That's a bet I'd take."

"Did you understand how it works? How it creates a resistance to the introduction of the vampire cell by cloning existing vampire cells into human antibodies and—"

"I don't care how it works." Dan swallowed some more of the wine. "Only that it works."

"It's still a long-range project," Marina said. "But theoretically we may have found a way where we could inoculate the entire world. Vampires wouldn't die out immediately, but they'd stop replacing themselves. Within a generation or two, if we continued hunting and killing them, they'd completely die out. Done and done."

"That's still a better chance than we've ever had." Dan refilled his glass again and topped off Marina's. He had never been so glad for her company in his life. . . .

By the time they got to the bottom of the bottle, Dan was sitting on the desk, back and shoulders hunched, his legs dangling between Marina's parted knees. He had rolled up his shirtsleeves and loosened his tie. Everything she said was hilarious, and he seemed to have the same effect on her.

And my God, she was *so* sexy.

"It's probably the wine talking," he said, aware of a little slurring. "But you are looking especially gorgeous today, Marina."

"Why, thank you, Dan. You're right, it must be

the wine. I didn't think you had ever noticed the way I look."

"Oh please. How could I not notice it? You're an . . . incredible woman."

She rubbed his lower legs, working her hands up to his knees. "Well, you're a pretty special man, Director of Field Operations Dan Bradstreet."

He leaned forward more, cupping her face between the palms of his hands. "You know, maybe I was wrong about you."

"Wrong in what way?" She continued moving her hands up his legs, his thighs.

"There have been times you've practically thrown yourself at me, and I've always pushed you away. But I was a fool to do that. I can see that now. It isn't just the"—his voice caught as her hand grazed his crotch—"the wine, it's you, Marina."

Her right hand took him firmly now, rubbing. He could feel his erection growing under her ministrations. "We should lock the door," he murmured. "We can use the floor or the desk, I don't care."

She smiled up at him, a pink wedge of tongue flashing over her lips. "I don't think so," she said quietly.

"What?"

She squeezed his erection harder, then released it. "I don't think so."

"You don't think what?"

She scooted her chair back, away from him, and stood up. "You know, Dan, you could be twice the lover in real life that you are in my imagination, and you'd still be miserable. Life's too short for bad sex. And all the wine you've had tonight will no doubt make you even worse than you are naturally. So let's just pretend that you never came on to me, okay? We'll keep it professional from now on, and I won't file harassment charges against you."

"You—charges . . . ?" Dan spluttered. He felt like he'd been poured into the wine bottle, shaken, and dumped onto the floor.

"That's right. Anyway, there's a helicopter waiting to take me to Montana. Seems there's been a report of vampiric activity there, and I know as my boss you'd want me to check it out."

"Marina, you . . . you can't. . . ." He let the sentence trail off. He had never understood what she was up to, but now, through the fog of alcohol, he thought maybe he got it.

He'd been totally, completely had, all along. She had outplayed him at the spy game, maneuvered herself into the position she wanted him in, and then triggered the trap. She probably had audio, maybe even video, of the whole encounter.

"See you, Dan," she said with a grin from the doorway. "This really has been a night full of good news."

The door closed behind her, and she was gone. Dan sat there on his desk, his erection already fading, his wine buzz fading, too. This was all becoming too much. That bitch! He was furious at himself for letting her get the upper hand. Now what was he supposed to do?

At least, he reminded himself, the news from the scientists had been real. Or might be real. He truly hoped they were right, if only so he could salvage some bit of grace from this horrible trip.

"There it is," Eben said. He couldn't keep a trace of awe from his voice, he realized. "It really is here."

"Looks like Andy and Marcus came through after all," Stella said.

"Did you think they wouldn't?"

"I think they're both scared enough of me not to take any chances." She pushed away a creosote branch blocking some of her view. "But I'm glad to see it just the same."

They stood on a desert ridge in northeastern Nevada, forty miles north of Ely. A half-moon hung low and yellow in the sky. A few minutes earlier, as they had been driving to this spot on the ridge, a helicopter had lifted up into the night and darted off toward the northeast, away from them.

In the valley below, completely surrounded by twelve feet of chain-link fence topped by coiled razor wire, stood Operation Red-Blooded's main research station, according to the research Andy Gray and Marcus Kitka had done. Guard towers anchored two of the corners. Inside the fence were a couple dozen buildings, one or two stories tall, with stretches of open area between them. Floodlights mounted on the guard towers spread a daylight glow all around its perimeter.

"Full circle," Eben muttered.

"What?"

"Sorry. I was just struck by how much it reminds me of Barrow. The way Barrow is now."

Stella snorted a laugh. "Got it. That's Barrow, and we're the vampires, massing for attack. Full circle."

"Right," Eben said. After all these years, sometimes he didn't even need to say that much. Sometimes she knew what he meant before he did.

Clear, quick communication was about to become more important than ever. This had to be pulled off with military efficiency, and neither one of them was the military type. Law enforcement, maybe, but there was a wide gap between being sheriff in Barrow and being a general leading an assault force.

"There are some differences," Stella said.

"Such as?"

"Such as that first time, the vampires practically sent out an open invitation to join them. We have, what, seventeen? They were going in for a feast, and they had plenty of time before the sun rose. We have about six more hours. But the biggest thing is"—she scooped up a rock, then hurled it to the ground—"the biggest thing is that they were going up against a town that had never heard of vampires, real ones anyway. Here we're going up against people whose whole job is knowing about, and killing, vampires. Imagine twenty of us trying to take down Barrow today. It'd never happen."

Eben was surprised to hear her sounding defeated before they had really started. "So, what? You want to back off?"

"Did I say that?" She picked up another stone, cocked her arm, and sailed it across the valley, toward the base below. "I thought you knew me better than that, Sheriff Olemaun."

21

THE TRAP IN L.A. a little more than two months ago had failed to net Dan Bradstreet or to do sufficient damage to Operation Red-Blooded to quench Stella's thirst for revenge.

Since then they had tapped their network—supporters and friends of Dane, mostly, although some were also vampires that Stella had met over the past couple of years. From those connections they drew recruits and recommendations. That had taken a couple of weeks. Another couple went by while they traveled around the country, meeting their potential comrades face-to-face.

From that group, they cobbled together their small band of dedicated disciples.

They couldn't work in L.A., not since what happened there, so they rented a farm out in California's Imperial Valley where they had plenty of space and privacy, and there they drilled, practicing shooting, fighting, running, climbing, any skill that might come in handy. During the warm spring days they stayed inside studying the aerial photos Andy had turned up, coming up with a strategy, refining it. When the sun went down they drilled some more.

The band ranged in age, gender, size, and race. The oldest was Mose, who had been a slave in South Carolina when he was turned in 1790. The smallest was Tina, just over four feet tall, fifteen years old in 1977. She still looked dainty, but Eben had seen her pitch a hundred-pound boulder almost twenty yards. There were Ruby and Paco and Ian, a mountain of a man called Crews, a wiry sneak named Felix. Keefer had munitions experience, from Vietnam, and there was still surplus stuff around that he knew inside and out. Brewer and Macafee also had military backgrounds. Jennelle and Grace had, oddly, both worked in the emergency room of the same Boston hospital, forty-four years apart. Carson, Anne, Denis, Krug, and Roach rounded out the team.

Stella was their drill sergeant, a role she hadn't played in a few years, when she was more concerned about bringing the fight to vampires in the name of her dead husband and shattered town.

If she spent too much time just sitting around, doing nothing, she began to slip toward madness again.

That completely terrified Eben—he didn't want to see what the end result of that journey might be.

She paced, she ranted, she broke things, she tore at her flesh with her own claws, slicing curling ribbons from her arms and legs. Eben had to distract her at those times, had to remind her that she had a goal, a task that needed to be accomplished.

But in charge of the others, putting them through

their paces, creating drill schedules and leading them, Stella forgot her heartbreak for a while, shrugged free of insanity's bonds, and became once again the Stella with whom he had fallen in love.

The battle among L.A.'s skyscrapers had been the first test of their miniature army. They'd had to use timing, wiles, speed, and strength to pull it off, and they had done it. Eben felt bad for the forty-seven innocent civilians who had lost their lives, and the hundreds of thousands of dollars in property damage . . . not to mention the very public display of violence; so much for skulking in the shadows. Any war had its collateral damages, though, and while he had not asked for this war by a long shot, he was determined to see it through—at least for the sake of his beloved.

Now they were here, outside some psychotic research facility, with an April moon shining down and something like sixty people inside. The facility was isolated, and most government documents revealed no clue of its existence. The people inside knew about the war—they were the ones who had instigated it, after all—but they thought they would take the fight to the vampires.

The idea of vampires bringing it to them had never crossed their minds.

They were about to be surprised.

The one thing Andy and Marcus had not been able to discover was what they would find inside. Research, yes, but what kind? Was it primarily a biochemical lab, studying the "immortal cell" that Andy told them a Dr. Felicia Reisner had theorized was responsible for vampirism—unkillable cells that spread like wildfire through any body into which they were successfully introduced? Was it a weapons lab, where new and more powerful antivampire technology was perfected? Or perhaps more of a think tank, where learned people sat around and debated the issues, hoping to reach some kind of reasonable conclusions?

Without knowing what waited behind those fences and walls, their ultimate goal was only guesswork. They could hope to take out everyone inside, disrupt their research, maybe destroy some equipment, fight fire with fire. But they just didn't know what to expect—it was their plan's weakest point, and standing on the ridge looking down at the daylight-bright perimeter, Eben hoped it wouldn't be their downfall.

"You ready?" Stella said.

"Sure, whatever."

She gave him a quick, firm kiss on the lips. Too much time working toward this, keeping her emotions pent up, trying not to go nuts while she waited. Now that it was here, she could let loose.

She turned to the rest of the undead assault force, behind them in surplus desert night camos, faces blackened. They carried guns, automatic rifles, and machine guns purchased on the black market. They had grenades on their belts. Their immediate goal was murder, not meals. "Everyone set?"

Nods and grunts in the affirmative came back to her.

"All right then. Let's do it."

At a certain point, any surprise attack would no longer be a surprise. Knowing that, they didn't try to hide their approach. They returned to the four trucks in which they had come this far and drove downhill toward the facility. Two hundred yards out they left the road and split up, two trucks heading in each direction around the facility, closing in on the guard towers. A hundred yards out they heard a verbal warning broadcast over powerful speakers. Ten yards closer, automatic weapons opened fire at them.

Twenty yards out they stopped and started firing grenades at the guard towers. They were mostly built for observation, not defense, and the explosions rocked them, killing many of the occupants. The one at the southwest corner, where Eben and Stella had gone, lost a leg and toppled into the fence. The searchlight exploded when it hit, flames licking up from its casing. The perimeter was plunged into darkness, broken only by muzzle flashes and a few handheld flashlights. Eben knew that once the soldiers discovered they were fighting vampires, TRU-UV lights would be brought into play, but so far that hadn't happened.

Alarm Klaxons blared. By this point, every soldier on the base was alerted to the attack, and they were taking up defensive positions. The invaders came under heavy fire. Eben and Stella abandoned the truck, and if the others remembered their drills, they did the same—at the moment, Eben couldn't stop to check, and Stella was too focused on moving forward to pay attention to anyone behind her.

He knew he just had to keep an eye on her. She had reached the point where she might just walk up to a tank barrel and dare it to fire a shell through her brain. Fire from the base kicked up divots around her but she just kept running toward the fence, heedless of any danger.

Eben dropped to one knee and laid down covering fire, trying to drive the soldiers back long enough for Stella to reach her goal. A bullet grazed his right hip, burning but not doing serious damage. He fell sideways, righted himself, kept firing until the weapon clicked on an empty chamber. He ejected the magazine, shoved in a new one, continued.

Stella had almost reached the fence. She fired occasionally, a burst here or there, but without any real plan. Eben had to strategize for both of them, pumping lead where it would do the most good. He dropped, fired, then advanced, dropped, fired again.

Behind him, others were doing the same. He heard the soldiers inside the facility shouting—sounds of near chaos—but his people were silent, determined, claiming a few feet of ground at a time.

Eben risked a glance back. Brewer had fallen, but so far that was all out of his group. He had no idea how the parallel attack on the other tower was progressing.

Then he saw Stella duck through the fence, where the falling tower had buckled one of its support posts and bent the wire. He fired a burst at the soldiers and raced after her, into a cloud of thick, bitter smoke.

As Eben pushed through the fence, broken points of wire clawed at his clothes, snagged his flesh. He ignored it and kept moving forward, looking for Stella in the dark and the haze. She had gone into the wreckage of the tower, or around it, into a warren of small outbuildings, storage sheds maybe. "Stella!"

If she heard him or responded, he couldn't tell. He heard great ripping bursts of gunfire and the disconcerting zing of bullets whizzing past him and the *thunk thunk* of slugs slamming into the steel and stucco structures. Voices broke through now and again, but he couldn't make out any words.

Blindly, he dashed in between some of the buildings. Bodies lay on the ground, blood soaking into the dirt. He still felt bad for these men and women, hired only to do a job. They must have thought they were safe here, safer than in Iraq, anyway, must have believed they'd pulled easy duty. By the time they found out that wasn't the case, it was too late for them.

He stepped over them and went deeper into the maze. He couldn't tell what the small buildings were for, but they seemed solidly constructed, windowless, each with a single door that had multiple locks. "Stella!"

he called again. This time his voice bounced around between the buildings. "Stella, where are you?"

A footstep on the ground behind him, a flash of motion at the corner of his eye. He whirled, bringing the barrel of his gun to chest height, finger tightening on the trigger.

Stella grabbed his arm. "Easy, big boy," she said. Her eyes gleamed in the faint light, a grin full of malice on her face. She looked turned on, which Eben found exciting and frightening at the same time. "You'll rile up the locals."

"Are there any unriled locals around?" Eben asked.

"To be honest, I'm not sure how easy the locals would be to rile up," Stella said.

"What are you talking about?"

She indicated the nearest of the small buildings, then beckoned him around to the other side of it. The door had been kicked in, the jamb splintered, the knob hanging half off. "You did this?" he asked.

"I was curious." She shoved the door open wider, allowing a pale band of moonlight inside.

Eben followed the light. It barely illuminated the building's far wall, lined with plain shelves mounted on steel brackets. On the shelves were bones. Human skeletons, one per shelf, dumped there like forgotten volumes in some ghastly library.

That's what he thought at first.

He took a step closer to the shelves, and saw the fangs in the slack mouths, the claws tipping the fingers.

Vampire skeletons, then. Six of them, in this building. And at least fifteen similar buildings arrayed around this one.

Eben shuddered and backed out. How long had Operation Red-Blooded been around? Over what period of time had they collected these? He really didn't want to see any more.

"Come on," Stella urged. "We have lots to do."

22

THEY HAD STOPPED for a snack at a roadside gas station/convenience store on the outskirts of Alamo, Nevada. There were a handful of people in the place—some tourists from Maine, a couple of truckers, and a woman working the counter—so everyone got a little something before they hit the road again.

Stella went first, drank deep, and then went outside, walking around the brightly lit building, looking out at the dark desert beyond the rim of light. She was buzzing. Had been, pretty much ever since Eben bit her. She knew about Dane's reaction to Marlow's bite, of course, and Eben had described something very similar happening when Dane bit him. A second bite, it seemed, bestowed great strength and endurance. She had wondered why it didn't happen more often—perhaps it was because vampires were always shifting allegiances and taking up pointless feuds, so no one wanted to make someone else stronger if that strength could later—in the vernacular, which didn't strictly apply here—come back and bite them on the ass.

When he did it, she had been surprised. Shocked. It had been wildly erotic. When she finally came to her senses, she felt ready to go for a run, maybe around the entire city of Los Angeles. Or play about six thousand games of racquetball, a sport she had never understood in the first place. She had energy to burn, that was the thing.

Since then, the high had faded but the sensation of great strength and energy remained. Sitting in the trucks with the rest of the little army they'd amassed—ragtag was too generous a word for them—bored her. She wanted to be hitting something. She couldn't wait until they reached the Red-Blooded facility she had scared Andy Gray into discovering.

Thinking about Andy reminded her of something else she had wanted to do. She was ready for action, hard and physical, but she had to remember strategy, too. The parts had to work together or none of it would work at all.

She went back inside and took a prepaid cell phone from behind the counter. Tina was feasting on the sales clerk. She smiled at Stella, her mouth rimmed in blood, teeth coated. Stella gave her a smile and went back out into the cool night. She dialed Andy's number, and he picked up on the third ring.

"Yeah?"

"Andy, it's Stella."

"Everything okay?"

"We're still a few hours away," she said. "We're going to hole up in Ely for the day, then hit it tonight."

"Okay. What's up?"

"I need you to do something."

"Where have I heard that before?" he asked.

"I give your life meaning, Andy."

"Yeah, I keep forgetting."

She watched a cloud scud across the moon, and ran her long tongue over sharp teeth. "I want your people to post two addresses online. Phone numbers, too. Everywhere. I want these plastered on the vampire boards, the blogs, the websites—everyone on the planet who is interested in the topic of vampires should see all this tomorrow night. I know the government will move quickly to get them down, but at least for a few hours I want them to be inescapable. You think you can do that?"

"You know I can."

"Good."

"Whose addresses are they?"

"You already know, Andy," Stella said. "You gave them to me in the first place. . . ."

Outside, the fighting continued. The participants, Stella's band of volunteers, understood that their main job was killing as many people as possible while distracting the rest. The rest of it was up to Eben and Stella.

There were satellite photos of the compound, but the facility's internal computers were tucked behind firewalls that thwarted even Marcus's most inspired attempts to hack them. As a result, they'd had to guess, from the physical layout of the buildings and apparent foot traffic, as measured by vehicles in the parking areas and wear on the ground around them, which building was the most important. That was the one they wanted to hit, to do the most damage to . . . to whatever it was Red-Blooded did here.

Whatever it was, from the number of vampire skeletons that must have been stored in those small buildings, they had been doing it longer than Eben had imagined.

They had settled on a building near the center of the facility. It wasn't the biggest building, but from what they could make out from the photos and plans, the biggest one housed the power plant that ran the place. The one they targeted was smaller, but it had a large parking area and clear routes of travel from various points around the compound. Eben and Stella ran at a half-crouch from the warren of little buildings toward the bigger ones that made up the bulk of the facility.

From these larger structures, floodlights still beamed down toward the ground. They dashed through some of them, then Stella hit the hard edge of light from one and shrieked, jumping back. "Damn!" she said, brushing a charred spot on her arm. "Watch it!"

Eben stopped short of the beam. "UV light. Either they've figured out what we are, or they use redundant security systems this far in. We've got to be a little more careful."

"Fuck careful," Stella snapped. "We've done that. I'm not playing their game anymore."

"It's not a game, Stella. It's all for keeps now."

"It always has been." She started walking toward the building, around the sweep of light from above. Eben walked with her, alert, gun ready to swing in any direction at the slightest sound. "We just didn't know it before."

A couple of soldiers running flat-out crossed about thirty feet in front of them. The soldiers didn't see them, didn't know they were there, but Stella unleashed a blast from her automatic rifle. The soldiers jerked and danced for a few seconds, chunks of them flying everywhere, before they fell. They hadn't had time to raise an alarm, but the sound of Stella's weapon might have accomplished the same thing.

Eben wanted to bark something at her for risking their lives to shoot two soldiers who would have passed right by, but he stopped himself. She wasn't in any shape to listen to reason. He had never seen her like this, living on the cusp of madness, driven by rage, half avenging angel and half demon bitch. Stella stormed across the warm bodies like they were shredded plastic bags in a vacant lot, litter not even worth noticing.

There would be more soldiers ahead, Eben knew. Regardless of the effectiveness of their two-pronged distraction, the people of Operation Red-Blooded wouldn't leave their headquarters unguarded. And now, assuming they heard the shots, they knew the perimeter had been breached. They knew someone was coming. They might even know vampires were coming. Every foot of ground gained would bring them closer to a violent confrontation—one that might end his unlife, or Stella's, or both.

His throat felt dry. He wished he could stop and drink from one of the downed soldiers without losing sight of Stella again, but settled for dipping the fingers of his left hand into a wound as he passed them, then licking the fingers clean, tasting the rusty metal flavor. Loving it, craving more. He had been this scared before, or close to it, in Norway with Dane, when they infiltrated Enok's slaughterhouse. But there, they'd been surrounded by vampires. Not his kind by choice, but his kind by circumstance just the same. Vampires could hate each other, could kill each other without a second's hesitation. Still, that ancient kinship existed.

Here, regular people—once his own kind—surrounded them. And these particular people made destroying vampires their top priority. They wouldn't look at him as a former person, but as a monster to be put down.

Would they be wrong?

That one I can't answer.

He jogged a few steps to catch up with Stella's long, easy strides. *Like she's taking a walk in the woods on a sunny Sunday afternoon.*

The structures in this part of the facility were older, wood-sided, as if Operation Red-Blooded had taken over an existing military compound and added to it, rather than building from the ground up. They circled around one, and Stella came to a halt.

"That's it," she said, pointing to the smallish building up ahead. A double handful of soldiers on full alert stood outside the place. Two more were flat on the roof, barely illuminated by the half-moon. They would be walking into a dozen guns; more if there were others they couldn't see from here. "We need to get in *there*."

Eben listened to the noise of the battle continuing on two fronts. It all seemed well behind them now. Too far back, and it had been going on too long, to distract these soldiers from their posts. "Any ideas?"

She drummed her fingers against her weapon, head bobbing slightly, like an electrical current flowed through her. "You think there's a back door?"

"If there is, it's just as heavily guarded."

"Element of surprise?"

"I think we lost that."

"Maybe we can get it back."

She turned around and headed back the way they had come, then turned left and passed between two of the dark, quiet buildings. Eben kept up with her, wondering what she had in mind. Dodging the UV floodlights, she went back to the large building they had identified as the power plant. Only two guards stood in front of it, and one of them held his rifle loosely in one hand, butt on the ground, and smoked a cigarette with the other.

Neither one saw Stella until she was a couple of

yards away, and she closed that distance faster than they could have imagined. The guard who had her rifle ready went down first, her neck snapped, and the other one was still struggling to bring his weapon up when she punched the cigarette into his mouth, then opened his throat with slashing claws. She stood in the arterial spray for a moment, head back like she was enjoying a hot shower, then toppled him. He landed on his back in front of the door. She stepped on his trembling body, over it, and shoved the door open.

From inside, Eben could hear cries of alarm. Stella ignored them, coolly taking two hand grenades from her belt, arming them, and tossing them inside. Then she slammed the door again.

"Better stand back," she warned.

Eben didn't need a second warning. He ran back to the shelter of the closest building, Stella beside him. The door to the power plant opened again, and a couple of people—technicians, he guessed—ran outside, but just an instant before the two grenades went off virtually simultaneously. Smoke and dust and debris blew out through the door, and the two techs were slammed off their feet. One of them stood up, blood running from his nose and ears. The other stayed down.

The door remained gapped open and smoke billowed from it. "Come on," Stella said. As the smell of smoke and fire reached him, Eben followed her between the buildings and toward the one they wanted. As they ran, he spotted some of the soldiers who had been standing guard racing toward the power plant by the more direct route.

When they got back, there were only three guards in front of the building, and the pair on the roof remained. These were more easily dealt with. Stella opened fire from the cover of darkness, and Eben joined in. The noise would no doubt bring some of the soldiers back from the power plant, if they heard it over the sounds of the fire there. By that time, however, they would be inside. One of the soldiers on the roof reared up and fell again, rolling off the edge like a stuntman in a Western movie. They all died under the barrage of lead.

Eben and Stella both stopped to switch out their magazines, then crossed the open space. Eben hit the door first and barged through. Inside, three Red-Blooded agents in civilian clothes were charging for the door, handguns drawn. One carried a flashlight, as well. Eben squeezed his trigger and dropped them.

For the moment, all was silent. They stood in a kind of reception area, with a high wooden counter. Behind it were a couple of scratched, worn wooden desks, one of which had a pair of monitors to which footage from outdoor security cameras was fed, standing among family photos and a magazine open to angel food cake recipes. A rack on the wall held literature generated by the federal government—pamphlets on how to report workplace discrimination, on employee health care options, and the like. The place seemed incredibly prosaic and he wondered if they'd been all wrong about it. Maybe this was just a human resources office—had they wasted time, effort, and lives for nothing?

Behind the counter a pair of swinging doors led deeper into the building. "Might as well see what's back there," Stella said.

They passed behind the counter and through the doors.

And there the illusion ended.

The front part looked like it had been built in the 1940s or '50s. Beyond the doors, though, it was purely twenty-first-century high-tech. Burnished steel walls lined a short corridor, at the end of which was a double steel door with an electronic keypad. The quick exit of the people Eben had shot had left the doors ajar. Recessed overhead lights provided a steady glow. It was quiet in here, with only a steady electrical hum making any sound at all.

"This is more like it," Stella said.

She was already in motion, pushing the doors open wider. She made it inside a few paces, then stopped short. Eben saw why when he joined her.

Operation Red-Blooded had built a facility that looked like the mad scientist's lair from a James Bond film.

From the doorway a set of widely spaced stairs led down, making a high ceiling without the necessity of raising the roof. This room alone looked bigger than the whole building did from the outside. In the center of the room, rising almost two stories tall, was a bank of equipment that Eben couldn't begin to understand. Some of it looked like computers, or parts of computers, but he wasn't a technical guy. *Marcus Kitka would probably wet himself if he saw this,* he thought. There were spiraling tubes and little boxes that weren't microwave ovens and racks of glass beakers and square refrigerator-looking things. Eben couldn't tell if someone would have used this stuff to cook dinner, brew moonshine, or map the human genome. Arrayed around the central altar to technology were various workstations, divided from one another by louvered glass walls and open shelving units. Some of these contained stainless steel tables or gurneys, like those found in morgues, and some of those tables were occupied.

It only took a minute to ascertain that those occupants were vampires.

"Eben . . ."

They had split up, each one wandering with wide eyes, aghast, through the big room. There was fear in Stella's voice—the slightest catch, a tremble. She was out of sight, on the far side of the central tower. He hurried around it, bringing up the weapon he had almost forgotten he still held.

She stood in front of a wall on which dozens of vampire skulls were mounted and displayed, as if in a natural history museum. Beneath some of them tags bearing cities and dates had been affixed.

"God," Eben said. His voice had no power behind it, his knees felt like rubber. The bones out in those storage sheds, the skulls in here . . . Operation Red-Blooded had been quietly doing away with hundreds of vampires, if not more.

And every one they got became grist for research. From the looks of this lab, he suspected an effort to find a medical "cure" for vampirism. But that might have been too charitable—the research might simply have been devoted to finding more efficient ways to murder vampires.

Once, this room would have brought joy to his heart. Now it chilled him to the bone.

Eben and Stella had thought this was their war against Operation Red-Blooded. But the war had been raging longer and harder than either of them had believed. And so far, Operation Red-Blooded was clearly winning.

23

"I . . . I NEED A MINUTE," Stella said. "To take this all in."

"Stella," Eben said, "we're in the middle of a place full of people who want to kill us."

"Where do you suppose everyone is?"

"It looks like this is primarily a research facility. Most of the people here are probably scientists. They were no doubt asleep in barracks or dorms when we hit, and once they heard the shooting they probably crawled under their bunks. I think we've already seen most of the people with guns. But I'd be willing to bet there are other agents around who are a little sneakier than the grunts we've seen so far, and they'll be on their way here to take us out."

She couldn't tear her gaze from that wall of skulls. Eben began inspecting a narrow shelving unit crammed with vials of blood, each vial labeled with some arcane code he didn't understand. "So many . . ." she said, her voice a hoarse whisper. "They've taken so many."

"It's what we wanted, remember? What we fought for. An end to all vampires."

"That was before."

"Before *what*?" He thought he knew, but he wanted

to make her say it. Maybe it would help pull her back off that cliff she'd been dancing on, the one with a thousand-foot drop down to looneyville.

"Before . . . before I met so many of them. Us. Before I found out that the only thing we all have in common is our diet. Before I learned that just as many of us are decent people as people are . . ." She looked toward the floor, away from the skulls at last. "I'm not saying we're an oppressed minority. Equal rights and all that. Obviously there's a pretty significant difference between us and them, and it's not easily set aside. But some kind of understanding could be reached, right? Or could have been, until they pushed it too far. Like a mutual nonaggression pact? They can't know"—she waved her hands, indicating the whole lab—"this much about us and not get that, can they? Have this much information and still just think of us all as ruthless bloodsuckers?"

Eben shook his head sadly. "'A mutual nonaggression pact?' What kind of people do you think we're dealing with? Ones who are willing to sit and talk . . . or listen? Did you want to when the shoe was on the other foot? I didn't have a lot of faith in humanity when I was part of it," he said. "I can't say that anything I've seen since has changed that. We should get out of here. We'll be surrounded any minute now, if we're not already."

"I know. You're right." She turned back toward the central tower, started toward it. "This place is just . . .

it just blows my mind. I mean, look at all this stuff. It must have cost millions. Billions. Your tax dollars at work." She stopped a few steps away from the equipment. "Eben, look. What is this?"

She was pointing toward a video monitor. At least Eben recognized that. What the monitor showed, though, was a different story. It looked vaguely familiar, but so out of context he couldn't place it.

The monitor showed an image from a camera mounted high on a wall, it seemed, aimed down toward a little enclosure that looked like a shower stall, if shower stalls were wired and cabled and tubed. The walls were glass or Plexiglas, it appeared, running red with blood. And there was someone inside.

"I don't know. There's someone moving, though."

"A vampire?"

"Can't tell, but that'd be my guess. Why else would the camera be on it? And all that blood—they wouldn't put a human in a box like that."

"Do you think it's close by?"

"There's no telling." He looked more closely at the screen. "Or maybe there is." He pointed at a time stamp in the lower right corner. 2:11 a.m., it showed, followed by B-104.

"You think that's a room number?" Stella asked.

"I don't know, but maybe."

"In what building?"

"There was a *B* beside the door of this one."

"But . . . all we saw were the doors leading in here."

"Maybe we missed something. Let's make a quick trip around the perimeter of this room. But we need to make this fast."

"I know . . . but would you want to be left behind in a place like this?"

They found the door just past the spot where he'd been, before Stella had called him. He might have missed it altogether if he hadn't been looking for it. It was made of the same emerald-tinted brushed steel as the room's walls, and there was no knob or handle showing, just a thin line around its edges and a control pad mounted on the wall beside it. He touched a softly glowing button on the pad and the door slid open with a *whoosh*.

Behind it was the room they had seen on the monitor with the little stall set against the back wall. Cables snaked across the floor into the snug enclosure; others coiled out of its ceiling. As they had seen, blood ran down the translucent walls in an incessant stream.

And there was, indeed, someone inside, barely visible through the crimson film.

The smell of blood was strong in here, filling the space, overwhelming the ventilation system that tried to whisk it away.

The thing was a holding cell and a life-support system in one.

He had to know who was inside. "Get ready," he told Stella. "This could be something pretty bad. Like Enok."

Stella nodded. Eben worked the latch and opened the door.

The woman inside—the partial woman inside—smiled at him.

Eben Olemaun. He heard Lilith's voice in his head. *If you ever compare me to Enok again, I'll tear your throat out.*

Mother Blood. The matriarch of vampires, the long-time mate of Vicente, who Eben had destroyed in Barrow.

He had last seen Lilith in Norway, at Enok's slaughterhouse, and he'd simply assumed that the destruction of that place had finished her off. New arrivals there had been encouraged to literally eat pieces of her as part of the initiation rites, biting them right from her body. Limbless, chunks of bone visible at her shoulders and hips, her only defense had been her fierce and agile will.

If anything, she was in worse shape now.

She was upright, not prone, held in place by steel bands around her forehead, beneath her breasts and over her hips. Her arms and legs had begun to regenerate; blunt, featureless stumps, the beginnings of new limbs, had started to grow. Tubes led into veins on her neck and her left temple. Wires carried data from other spots. Her flesh was scarred and torn, as if her current captors had carried on Enok's tradition. Once beautiful, that beauty had now been marred; a recent gash from her left eye to the corner of her mouth revealed the glistening white of muscle and bone.

They do not feed from me. Lilith's voice continued Eben's thought process, her voice coming as clearly in his mind as if she'd been speaking aloud. *But they still take from me. They experiment. They never seem to tire of that.*

"Oh my God," Stella murmured.

There is no God here, Stella Olemaun. You most of all should know that. The blood that ran from overhead splashed throughout the enclosure, keeping Lilith wetted down. It was the blood poured across her body that allowed her wounds to heal, that kept her functioning. And she could drink simply by opening her mouth and catching some of the spray.

"But how did you survive? And how did you get *here?*"

Lilith didn't answer verbally, but instead projected her memories into Eben's mind. From the shocked expression on Stella's face, she was receiving the same signal.

Eben was back inside Enok's abattoir, with the smell of blood everywhere, permeating the wood from which the multilevel structure was built. Enok had built down, deep into the earth, and furnaces kept the place at a constant temperature, but the metallic tang of blood overwhelmed the odor of burning wood and the dull stink of sweat and shit from the humans kept for food on the bottom level. Vampires, somewhere around a thousand of them, roamed freely through the upper levels, feasting from troughs or barrels or mugs.

But Lilith was confined to a slab in the Lilith Room—on display as a constant reminder of the relic she was, of the old world order she represented. She was regularly visited by vampires—mostly new ones, having made the pilgrimage to Enok's hell on Earth for the first time—who bent down or knelt beside the slab and tore bits of her loose with their teeth. Illuminating the scene were burning words inscribed on the wall above her: *THE OLD WAYS HAVE PROVEN WEAK. NOW IS THE TIME OF THE VAMPIRE.*

The place was falling down around her. The epic battle between Eben and Enok had rocked the structure's very foundations, and with the collapse of supporting pillars and walls on the lowest levels, the ramshackle nature of the whole building revealed itself. Dust plummeted from the ceilings, pipes that once channeled blood to feeding stations split and flooded rooms, weakening them more. The cracks of splitting wood echoed over the screams and thundering feet as *nosferatu* tried to escape with their lives—many of them rushing straight into the first rays of the rising sun.

Fear rose in Lilith's broken throat, and she too screamed, but soundlessly. By casting her mind out about the place, she could follow what was happening, but as much as she tried to beg silently for help, none came. No one was willing to try to carry her up the crumbling stairs and out to possible safety.

Finally the walls of the Lilith Room collapsed. A beam struck her slab, tipping it over, and she slid off, onto the debris-caked floor. The roof caved in over her. Her terror had grown unbearable. She could no longer reach out with her mind, could only imagine the same thing over and over, wishing that a large enough piece of rubble would fall, crushing her skull, destroying her brain and ending the agony her unlife had become.

It didn't happen.

Lilith lay there in the building's remains, unable to move.

With no one to pour blood on her, her wounds didn't heal.

With no one to feed her, her hunger grew, twisting her guts in painful knots.

The fires burned for a while, but then went out, and Norway's winter cold settled over the place's ashy bones. Rats came in seeking shelter from drifting snow, feasting on the bodies of those who had not made it free—including Lilith. She tried to writhe away from them, but they nibbled at her flesh just as the *nosferatu* had, tore at veins and muscle.

She had no way to keep track of the days, the weeks. Time passed. Immortal, she couldn't die unless she was killed, and no one would grant her that favor.

She eventually heard the voices, the thunk of shovels

digging through snow, the clatter of people climbing down on ropes and ladders.

Her first thought was that they must be vampire. Followers of Enok, come to rescue him if possible—or better, others who had come to celebrate his long-awaited demise. For the first time since that last day, the day of destruction, she cast her thoughts out, touched a mind—

And it was human. Curious. She skated carefully through it, and then others. There were a dozen of them, with more waiting on the surface.

They were, she learned, agents of a clandestine organization of the United States government. Operation Red-Blooded. From their thoughts, and soon enough from overhead snatches of conversation, she learned that they had heard rumors of this supposed undead paradise, but had never been able to find out where it was. Satellite photos of the sawmill's collapse, however, showed a sinkhole much bigger than the mill would have left. By enhancing those photos, they had discovered the bodies of some of the vampires who had tried to escape, only to be caught by the sun. Word had filtered up through the ranks, and the decision had finally been made to send in a search team. They didn't expect to find any unliving vampires at this late date, but they were constantly in quest of information about the *nosferatu*.

If anything could have scared Lilith more than an eternity here without blood, it was this. She couldn't hide, couldn't scamper away from the searchers. If they came upon her here, undead, helpless, they would take her. She might be lucky enough to have them destroy her at once, but that seemed unlikely, from what she could garner. They were after data, after knowledge, and she would certainly be a prize.

They would, in short, do just what they had done.

She tried to avoid that fate. She tapped into the mind of one of the search party, learned that he had a gun, and bade him use it on his comrades.

He turned it toward a woman below him on a ladder going deeper into the complex. Lilith watched through his eyes as the woman sensed his motion, looked up at him, eyes saucering in fright, spittle flying as she tried to beg. Then he pulled the trigger and her head exploded like a melon hit with a hammer. Lilith could hear the shot through her own ears as well as his, and she smiled.

Then she made the agent turn his gun upward. One of his comrades came to the hole's edge. "What was that?" he asked. "You see something?"

Lilith's puppet fired again. The first shot missed, rocketing high into the air outside the pit. But the man only drew his head back a few inches, and the next shot punched through his throat. He pitched forward, blood fountaining onto the man Lilith controlled.

Others reacted, and one of them shot Lilith's puppet. She felt the searing heat of the bullet enter his back, tear through his heart, and blow out through his chest.

The next one she took over was the one who had shot him. This one was a woman, busily congratulating herself on her accomplishment when Lilith made her aim her gun again and pull the trigger.

Four more died the same way, Lilith controlling one after another, before she touched a mind that had figured out what must be going on. They all retreated from the pit, and she allowed herself a smile of satisfaction. She had driven them away. She remained trapped inside with the rats and the insects gnawing on her, but at least she had not fallen into the hands of these disease-minded humans.

More time passed, but not much. A day, two, she couldn't tell. She heard trucks outside, heard the muffled voices and footsteps of more people. She made ready to reach out to control these as she had the last set.

But then something—not a sound, at least not on any frequency her ears could hear, but like a sound, in her mind—began to nag at her. It was loud and repetitious, a keening sound that faded and grew, faded and grew. It blotted out all other thought, made other thought impossible. She tried to ignore it, tried to send out her mental tendrils, but she couldn't. They had rendered her as helpless mentally as she already was physically.

Finally, they found her.

Through panicked, bleary eyes she saw them come

into what was left of the Lilith Room, wearing heavy clothing, boots, gloves, and protective headgear. So they could work through what she couldn't, she guessed, through the noise they generated that rendered her helpless. She didn't need rational thought to know they thought her pathetic, limbless, dehydrated, and pale, like a half-dead queen sitting alone inside an anthill after pesticides and termites have eliminated the rest of the colony.

Someone dared to kneel beside her and hold a pressure hypodermic to her naked flesh. She felt the quick rush of something being pumped into her. A few minutes later, the not-noise faded away. But so did everything else. Her fear, her hunger, her humiliation, her surroundings, all of it vanished into the gray soup of unconsciousness.

She came to here, in the small enclosure. They kept her supplied with blood, but in return they tested her, studied her, sampled her at will. They kept just enough of the drugs with which they had dampened her psychic abilities back at Enok's running into her through the tubes that were joined to her veins, so that she stayed conscious but unable to reach out with enough force to control any of her captors.

At least, that was their plan.

But she was Mother Blood, Lilith, first among women.

She had not survived the ages without using her wiles, her intelligence, and every other skill at her disposal. She was smarter than almost everyone.

And she found someone she could control.

He brought it on himself. A scientist named Darrel Keating. He had no family, no wife, not even a girlfriend. He hadn't since his first year of college, when Amy Clarkdale, the girl he dated—the girl he thought he loved, although that love still had not escalated into physical intimacy beyond a few chaste kisses and some occasional hand-holding—had allowed him to walk into his room while she was on her knees with his roommate's cock in her mouth and three more guys standing around waiting for their turns.

That sight had spoiled romance for him. He dreamed of it—and dreamed of Amy taking him in her mouth instead of his roommate—but he had never again worked up the nerve to act on it.

Keating considered Lilith beautiful beyond words.

She caught him staring at her sometimes, his eyes liquid, his lips slightly parting, nostrils flaring as if hoping to breathe in her essence. The time she saw him rubbing the outside of his pants, she knew she could have him. Even as weak as her mental abilities were, due to the drugs, when she reached into his mind she found it ready for her, as open to her penetration as she would have been to his, had he dared approach her physically.

Tasting his mind, she learned that he wasn't only interested in her body, but that his attraction worked on many levels, some twisted. Since her arms and legs had not fully grown back yet, she couldn't push him away or escape him, and he fantasized about taking her into his bed. She might protest verbally, but she couldn't stop him. For once, he would have found a woman he could have, any way he wanted her.

He was also drawn to her power. She had lived what was essentially forever, in his view. And she would continue to do so as long as her brain stayed intact. As a biologist this fascinated him. It held vast potential for fighting disease, for reversing the aging process.

All these things worked together in his mind, and made him lower his resistance to her psychic probing.

Once she discovered a way in, she had him.

Controlling him, she made him cautiously reduce the mind-dampening drugs they kept her on. She didn't cut them out all at once, much as she would have liked to, because she was afraid that would be too noticeable. Instead, she eased back, little by little. The less drugged she was, the easier it was to manipulate Darrel, the poor fool. She had begun the process of enlisting some of the others, too, but hadn't yet reached the point where she could get them to kill each other, to free her.

And what good would that do her? Until she regenerated her limbs completely and regained her mobility, she needed slaves she could command. It would be far easier if they were vampires who served willingly, rather than humans who would have to be watched at every moment.

Tonight she had heard the sounds of warfare, felt

the anxiety that gripped Darrel and the others, and wondered who was coming this time. She had almost given up hoping for rescue. Nobody knew where she was, except Operation Red-Blooded agents.

And then Eben had opened the door to her enclosure.

So what is it to be? Lilith inquired. *Salvation, or destruction? My fate is in your hands now.*

Eben stepped into the enclosure. The blood spraying around it soaked through his clothes, but it was fresh and pure, filtered somehow, and if she was right that the drugs were only introduced intravenously through the tubes, it should be safe. He drank deep as he unfastened the steel straps that held her in place.

"Stella, get me one of those gurneys from the other room."

By the time she returned, wheeling a stainless-steel gurney, he had freed Lilith from her bonds and torn away the tubes and wires connected to her. He couldn't deny the strange erotic thrill he got, clutching her body against his, her naked flesh slick with blood. Her head lolled against his shoulder, and he felt her tongue lapping blood from his neck.

"Well," Stella remarked, "isn't this cozy?"

24

EBEN SET LILITH DOWN on the gurney, still feeling the heat of her tongue on his skin. Stella stood at the gurney's far end, hands on her hips, glaring at them.

"Come on, Stella," he said. "I was just taking her down."

"And pressing her against you. I saw the tongue action."

"Stella—" he began. Lilith's "voice" cut him off.

I hope you do not think I have forgotten how I came to be here in the first place, little Stella. It was you, after all—your betrayal—that weakened me enough to allow Enok to overwhelm me.

Ah, yes, the betrayal. In Los Angeles, Lilith had offered to trade Eben's ashes to Stella, in exchange for what was believed to be the only copy of a disk containing video evidence of Vicente's first assault on Barrow. Stella had delivered the disk, taken the ashes, and blown up the house Lilith was staying in with a cocktail of high explosives. Lilith had barely survived, and apparently Enok had been able to track her down and take her.

Eben was glad the bargain had been made, since it

had given Stella the means to resurrect him. But he also understood why Lilith might still be a little peeved.

"Look, *bitch,*" Stella snarled. "I heard you maybe helped Eben and Dane out in Norway, and it's appreciated. But it doesn't mean I like you, and I damn well don't think it entitles you to be sticking your tongue on him."

I aided them, they aided me. We set aside past trespasses and came to a mutually beneficial arrangement. I see the pain that plagues you, little Stella, your loss . . . the infant . . . how tragic. You have your vendetta to settle with these cattle, and I have mine. In particular, there is a pitiful human here who seems to be in charge of this operation. Should I have the opportunity, particularly when my limbs are fully regenerated, I should dearly love to tear him to little pieces.

For now, though, I need you both, and I believe I can help you. I suggest we put aside our differences, Stella, if you can find it in yourself to do so.

Eben wasn't sure how Stella would react to the offer. She had been so nuts lately, since the baby's death, he rarely knew what to expect from her at all. An olive branch extended by a mortal enemy? He braced himself for the coming explosion.

But, as always, his wife surprised him. She had seemed more subdued since they'd penetrated deep into the Red-Blooded facility, except for those few moments when she had found him and Lilith locked in their grisly embrace. Perhaps her madness had passed as her grief shifted into another phase. He hoped. "So in other words, the enemy of my enemy is my friend? Okay, I can buy that. We definitely have that in common. Besides, when we met before, when I failed to blow the shit out of you, I was still human. We were as different as could be—I had every vampire in my sights, and you were the queen of the bloodsuckers. I've been through some major changes since then, as you pointed out. I guess you have too."

So what are you saying, little Stella?

"I'm saying that forever is a hard time to hold a grudge. Maybe it's easier for immortals to forgive, because if I was still human I'd be kicking your ass right now."

Perhaps. But you are one of us now, undeniably. Whatever else has happened, I am still your mother.

Lilith held out the stumps of her arms. *Come to me, child. Let me begin to heal your grief.*

Stella didn't look at Eben but kept her gaze glued to Lilith. There might have been wetness in her eyes, but he couldn't tell for sure. If she and Lilith were still communicating psychically, he had been cut out of the loop.

Stella leaned over the gurney and embraced Lilith, heedless of the blood that still coated her, or of Lilith's nudity. Lilith returned the embrace as best she could. They held each other like that for a long time. After a while, Eben saw that Stella's back was shaking, although if she was sobbing she managed to do it without sound.

"Stella . . . hey. We should really get out of here," he said after a while. "I'm sure they know we're in here by now."

As if in response, he heard a noise in the big command center. "Damn," he said, "here they are."

No, Eben. Those are our kind.

Weapon at the ready, he went to the door and looked. She was right. Mose, Crews, Tina, Macafee, Paco, and Keefer were walking through the big room, gazing in wonder at the same things that had enthralled Eben and Stella. They had all been shot at least once, bullet holes and burn marks visible on their clothing and skin.

"We're in here," Eben called to them.

Crews glanced toward them. The big man looked morose. "Hey, Eben. We made it through. Some of us, anyway."

"The others?"

"Gone. Pretty hairy out there. It's a plus when you can get shot and keep going."

"Y'know," Keefer added, "if we had embraced the concept of high-tech weapons, Enok could have had his war a long time ago, and maybe won it."

"The only way to win such a war is through the complete elimination of your enemy," Mose said. "And that wouldn'ta served anybody's purposes. Long as we're outnumbered and we haveta quit fightin' 'fore the sun rises—"

"Everybody knows that, Mose, Christ!" Tina interrupted. "He was just saying."

Keefer bobbed his head loosely, like one of those old automobile rear window nodding dogs. "I was just saying. You can kill a lot of people with 'em, fast."

"That's gospel," Mose agreed.

"Glad you guys came through," Eben said.

"What is all this shit?" Tina asked. "Looks like Bill Gates's playroom in here."

"Screw what it is," Crews said. "Can we bust it up?"

"Be my guest," Eben answered. At his invitation, the giant Crews and the almost dwarfish Tina both barked laughter.

They and their comrades began doing just that, using hands to knock over shelving units and gun butts to smash the instruments and appliances on the tower of tech. Macafee took one of the wheeled gurneys and ran it into everything he could, cackling like a madman the whole time. Eben watched from the doorway, enjoying the chaos and destruction. *Serves these bastards right.*

He was still watching when the TRU-UV lights clicked on overhead, and the *nosferatu* started to burn.

Dane's death—big Dane, in Norway—had hit Stella harder than she'd let on to anyone, even Eben.

Although he'd been an all too brief part of her life, he was an indisputable link between the days before she became undead and those after. It was fairly simple given that he was largely a human sympathizer. She had even slept with Dane once—a desperate and needy act, in retrospect—before she resurrected Eben. For some reason, she had felt herself untethered from reality for a time after Eben brought her the news from Norway, as if Dane's philosophy had grounded her in some way, and without it she floated free, clutching now and then at treetops, hoping to reel herself back down to earth.

Before she had been able to do so, little Dane was murdered. He hadn't been with her nearly as long, but the three of them—Dane, Dane, and Eben—were like the three legs on which her life balanced, and with two of them gone suddenly and violently, she was at a loss. She went through the days tender, emotionally as well as physically. The sleeves of a jacket rubbed too coarsely against her arms, so she went without one. Certain smells, among them talcum powder, cinnamon, and chocolate, brought tears to her eyes. Every sense seemed too close to the surface, too fragile. It was like every nerve ending she had was hypersensitive, and she shied away from touch. Even her husband's touch.

She had put little Dane in danger, and for that she didn't think she could ever forgive herself. Forgiveness had never been her strong suit anyway.

But somewhere during the attack on the Operation Red-Blooded base, she had come back to herself.

She didn't know if it was the physical nature of the confrontation, at last putting to use the increased strength and stamina she'd gained from Eben's bite, or the simple emotional catharsis of working through rage and terror and sorrow, but one minute she had been her new, prickly self, and then she was old Stella, more even-keeled. Steady, if not precisely sane.

When Lilith had suggested a truce—*no, be honest, Stella, she was suggesting more than that. She wanted mutual forgiveness, and that's what tweaked you at first*—Stella had balked. Because she was on her way back to sanity, though, she had considered it. In truth, she had hurt Lilith far more than Lilith had her. If Lilith—so completely violated—could so readily forgive, Stella was hardly in a position to deny her the same.

So she was standing beside Lilith, silently communing, gently massaging Mother Blood's ruined arms, when the Operation Red-Blooded counteroffensive came.

She knew some of the vampires from their little army had come to the big command center, and that Eben had given them leave to destroy the place. They were doing so with gusto, laughing and shouting and smashing. All at once, they stopped. She heard cries of pain and rushed to stand beside Eben in the doorway. UV lights had blasted on in the main room, and the remnants of their group began to fry.

Crews was near the door to the side chamber in which they'd found Lilith, and he dove for it. Eben caught him, turning and helping the big man through the doorway. Then he stepped into the big room, into the lights. "Eben!" Stella called. She reached for him, but as soon as the light fell on her arm it started to smolder, and she withdrew it.

Eben didn't go far. He had left his weapon out there when they had entered the other room, lying across one of the bolted-down autopsy tables. He snatched it up, then retreated quickly. Even so, his flesh was already sizzling, smoke rising from his hairline. He shook off Stella's hand and aimed the gun up at the lights. When he pulled the trigger, the roar was deafening, but the offending bulbs shattered one by one, plunging parts of the command center into darkness.

Little Tina was gone. Macafee was gone. Keefer was gone. Crews was badly injured. Mose dragged himself, with difficulty, toward Stella and Eben in the doorway. Only Paco, who had ducked under one of the steel tables, was whole. As Eben blasted out the lights, Paco emerged from his shelter and dashed toward them, stopping to scoop one arm around Mose and helping him to safety.

Stella, shaking with rage, reached out. Together they helped Mose to a corner and sat him down. He was seriously burned and trembling uncontrollably. Bloody drool ran from the corners of his mouth. On the left side of his head, where thinning hair didn't provide enough protection, she could see the pale white of his skull beneath the blisters.

He might make it, but it would be close.

Then she remembered Lilith's regeneration chamber. "Not here," she told Paco. "Help me move him again. In there."

That will help him, Stella. Lilith, in her head. Maybe she had never left.

I haven't.

That's creepy, Stella thought back at her. *But kinda cool at the same time.*

She and Paco hoisted the quaking Mose again and put him on the floor inside the little enclosure. Whatever damage had been done to the control center had not shut off the flow of fresh blood, which still sprayed throughout it and ran down the walls. Mose tilted his head back, trying to catch some of the spray in his mouth. As soaked as Lilith and Eben had been earlier, Stella and Paco were now as they backed out.

"Whoa," Paco said. "Gotta get me one for my bathroom."

"If we get out of here," Stella said.

"Yeah, if."

Eben's gun went silent. She hoped it meant he had shot out all the lights, and not that he'd run out of ammunition.

Turning around, she saw that it was the latter. Her own weapon had been abandoned across the room, by the wall of skulls. Eben patted his pockets, hunting for another magazine and coming up empty.

"I'll get mine," she said. She didn't have any more clips either but her gun wasn't out. She squeezed past

Eben and started into the room. Most of the lights were out, and she could avoid the remaining ones.

She was almost to the center tower when the doors burst open.

"That's far enough," a voice called out. Dan Bradstreet, in the flesh. Behind him were eight more agents, all armed with automatic weapons and TRU-UV flashlights. "You've reached the end of the line."

25

EBEN SNAPPED HIS HEAD toward the door, saw the blocky guy standing there in a dress shirt and tie under a Kevlar vest. The other agents wore helmets and combat gear, but not him. "Bradstreet."

"You recognize me. Should I feel honored?"

"I recognize dog shit when I step in it," Eben said. "So don't bother."

Bradstreet forced a laugh. "I was hoping I wouldn't like you. Thanks for putting my mind at ease so quickly."

Eben had instinctively aimed his weapon at the man, but it would do no good. Bradstreet knew it. "You're running on fumes," he said. "So do us all a favor and just toss that thing down."

Eben almost hung on to it out of sheer stubbornness, but the agent was right. Empty, it was worthless. He flung it across the room, and it skidded and twirled on the tile floor until it hit wreckage from the brief demolition spree that had taken place. "I've never needed guns to take care of people like you," he said. "And that includes when I was alive."

"Maybe you've never met anyone quite like me," Bradstreet said.

"Oh, I'm pretty sure I have. Officious pricks with badges and tough guys backing them up aren't hard to come by."

"You don't like me. I find that pretty funny. I don't much care for you, either. But I'm fascinated to finally meet the famous Stella Olemaun. Your wife and I are going to have lots to talk about."

Eben felt the heat rising in him, his hands clenching into fists. The fact that Stella had always been able to take care of herself didn't enter into it when the protective instinct came over him.

Before he could protest, though, a thickset man with thinning red hair bulled through the uniformed agents and stumbled down the wide stairs. Terror threatened to bloat his eyes right out of his head. "My God!" he cried. "All our work . . . you barbarians have no idea what you've done!"

Eben would have figured him for a test-tube jockey even if he'd kept his mouth shut, if only from the piss-yellow shirt he wore.

"Relax, Dr. Keating," Bradstreet said. "We'll up the budget next year and rebuild it better than it was. Just like the six-million-dollar man. You'll be fine."

"You don't understand," Keating protested. "The data . . ." He had reached the center tower now, and he stared at the rubble like his life had been dashed to pieces.

"Just stand back and shut up!"

Eben remembered why the name Keating was familiar. This must have been the scientist who had become infatuated with Lilith.

He half expected to hear Lilith's voice in his head, but she was silent. He risked a glance over his shoulder toward her. She remained on the gurney, clearly paying close attention, her forehead furrowed in concentration.

"If you've caused Lilith to be hurt . . ." Keating said.

"Keating, if you don't step out of here," Bradstreet said, "I'm going to have you thrown out."

Instead of leaving, Keating knelt before the ruins of his technological temple. Tears spilled from his bulging eyes. He swept listlessly at the shards and chunks and scraps.

"Get him out of here," Bradstreet remarked. Two of the agents crowding the doorway started down the steps toward Keating. As they neared him, Eben saw Keating tense. With awkward fingers, he picked up a big shard of glass from a broken video screen. Clutching it tightly enough to slice into his hand, he rose and turned stiffly toward the agents.

"Let's go, Dr. Keating," one of them said.

Keating took a lurching step and slashed out, straight-armed, with the shard of glass. The agent brought his left arm up to block, but he was too late. The shard sliced through his throat, above his vest and below his helmet's face shield. He released a gurgling shout as blood sprayed several feet in front of him.

Keating swiveled toward the second one while the first was still upright, knees buckling, about to go down. The second had a moment's more warning. He aimed a Glock nine-mil and pumped a round into Keating's midsection. It tore through the scientist and billowed out his ugly yellow shirt in the back.

What it didn't do was slow him down. He shouted "Lilith!" and swept the shard up, his fingers pouring blood now where he gripped it. The jagged point entered the fleshy area behind the other man's chin, kept going, and burst out between his upper lip and his nose.

"Take him out!" Bradstreet ordered.

With blood-drenched hands, Keating snatched the Glock away from the agent, who released it in order to paw with both hands at the slippery chunk of glass bisecting his face. Keating was spinning around to aim it at the agents on the steps when they opened fire. "Lilith!" he cried again as he squeezed the trigger. A bullet ripped through his upper chest, beneath the right collarbone, and another hit his stomach. Kevlar stopped his first slug—the agent it hit went ashen and staggered but remained upright.

"Amy!" Keating called. He fired again, this shot scraping Bradstreet's left upper arm before punching through another agent's helmet.

"Shit!" Bradstreet shouted, clapping his right hand over the wound.

Keating took two more bullets but kept going.

"Lilith! Amy!" he shouted as he closed on another of the agents, shoving the gun barrel up against the woman's throat and jerking the trigger. His movements were spastic now, his steps halting, left arm thrown out almost straight, away from his body, like he was walking a tightrope. He had taken at least six bullets, so Eben wasn't surprised he was barely functional. Tears ran down the scientist's cheeks, and while his mouth kept moving, his words were no longer audible.

As he tried to lift the gun again, the remaining four agents opened fire on him all at once. He flailed around as the bullets pelted him, the Glock flying from his hands, and finally he went down, bleeding from a dozen wounds.

Eben had enjoyed the show, but when Keating went down, it appeared to be over. *Did you do that, Lilith?* he thought.

Yes, Eben Olemaun.

I didn't think he could have kept going on his own. I didn't know you could do that, though.

The will is stronger than most ever imagine, her voice came back. *Far stronger than the physical body, in most cases. As it was in his.*

Eben prepared to rush Bradstreet, to tackle him before the UV lights were brought into play, but before he could, the agent who had been shot in his Kevlar vest aimed his gun at the agent next to him and pulled the trigger. The bullet shattered the agent's faceplate and smashed into her left cheek. The agent kept turning and firing, dropping two more before Bradstreet shot him four times in the head, penetrating his helmet and killing him. The agent, whose cheek had turned to hamburger, sat back against the steel doorjamb, bleeding, eyes open—alive, but barely, and in shock.

"Very impressive . . . *Lilith,* is it?" Bradstreet said. But his voice had lost its cool command, and there was a hesitation when he spoke Mother Blood's name. "At least I presume that was your doing. Apparently you h-haven't been taking your meds."

Not for some time. Eben heard her, and he could tell that Bradstreet and Stella did as well.

Bradstreet hefted an automatic pistol and a TRU-UV flashlight, but he couldn't quite control the trembling of his hands.

He was genuinely afraid now.

Lilith, without budging from her gurney, had managed to kill eight federal agents, and to spook Dan Bradstreet in a way nothing else had.

"I hope you don't think you're getting out of here," Bradstreet said, his voice shaking. "Our people have . . . killed the rest of you, and they've got this building surrounded."

"I'm not so sure I believe that," Stella said. "If they're out there, why haven't they come in? How is it you're supposedly communicating with them? I don't think you have anywhere near Lilith's abilities."

"L-let's just say I kn-know my people," Bradstreet said. "They're out th-there all right, believe me." He sounded like he was trying to convince himself. The quaking of his hands and his voice were accelerating, as if each stimulated the other.

"You want to know what I think?" Stella asked. "I think you're scared shitless. You didn't really have as much as you thought—you had some expensive equipment and some geeks to run it, and you had Lilith, and you had a pocketful of hunches. Now that's all gone. Now all you have is the knowledge that the world is full of more of us than you can ever cope with. What you don't know, but you should, is that by now all of them know who *you* are. They have your home address, your office address. If you want to check your messages, you'll find that they have your phone numbers too."

"You're lying."

"Try it, then. Here's the thing, Danny boy . . . you've hunted and harassed our kind long enough. Now it's our turn. When you're trying to sleep at night, you'll always be wondering if we're right outside your window, looking in. When you drive to work on those dark early mornings, who'll be in the car behind yours? Or working late? Or coming home after dark? Never mind going out for a movie, or running to the store because you're out of beer or milk at home. If we should let you live long enough to get married, pump out some sprouts, you think they'll be safe? Not for a second. You made the rules, Mr. Bradstreet. Now you get to live by them."

He stood on the stairs with his gun drooping toward the floor, shaking like a kid with stage fright on the night of the Christmas play. His jaw dropped as he tried to formulate some response to Stella's news, then his mouth clamped shut again, lips pressing together in a thin white line. "Bullshit," he snapped at last.

Stella just shrugged.

Bradstreet had given up threatening the three *nosferatu,* and Eben was anxious to leave, to make it back to at least one of the trucks and get Lilith out of there. But Lilith wasn't done with the Operation Red-Blooded agent, even if she couldn't physically tear him apart.

A puzzled look flashed across Bradstreet's face, and he came down off the steps with jerky, unsteady motions that reminded Eben of Keating's. "Wh-what . . . are . . ." Bradstreet managed, then his mouth went slack. His eyes were the only animated part of his face, shifting and darting all over as if they were trying to escape his head.

Lilith lay on her gurney, a few beads of bloody sweat on her brow, but otherwise appearing perfectly relaxed.

"Don't . . ." Bradstreet said. His mouth fell open again, and a thin line of saliva ran out from one corner.

His fingers straightened and his gun dropped to the tile floor.

His right hand snapped over to his crotch, squeezing himself hard. Startled, his eyes popped. He swallowed hard and released himself. It was evident from his eyes that he didn't appreciate what Lilith was doing to him.

And just as evident that he couldn't do anything about it.

Bradstreet took one intentional, noisy step toward Lilith, landing with his foot flat. But then he backed up two steps and performed an ungainly pirouette, which ended with him losing his balance and falling hard onto the cluttered floor. There he drew himself up into a sitting position.

"Nnnnnn . . ." he said. More drool spilled from his mouth. His hands rose from the floor, right palm bleeding from a glass cut. He gripped his arms and held on tight, like he was trying to keep them from flying away—or maybe prevent his hands from doing something else.

Inch by inch, those treacherous hands slid up his arms. His eyes showed pure panic now, and his mouth flapped like a stiff breeze blew it. "Nnnnn . . ." he said again, some sort of negative plea. "Nnnnuuuh . . ."

His head started to jerk to one side. He was trying to shake it, Eben believed, but Lilith's grip on him was too tight. His hands crept to his shoulders, and his pathetic mewling became more frequent. "Nnnnuuuuh, nnnnnn, nnnaa . . ."

Stella caught Eben's gaze, raising an eyebrow questioningly. Lilith wasn't in Stella's head anymore either, so she had no more idea what was coming than he did.

All Lilith's attention must have been focused on Bradstreet.

"Nnnnnuuh!" Bradstreet said, louder and more frantic than ever. *"Nnnnaaa!"*

His hands released his shoulders and flew to his face, clapping his cheek and jaw. He trembled like a Parkinson's victim in hurricane-force winds. His skin had gone as white as any vampire's. The fingers of his right hand inched up his cheek, distorting the flesh around his left eye as they went *"Nnnnn! Nuuuuhhh! Nuuunnnn!"*

Bradstreet's suit pants darkened at the crotch, and the rank ammonia stench of his urine filled the room. His right hand climbed higher, index finger pressing at the corner of his eye. Now his wordless keening was a constant, "Nnnnnnnnnn" that never ended. The pale flesh around his eye went even whiter under the pressure of his fingers. He kept pushing, even as his left hand slowly slid across the front of his face, as if trying to reach the right hand in time.

But that left hand moved like it was adhered to his skin, crawling at less than an inch a minute, and even that seemed a nearly impossible strain for Bradstreet. As it made the fruitless voyage, the right hand's fingers pressed in ever deeper, eventually hooking behind the eyeball. Blood spurted out around his fingers, then some milky white fluid. His teeth were pressed together, grinding, and the "Nnnnnn" sound had changed to a soft whimpering, but he kept digging with his fingers.

Finally, he managed to tear the eyeball out. It dangled on his cheek for a few seconds, held there by the optic nerve sheath, but he swatted at it and tore it free. It landed on the floor with a faint *plop*.

Bradstreet sat on the floor, shivering and stinking.

Stella and Eben turned and clattered the gurney across the debris-filled floor and hoisted it up the wide steps. Crews hadn't made it, and neither had Mose, but Paco hurried alongside them. Outside they met no soldiers, no agents of Operation Red-Blooded. They were almost back to the trucks, passing between the vampire mausoleums, when they heard a loud hiss. Eben turned to see Felix capering toward them, blood coating his face. "I've been busy," he said as he caught up. "And I'm full. It's kind of fun feeding on folks who'd happily stomp my brain to bits, but I think I've had plenty."

"Crews said you were all destroyed," Stella said. "Is there anyone else left inside?"

Felix shrugged. "Don't think so."

Eben trusted Felix about as much as he did Dan Bradstreet, and if he hadn't had Crews's word that the others were gone, he would have insisted on a last sweep through the facility.

That will not be necessary, Eben Olemaun. Lilith's voice in his head sounded weaker than before. *Some of the humans still live, but they cower in the buildings, afraid to show themselves. None of our kind remain except those with us here.*

Her grim message confirmed his worst fear. This had been a suicide mission for most, but they had undertaken it because they believed it to be worthwhile.

What impressed him all over again was how powerful Lilith's psychic abilities were—and he felt awkward even thinking about that when she could dip into his mind with ease and catch him. Was it simply because she had survived for so long? Would the same evolution happen to all *nosferatu* who could dodge the bullets, blows, and sun?

If so, then in generations yet to come, the war that Enok wanted might still come to pass, and the result could be far different than it would be now.

On the way to the truck, Felix showed Eben a remote control device. "Keefer wanted me to hang onto this," he said. "He planted some charges. He said to push this button here and—"

"Well, don't press it until we're out," Eben said.

"No, course not."

Eben and Paco lifted Lilith into the back of the truck. Stella climbed in beside her. "You drive," she said. "And make it fast—we've got to put some distance between ourselves and this place, and there's only another couple hours of darkness left."

She opened a container of blood and started pouring it over Lilith's body, into her mouth, trailing it down her flesh. Lilith's appreciation showed on her face, and Eben left them, closing himself into the cab with Paco. Felix stayed in back with Stella and Lilith. Eben started the truck, and floored it away from there.

Distance would be a good thing indeed.

They had gone less than a quarter mile when Felix must have pushed his button, because explosions ripped the night, flaring bright against the dark sky, rumbling like nearby thunder. Eben didn't know how many charges Keefer had managed to set, but from the sound of things a good bit of the facility was being blown across the Nevada desert.

Just picturing it made him smile.

26

IN THE WEEKS that followed, Eben and Stella dropped off Paco and Felix and took Lilith to a safe house she knew of on the Arizona strip, that wild stretch of Arizona wedged in between the Grand Canyon, Nevada, and Utah. The long reach of the United States government barely penetrated the area, and it was so remote from law enforcement that Mormon polygamists had long since settled there instead of in Utah.

At the safe house, they kept her well fed and bathed in blood. It seeped into her pores, aiding her recovery. Her body regenerated to the point that, within a month, she was hobbling around the place on crutches, going outside on the cool nights to take in the sharp scents of the desert in spring. One night Stella found her there, head tilted back, staring up at the sky.

"All those stars," Lilith said. Stella still wasn't accustomed to actually hearing her speak out loud, but her physical condition kept improving. Her voice had a faint rasp to it but was almost back to normal. "You do not always see that anymore."

Stella followed Mother Blood's gaze. The sky was indeed impressive, filled with bright pinpoints of light, like some mad artist had flung billions of tiny bulbs against a black canvas and let them stick where they fell. In Alaska such views were commonplace, sometimes enhanced by the aurora borealis, but in Los Angeles and other big cities it was easy to forget that so many stars had ever existed. And as a captive deep in the bowels of Enok's slaughterhouse, then inside the Operation Red-Blooded facility, Lilith might have been forgiven for wondering if she would ever see a star again.

"There definitely are a lot of 'em."

"Like us, they come out in the dark of night," Lilith said. "Like us, they are legion. And they have learned, as we should, that the daylight is not for them. They are not gone, only hidden."

"Let's go inside," Stella said. "If you have something to say, Eben should hear it too."

"What are you saying, little Stella?"

"I'm saying that Eben's been thinking that maybe Enok was right after all."

"Enok was wrong. If Eben has been swayed, then he is wrong too." She planted one crutch and swiveled on it. "Come, Stella. It is time we all spoke."

Inside, they found Eben and settled into old but comfortable chairs arrayed around a coffee table. The house had been furnished sometime in the early twentieth century, but Lilith had kept it updated with modern conveniences even while preserving its original rustic charm. Eben had started a fire in a cast-iron stove, more for ambience than heat, and the tang of burning mesquite logs filled the room.

"Stella tells me you have been thinking about the future," Lilith began.

"That's right." Eben crossed his left ankle over his right knee and steepled his fingers. "Stella and I have been living two lives, and it's all been a big stupid lie. We've been trying to act like we're still human beings. But we're not. We're vampires, and maybe it's time we accepted that."

"Humans and vampires are two different things," Stella said. "I'll grant you that. But it doesn't have to mean all-out war, Eben. Now, or ever. It can as easily mean a peaceful, if occasionally confrontational, coexistence. We need them to provide food. They need us for . . . I don't know. To scare their children into behaving? To remind them that dangers lurk in the dark?"

"They could live without us," Eben said. "But not vice versa. That's why we are always at a disadvantage. They would happily destroy every last one of us and they'd still have the stories to scare them, but we have to leave many of them alive. Absolute extinction is far easier to achieve than absolute domination. But in years or decades to come? What if Lilith's brand of mental powers have spread, become the norm for us? Then their advantages will seem trivial."

"That may happen," Lilith admitted. "But over the course of millennia, not years or even centuries. Until then, declaring war is the surest way of spurring the extinction you mentioned. What we need most is for humanity to forget that we exist, not to be constantly reminded that we are real. We need to fade back to the status of myth, of terrifying legend. If the day arrives that every *nosferatu* has power like mine, who knows what the definition of human will be? They will continue to evolve as well. If they do not destroy the planet first, that is. Perhaps by then the chasm that separates us will not be so wide after all."

As they talked, Stella watched a spider spinning an ever more elaborate web at the junction of wall and ceiling. None of them had felt compelled to clear it out, and while the house sat empty the spider, or perhaps a series of them, had covered several feet with thick webbing. Dozens of dried insect carcasses hung suspended inside it; no doubt dozens or hundreds more had been fully consumed. It was big enough, Stella believed, to hold a small dog.

"Enok's way can only bring about our final destruction," she said after a few moments of consideration. "You're right, Eben, in thinking that things may change. And if they do, and if we're still here to see it happen, we can reconsider. But we cannot speed that future up. We can only deal with the here and now and hope that our efforts affect the future in some positive way."

"Positive for who?"

"For us. Vampires. Ideally, what's good for us will

also be good for them, for humans, because obviously we need them around. But we have to stop pretending we are part of their race. We are different, separate, and we have to accept that."

"Vicente was right," Eben said. He turned to Lilith. "Had I understood then—well, I still would have done what I did, because I was trying to save Barrow. I was human then, after all—or, to be more precise, at the end there I was more recently posthuman, and I still had a human's urges and instincts."

"Vicente was right," Lilith echoed. "I understand why you had to destroy him, Eben. But I regret it with all my heart, and I miss him terribly. Imagine how Stella felt without you, how you would feel without her. Then imagine if you had been together for a thousand years before you lost each other."

"The pain . . ." Stella said.

"Indeed." Lilith was quiet for a bit. She was very beautiful, Stella thought, when you really looked at her, and when she hadn't recently suffered abuse at the hands of various sadistic captors. "But at last we can put Vicente's beliefs into practice. The two of you have a certain . . . *credibility* in the vampire world, a certain fame, is it? I would not say that you are universally adored, but you are respected by most and feared by many. If the three of us present a united front, we will certainly be hard to ignore."

"What do you have in mind?" Stella asked, shifting forward in her seat.

"We have a fresh opportunity," Lilith said. "A blank slate, of a sort. With this government organization either shut down or severely crippled, we can take advantage of the opportunity to fade once more into the shadows."

"We've kind of been working toward the opposite goal," Eben said. "Stella's book, our websites . . ."

"That is true," Lilith said. "I imagine you will have to make some strategic shifts."

"*30 Days of Night* is due to go into a new printing," Stella said. "Even though it's categorized as fiction, it's won many fans who recognize the truth in it. If we want to suppress that conversation, we should find a way to stop the new printing and let the copies that are out there disappear into private collections."

"I'm sure the publisher can be persuaded," Lilith said.

"There's probably a way to do that," Stella agreed.

"What about the websites?" Eben asked. "Everything we've had Andy and Marcus working on. That's all got to go away."

"Andy Gray is a reasonable man," Stella said. "But he's become a bit of a crusader. I don't know if he'll be easily dissuaded from continuing his efforts."

"You must try," Lilith said. "In all my time on Earth I have never seen a medium that can disseminate information as quickly and efficiently. We thought Gutenberg's printing press was a major innovation—and for its day, it was. But compared to the internet . . . your 'friend' Mr. Gray cannot be allowed to continue spreading the word about vampires, and he must find a way to keep his acolytes from doing so as well. Whatever it takes, this must be done."

"Whatever it takes," Eben repeated.

"I mean that explicitly," Lilith said. "*Whatever* it takes. Even the book is not nearly as important."

"This can't all be done overnight," Stella said.

"Not at all," Lilith said. "It will take time, certainly. A great deal of time. But we have an opening, while Red-Blooded is rebuilding, and we need to take it. Perhaps by the time they reach full force again, they won't be able to find any of us to destroy."

"Okay," Stella said.

"Okay what?" Eben asked her.

"Okay, I'm in. We kill the new printing, we squash Andy's web network. Anything else we can do to send vampires back into the shadows, we do. I'm in, Eben, what about you?"

"Stella," Eben said. "I thought I'd already made it clear. Where you go, I go. No matter what."

She pushed up out of her chair, crossed to her husband, and kissed him hard on the lips. When she felt his tongue press against her, she opened her mouth and greedily sucked it in. After a minute or so, she released him, smiled at Lilith, and returned to her seat. "Sorry," she said. "I know public displays of affection may be inappropriate in front of a widow. It's just that sometimes he's so damn cute."

Lilith was smiling back at them. She shrugged her shoulders, then held out her hands—fingers still webbed together, but taking shape bit by bit—and examined them. "Not at all," she said. "You are free to do whatever you want, little children. I am only pleased you are both in accord about what must be done."

Stephen Edgerton sat at his desk on the seventh floor of the building that Kingston House Publishing leased in midtown Manhattan. The sky had gone dark, but it was Thursday night and he still had some print runs to set before Friday. Kingston House had been acquired by the Monument Group thirteen months before. The huge publicly owned conglomerate, which had fingers in entertainment, liquor, aerospace, energy, defense, and a dozen other businesses, didn't pay much attention to individual books—if Edgerton wanted, he could publish an exposé of the Monument Group's war profiteering in Iraq, and even if they noticed they wouldn't object, as long the book made money—but they paid attention to schedules and to numbers. And they wanted Edgerton's numbers by noon on Friday. So Stephen Edgerton burned the midnight oil, as they said, that Thursday.

He was so immersed in his work that he didn't hear the man enter his office. He glanced up from the screen, blinked a couple of times, and there the guy was, standing in front of Edgerton's desk, tall and gaunt with skin like parchment and eyes that sat deep in his skull. "Can

I help you?" Edgerton asked. Guy was obviously lost. His clothes were pretty nice, though, a dark suit, an off-white shirt that looked like silk, even a black-and-red striped tie. And there was a guard in the lobby who would have stopped him if he was a homeless guy.

"I'm here about *30 Days of Night,*" the man said. His voice was a deep baritone, without accent.

"You really should have made an appointment," Edgerton said. "I'm kind of in the middle of some stuff right now. What's your interest in the book, anyway?"

"I suppose you would say that I'm a neutral third party." The man's smile revealed a mouth full of too many teeth, yellow and pointed and too large. A crocodile's teeth crammed into a human jaw. The carryout Chinese Edgerton had eaten for dinner turned to liquid in his guts. "That is, I don't have a financial interest of any kind."

"Then what—"

"I would prefer that the book not be reprinted. That is the author's wish as well. We would like it to go quietly out of print."

Edgerton had received an e-mail from Stella Olemaun the day before, and she had made the same request. "It's not up to the author," he said. "Or to neutral third parties. There's been a sales bump. We're not talking an Oprah bump, but still—significant enough. I'm ordering a thirty-thousand-copy printing in trade paperback."

"And I'm suggesting you cancel that order. While there's still time."

Edgerton remembered Carol Hino, the book's original editor. She had been run over by a cab. The *Post* had a field day with it, because the cabdriver only worked at night—"Vampire Cabbie Kills Vampire Editor," the headline trumpeted, even though Carol had edited dozens of books in her time at Kingston House, and was gone from the company well before her death.

Before she died, though, she had been increasingly anxious, drinking too much, partying too hard. In an unguarded moment, when Edgerton had bumped into her at a seedy bar on Eighth Avenue that he had gone into precisely to avoid publishing people, she had confessed to him that she was scared, that she never should have acquired what she called "that fucking vampire book," and that if anything happened to her, it was the fault of *30 Days of Night*.

So for this guy with the crocodile mouth to stand in front of his desk and make demands about the same book was unnerving, to say the least.

"Look, we're owned by a huge conglomerate," he explained. "We answer to the stockholders. If we have a book that's making money, we have to milk it. Otherwise it's my job, it's maybe the job of several other people around here. Do you have any idea how many books don't make a dime? We need the hits to make up for the misses."

"You keep talking," the man said, "but I don't hear the right words coming out of your mouth."

"And what are the words you want to hear?"

The man leaned over Edgerton's desk. His breath was hot and foul. It smelled, Edgerton realized, like his basement in Connecticut had when his wife's cat had had a litter of kittens, and one of them died only nobody knew it. After about a week, they knew something was amiss, but it was another nine days before they found the tiny, decomposing body swarming with maggots. "Cancel the order."

Edgerton had not, in fact, placed the order yet. He had only entered the number into the spreadsheet he would pass on to his boss, who would pass it on to the powers that be at Monument.

He knew he should make a stand, kick this freak out of his office, and call building security to remove him from the building.

Instead, with a hand shaking so hard he could barely tap the right keys, he deleted the number, then deleted the whole title from the document. He had to clench to keep from releasing his bowels right on his desk chair. "There," he said. "It's done. You want to check it?"

"That won't be necessary," the man said. "You know I'll be back if you've lied to me, don't you?"

"I get that. Don't worry. We've got a new celebrity bio by a guy who dated Anna Nicole and Paris."

"Both?" the man asked.

"That's what he says. It'll do enough business to make up for losing *30 Days*."

"I'll come by and pick up a copy when it's out," the man said. "And we can look back on tonight and have a chuckle together."

Edgerton didn't want to see the man again, ever. Ever.

"Come back tomorrow night," he suggested. "And I'll leave a bound manuscript for you at the security desk downstairs."

"Just take it home with you tomorrow night," the man said. "I'll pick it up there."

He left as quickly and quietly as he'd come, out the door in a blur.

When he was gone, Edgerton wept.

27

They had to work fast. Fortunately Andy Gray and Marcus Kitka had been a team long enough now that they often anticipated each other's needs. Marcus could answer questions Andy hadn't finished asking. They were almost finished, though—would finish in the next few hours, Andy believed. And just in time.

His last few phone conversations with Eben and Stella Olemaun had been strained and awkward.

Something was up.

He didn't know precisely what, but he didn't expect it to be good news. He had enjoyed hearing what had become of his old nemesis Dan Bradstreet, but that was the last happy thing either of them had said to him.

As they had agreed, Marcus and Andy put their contingency plan into effect. They had a few days, Andy reasoned, since Stella and Eben were still in Arizona. Or they said they were. With mobile phones, Andy couldn't be absolutely sure, and that was what worried him the most.

It was after midnight, and he had sent Marcus home. The kid had had a rough time getting acclimated to life in Barrow—he seemed to enjoy setting up the War

Room and working there, but he was just a kid and he should be doing teen things, not spending all his time worrying about vampires. His dad, Brian, was a good guy, and Andy knew he'd like to be able to spend more time with his son.

Anyway, they were basically finished. Andy was about to watch the edited version of his video one last time. Then it was just a matter of a few clicks and he was done.

There was nothing fancy about the video, no sophisticated production values. They'd shot it right here in the War Room, Andy sitting in his usual swivel chair, looking straight at the camera. He still didn't quite recognize himself; after having been one person for most of his life, he had become another, and the muscular, bull-necked, shaved-headed guy staring at him from the screen seemed like a stranger.

"Here's the deal," that Andy Gray said. Even his voice rang odd to Andy, like someone trying to imitate him and not quite pulling it off. "My name is Andrew Gray. I used to be an FBI agent. Here, wait." He reached into his pocket—he'd meant to have it ready, but forgot—and pulled out his leather ID case. He opened it and held it up to the camera, badge on one side, photo ID on the other. Marcus zoomed in on them and then back out again, the camera moving fast enough to cause vertigo.

"See, FBI," Andy continued on-screen. "And what I'm going to tell you—the reason I wanted you to see that I was a special agent for the Bureau is so you'd understand that I'm not just some wack job, and also so you would know how I first found out about what I'm going to tell you. Because I know your initial reaction will be the same as mine was, same as anybody's. You're going to think I'm full of crap. So all I'll ask of you is to keep an open mind while I show you the evidence. Once you've seen it, you can decide if I'm telling the truth, or if I'm one of those conspiracy theorist lunatics."

The Andy on camera paused for a second. Andy remembered that he had glanced at Marcus, who had given him a nod. With that encouragement, Andy had kept going. "Here's the thing. The reason I'm doing this is to tell you that vampires are real, they're not monsters from bad movies but real things, bloodsuckers, and they are genuinely dangerous. If you know about them, you have a chance to protect yourself. You'll want to know how to do that too, and I'll get into that later on, but the main thing to know is that they burn up in sunlight, or if you can destroy the brain, you kill it."

God, I'm not very articulate, he thought. He'd had notes to remind him of the main points but he hadn't wanted to read from a script because he wanted to come across as natural as possible. *A natural doof, more like it.*

"So I know it sounds crazy. Dracula's a guy in a shiny cape and slick hair, right? He talks funny. But vampires aren't like that—real ones, I mean. They might look like your neighbor. They might be your neighbor. That doesn't mean if your neighbor works nights, you should destroy his brain, or even report him. But if you see him running inside before the sun's rays can reach him, he might be worth keeping an eye on.

"Anyway, I promised you some proof, so here it is. First up is some video shot from a helicopter, back in 2001. I'll warn you, this stuff is pretty graphic. What you'll see here are vampires in Barrow, Alaska, where they went because the sun goes down up here, north of the Arctic Circle, in November, and it doesn't shine again for a month."

The image switched over to the video footage Taylor Ali had shot from the chopper and transmitted to Judith Ali, before vampires had brought the helicopter down. It showed a town in ruins, smoldering buildings, bloodstained snow, bodies everywhere, and moving through it all, the vampires. They caught a human, a young girl, and one of them bit her neck. They passed her around like a joint, each one taking a big hit. Finally, they noticed the helicopter overhead, and with an impossible leap, one of them—later identified as Vicente, whom Eben Olemaun had killed—latched on to the chopper's windshield, then tore his way inside and killed Taylor Ali.

"They decided to use the dark time to stage a full-scale invasion," Andy said over the silent video footage. "As you can see, they systematically destroyed most of the town. People tried to hide, but the vampires sniffed them out and hunted them down. The brave young man who shot this tape was murdered, but because he had managed to send a digital copy to his mother in New Orleans, we have it."

The video stopped, and then still images that Marcus had captured from the video and enhanced came on the screen, each one staying for about ten seconds before dissolving into the next. Andy's voice continued over the images. "Here is some of what appeared on that video, in greater detail. Look at the bodies, stacked up in the cold, drained of blood. Look at this poor woman's neck, opened up—it looks like a bear did it, but those were vampire claws, not bear claws. Look at this guy's teeth, and that tongue. They don't look human, because they're not. They're undead, *nosferatu*. Vampires."

Other still images replaced the Barrow ones. These were taken by Stella Olemaun's band of vampire hunters during her abbreviated *30 Days of Night* book tour—cut short the day it began by her publisher. They had managed to catch a couple of vampires in action, and again Marcus had improved the pictures, making them clear enough to see. Barrow residents had taken more photos during the second invasion.

"Vampires don't always bite," Andy's voice announced. "Sometimes they use their claws, or even knives or other weapons. The idea is to get to the blood as fast as they can. Usually to drink it, but sometimes to bathe in it, shower in it—they need it to survive, but some of them just plain like it. It becomes like a fetish to them, their version of water sports. Here you see some pictures from their second trip to Barrow, in 2004. This time they got their asses kicked good, because Barrow was ready. They had learned how to kill vampires. They set up lights—we call them TRU-UV lights, because they duplicate the photochemical makeup of the sun's rays, and they're fatal to vampires. They had explosives. They had large-caliber firearms. All these things are excellent vampire-killing weapons."

Those images dissolved into another series—vampires after they had been destroyed. Some were of skulls, showing their horrible teeth, and others showed more recently defeated ones with their tongues held out at full length, their mouths open, their claws on display. A couple just showed close-ups of vampire fangs.

"Vampires can make themselves appear human," Andy's voice said. "They can warm their skin until it passes for living flesh. They can reformulate their mouths. It's hard to do and they can't hold it indefinitely, but if you only saw someone for a couple of minutes at a time—and usually at night of course—he or she could be a vampire and you'd never be able to tell. But when the masks come off and they're showing their true faces, they are ugly fuckers.

"Something else you should know about them. That stuff you saw in the movies, about crosses and stakes through the heart and not showing up in mirrors and sleeping in coffins? Forget it. That's fiction, and if you bank on it, you'll end up dead."

Andy came back onto the screen, holding a copy of Stella's book. "Now here's the part that'll take some doing on your part. You've been watching this video, and that's great. But there's a book written by a lady named Stella Olemaun. She and her husband were the law enforcement in Barrow in 2001, and she survived the attack and wrote about it. It's called *30 Days of Night*. You might have a hard time finding it in bookstores, but at the same place where you got this video—and lots of other places on the web, too—you can download a PDF of the whole thing. It tells you what you need to know to survive—what you need to believe, and what you need to tell your friends. Read it. Pass it around. Put the files up on your own website. We need to spread the word, people, and fast, because the vampires want to kill us and we don't want to let them.

"Be safe. Learn the truth. Spread the word. This is going to make a lot of vampires very pissed off, so by the time you watch this, it might be too late for me. But if you're watching this, it's not too late for you."

The on-screen Andy gave an awkward salute, and the screen went black. He considered going back in and editing out that salute, but decided not to bother. It looked stupid but at least it was something, and he didn't have another close to replace it with.

Marcus had set it up so all Andy had to do was save

the video if he was happy with it. Marcus would combine it with the PDF of the book and send it out to multiple .torrent sites from which anyone with internet access could download it. The video would be uploaded to YouTube and other video-hosting sites as well. If any one site took the stuff down, it would remain up on dozens of others—as the word spread, Andy hoped, on hundreds or thousands of others. Sweating, his stomach fluttering, he clicked the mouse to save it all.

When that was done, he sat back in the chair, rubbed his palms over his scalp, and blew out a sigh of relief. It was done. He had been working toward this for a long time, but in bits and pieces, never all-out. Most big decisions were a kind of journey, a trip during which there were various stages where a person's mind could change, the destination could shift. At some point, though, one had to make a commitment. Andy had taken that last step, the one from which there could be no going back. The nervousness that had accompanied the earlier steps vanished as the finality of it set in. No matter what happened now, he had done what he could.

Andy was shutting down the machines and switching off lights when the door swung open.

Stella Olemaun stood there wearing a black leather jacket, jeans, boots, and a frown. Surprisingly, Andy's sudden sense of calm held. "I wondered when you'd show up, Stella."

"I'm here now. What's going on?"

"Something that would have made you happy, once. Now, I'm not so sure."

"What, Andy? What have you done?" She crossed the room, pulled out one of the rolling chairs, spun it around, and straddled it, resting her forearms on its back.

He gestured toward the computer he had used to save the video on. "It's all out there, Stella. Everything we've got."

Her voice took on a new tightness. "What do you mean?"

"The video, still pictures, the book, all with me making my small-screen debut and introducing it. Pretty much everything we've got. And it's been sent to so many different places, there are no doubt already people downloading it and reposting it." He was lying, hoping she wouldn't catch on. It had been saved but it hadn't gone out yet. Marcus had to do that part, and the kid wasn't there.

"Oh, Andy, Jesus. Wow. What a stupid fucking thing to do."

"You haven't always thought so."

"Things have changed."

"Not everything. Or have vampires gone extinct while I wasn't looking?"

"Of course not. But the whole situation is in flux. There's not going to be a war, Andy, unless your stupid, thoughtless act starts one. We plan on going back into the shadows, and you just turned the spotlight on us."

Her mood was somewhere between angry and grieving. "That's the whole point," Andy said. "I've played along with you, but only because it seemed like we wanted the same things. Lately, whenever I've talked to you or Eben, I've had the sense that you were changing your tune. But that doesn't affect *my* goals. I want vampires wiped out, if possible. When I thought we were on the same page, I was happy to work with you . . . even let you run the show here and there."

She had bunched her hands into fists while he spoke. He didn't like the looks of them, or of the way her eyes had narrowed into slits. "I really can't believe how stupidly thickheaded you turned out to be, Andy. I thought you were a smart guy once . . . but a smart guy would have waited, would have talked to me before doing something like that. A war will do nobody any good—peaceful mutual existence is the only way to limit loss of life."

"In the short run, maybe. In the long run? I think we're better off without vampires than with them."

"That's pretty arrogant, isn't it? Would you kill every shark because they might eat a person sometime? What about mountain lions, or grizzly bears? Would you close all the liquor stores, shut down the tobacco factories, and put governors on every car to keep the speed below forty? There are lots of ways to die, Andy Gray. Heart disease kills more people every year than vampires do."

"If someone wants to eat a triple cheeseburger," Andy

said, "that's his choice. No one asks to get drained by some bloodsucker."

"You might be surprised," Stella said.

"Don't give me that bullshit. Being killed by vampires tends to be involuntary."

"So does being killed in war."

"Right, but—"

Working herself up, Stella talked over him. "So does going to work on a bright Tuesday morning in September and finding that someone has flown an airplane into your building. So does living beside power lines that turn out to give you cancer, or being caught in a mine cave-in because you work for a company too cheap to fix their safety violations, or taking prescription drugs that turn out to be fatal. There are any number of ways people can die in this world, Andy. For the most part, if you dig deep enough, you'll find that someone rich and powerful is benefiting from whatever it is that's killing them. The CEO of the energy company gets a ten-million-dollar bonus instead of five, because his company managed to go another year without installing new safety equipment in the coal mine. Those people running tobacco companies talk a lot about personal responsibility, but it's no accident they keep increasing the amount of nicotine in cigarettes."

"All right, I really think that you—"

"We don't even know how the vampire cell or whatever causes this started in the first place, Andy. But it's apparently natural, or God-given, or something.

I mean, it's not like it was created it in a lab or anything. Which makes it some sort of evolution, right? There's nothing unnatural about what we do, and who knows what'll happen if you do succeed in eliminating it? We've found that extinctions of any kind can have unforeseen consequences, and who can even imagine what wiping out a potential new shoot in the tree of human evolution could mean? Humans have fucked the world over royally, in case you hadn't noticed. Turned it into a giant solar oven. Maybe we vampires are the only ones who can turn it around. We're taking the race to new heights, Andy, and you want to cut us down before we even show what can be achieved."

The phone started ringing. He reached for it, but Stella shook her head. "Leave it."

Andy left it.

He couldn't quite believe what he was hearing. He'd read Stella's book, and met her not too long after it was published. She had gone from being a vampire hunter, one of the toughest fighters out there, bitterly antagonistic toward the entire breed to a champion of vampire rights, some sort of undead Messiah who viewed the hand of God behind creatures who murdered humans and drank their blood to survive. What the hell?!

His former partner, Paul Norris, had gone mad too, after he became a vampire. Maybe it was just part of the process, and it happened to different bloodsuckers at different speeds. Maybe no human mind could take living in the darkness and embracing the concept of perpetual murder without snapping.

"Don't give me that pitying look, Andy!" Stella snapped.

"I didn't know I was."

"Don't think you're superior to anyone else. I'm stronger than you, and faster, and I can live longer, and apparently now I'm smarter."

"I don't think—"

"The blinders have fallen off my eyes, but you're still hanging onto yours like they were water wings and you're afraid of drifting out of the kiddie pool. Look, if you're so concerned about human life, do the math. How many more humans have died since . . . well, since Barrow? When vampires started to become more widely known?"

"Your book—"

"I know, *30 Days of Night* had a lot to do with exposing us. Writing that was a mistake I wish I had never made. It opened up a whole can of shit that I can't shovel back in, and everyone associated with it has died—Carol, my editor, Don Gross, my ghostwriter, and who knows how many others? Plus your old partner Paul Norris, and whoever he killed. Whoever was killed while you tried to find him. All those who died while I was waging my own sanctimonious anti-undead campaign. All who died in the second attack on Barrow, and even those we killed in Operation Red-Blooded. The blood spilled and body count since this all started is beginning to look like a world war, and if we can't put a lid on it it's only going to get worse. And what you've done will definitely make it worse. How many widows do you want on your conscience, Andy? How many orphans can you carry on those shoulders?"

The phone rang again. Once again, Stella shook her head. Andy didn't bother arguing. "Even if I wanted to, I can't undo it, Stella."

"You could. You could just follow up with another e-mail telling whoever received your last one that it was a joke, a hoax, a lie. Pull those files down from the servers. You've done a lot of damage, but you can still limit it."

Stella's voice had changed, the timbre becoming higher, shrill. She was on the verge of something—attacking him, maybe. He backed up against the bank of electronics equipment at the far end of the room from her. As far as he could go. "No."

"I'm asking you, Andy. We've helped each other a lot. We've been friends, right?"

"I'm sensing an 'or else' in there, Stella."

"I don't think you're telling the truth. I don't think you have the slightest idea how to get all that data out there. You've got your network, I suppose you could send some e-mails, but that's about it. You're not the tech genius, are you?"

"If you think I'm telling you—"

"I'll just have a look for myself then."

"No you won't."

"You seriously think you can stop me?"

"I can try."

"Andy, you knew this would happen someday, didn't you? You ran with the big dogs for a while, but sooner or later you were going to get trampled."

"Maybe. I didn't think it would be you, though. I thought maybe Eben, maybe someone else. But not you."

"Sorry, Andy." She got up from the chair and gave it what looked like a gentle shove. It rolled into a workbench with a ferocious crash. "You're the one making this happen. You can still stop it. Last chance."

He couldn't deny his fear of her. He was more afraid, however, of what might happen in the long run if her point of view prevailed. "Not gonna happen. So why don't you just fuck off."

He dropped his hands to the work surface behind him. He felt the pressure of the tabletop's edge on the backs of his thighs. Stella advanced on him slowly, giving him time to change his mind, but he knew if she wanted to she could spring across the room like a shot and tear his head off before he could even react.

So he didn't give her time to do that. He hit one of the panic buttons Marcus had installed all around the War Room.

TRU-UV lights flooded the room. They were mounted on the walls, the ceilings, beneath the tables, all hidden behind thin scrims that protected them from view without blocking their rays.

Stella screamed and doubled over, instinctively trying to hide her face behind her arms. Smoke wafted from her scalp. She dropped her arms and glared at Andy for a fraction of a second, a look of pure hatred, and then jumped to a workbench and sprang off that, through a high window, crashing through glass and an iron security screen.

Andy grabbed a gun cached beneath his table, but by the time he reached the window she had vanished into the night.

Sweating and shaking, he sat down in the chair she had so recently vacated. The strut that held the back on had broken when she slammed it. *I suppose I can always buy a new chair,* he thought.

If I live long enough.

28

ANDY WAS STILL SITTING in the broken chair five minutes later. His gun lay on top of a table, next to an external hard drive. He was bathed in hot UV lights, but he didn't plan to turn them off anytime soon. Maybe never.

He tried to figure out his next move.

When the sun rose, he'd be relatively safe outside. But he didn't want to spend the rest of his life fearing the dark. And she would be back for him, he knew. Either Stella or Eben or maybe someone else entirely, but probably them. They were revered in Barrow, admired, even though they were bloodsuckers. Trying to warn a town they had saved twice would be like some newcomer talking smack about royalty.

And they couldn't accept what he had done without retaliation. When his efforts started to take effect, when the global conversation turned to what could be done about the vampire menace, everyone would know that he was the one who had amassed the information and ratted them out. They would have to move against him, if only to preserve their own reputations. They might not come for him tonight, or tomorrow, but it would happen sooner or later.

Not without a fight, though. He knew how to kill them. He knew their weaknesses and their habits as well as any human being alive. When they did come, they'd find him ready.

First things first, though. He reached for a phone to call Marcus. He had to wake the kid up, make sure he was safe from Stella, get him busy sending out their data packets.

When the door scraped open, he dropped the phone and snatched up his gun—loaded with hollow-points that would expand when they hit the brain, and swiveled around in the broken chair.

It wasn't Stella.

The woman who walked in blinked in the bright light but was otherwise unfazed by it. She could have stepped out of a porn video. Her hair was long and straight, as black and shiny as raven feathers. Her body was strong but still womanly, with generous curves. She wore a hooded red parka and somehow made that sexy. It hung open over a tight black corset with red laces that snugged in her waist and plumped out the tops of her breasts. Beneath that was a short black leather skirt, with red-and-black striped tights clinging to long legs. Her boots were black and sturdy. Stomping boots. On her they still managed to be sexy, like the parka. There was a black leather bag slung over her left shoulder. Looking at her reminded him how long it had been since he'd been with a woman. Since Paul had killed Monica, his wife. Before that, there had been one time with Sally, Paul's widow. Since then? Well, he'd been busy.

Like Stella had said, there had been a lot of death since then. He could only hope his efforts had saved some lives, too. This woman made him realize he didn't want to have given up sex for no reason at all.

"You're Andy Gray."

"That's right." He put the weapon back on the table. "Sorry," he said. "Had some trouble here earlier. What can I do for you?"

"My name is Marina," she said. She reached across her torso, right hand going toward the bag. The motion popped her breasts even more. "I'm the new director of field operations for Operation Red-Blooded."

Andy's eyes popped wide with the realization.

"Easy now, I'm just going to show you my ID," she said. Her hand went into the bag.

And came out holding a blued .45. "Changed my mind," she remarked, raising the gun and squeezing the trigger at the same time.

The first slug plowed into Andy's shoulder. It spun him in the chair and rolled him backward, away from his gun. Before he could lunge for his weapon, another shot burned into his gut. He slumped back into the chair, clutching at himself. Blood coated his hands. He started to feel a chill. Had she left the front door open?

That broken window. Stella broke the fucking window. No wonder it's so cold in here.

Marina kept smiling at him, holding his gaze with

hers, like she intended to kneel down and blow him. He would have been fine with that.

As the world blacked in around him, he began to think that wasn't going to happen.

He heard the shuffle of other feet, the murmur of other voices. She hadn't come alone, then. Although he felt like he was sinking in a pool of black tar, he picked up snatches of conversation.

". . . traced the calls between them . . ."

". . . that window there? That's an iron security screen and it's bent like . . . was here, and not that . . ."

". . . wanted this moke for a long time—I guess he shot Dan once and Dan always said . . ."

". . . tell him next time I visit. Not that he knows anyone's even in the room with . . ."

". . . put a bunch of crap online. If he did it'll take us a while to get a lid on . . ."

Finally he couldn't stay in the seat any longer, and he slid off it, landing in a heap on the floor. Something nudged him. It might have been an unexpectedly sexy black stomping boot, but it could just as easily have been a cordovan wing tip. He tried to focus, but couldn't. The world swam around him in shades of dark.

"I hope . . ."

"He's trying to say something." That was the woman's voice. *Marina,* he remembered. *Nice name.*

"I hope you get what you want."

"What a guy," she said. Then he heard a steely click.

By the time the next shot rang out, the one that put

a bullet in his skull and punched his brains out onto the floor, Andy Gray was already dead.

Marcus Kitka had a bad feeling. He didn't like being outside—the predawn air felt cold and menacing somehow, as if there were eyes on him, and teeth in the deep shadows. But he had awakened from a deep sleep, feeling instantly alert and panicky. In the dark of his room, he fumbled for his cell phone and tried to call Andy Gray. No answer at the War Room. He tried again, just in case.

When Andy didn't pick up, Marcus clicked on a light and tugged on the clothes he had been wearing before he went to bed. Creeping from the house, he saw that his father had come home and fallen asleep on the living room couch with the satellite TV on a movie channel. That happened a lot these days. Dad escaped from the life of a Barrow sheriff—boring ninety-nine percent of the time, unless a vampire invasion was under way—by immersing himself in stories of other people's adventures.

Halfway between home and the War Room, Marcus decided his own adventures were more than enough for him. His knees threatened to give way with every step. He had been running, but he kept thinking he heard heavy breathing right behind him, so he slowed to a brisk walk, the better to keep track of his surroundings. Now he didn't hear the breathing, but the back of his neck prickled. Something was out there. He was convinced of it.

He could have used someone like John Ikos now—a fearless motherfucker with a big gun and a burning hatred for the undead. Or the Olemauns, Stella and Eben, who had been his guardian angels during the second Barrow attack. He'd just been a kid then, but they had saved his bacon, no two ways about that. With each block he covered, he was a little amazed that he hadn't been attacked yet. Finally he could see Andy's building ahead, the burned-out hulk he had renovated—with Marcus's help—into the most technologically sophisticated spot in Barrow.

He felt the vise crushing his heart start to relax a little.

Then he saw people walking into the building. Six of them, most wearing black clothing. They had gotten out of two big black SUVs still idling outside with their running lights on, steam from their exhausts rising around them in billowing clouds.

People?

Or vampires?

Probably the latter. They carried themselves with that smug, superior air that vampires often adopted. They weren't sneaking around, but walked right in like they'd been invited to an open house.

Marcus stopped, pressing himself up against a parked truck, watching. He didn't think they had seen him. Vamps had some hella night vision, though, and he didn't dare get any closer.

He wondered if they were there for Andy, or for the data they had amassed. He supposed it didn't really matter if they were bloodsuckers or the other, the government people Andy said had been after him ever since his ex-partner framed him for murdering his own family. Either way, it was bad news. Seriously bad, the kind that Andy might not walk away from.

He and Andy had discussed what to do in a case like this. They had covered every kind of emergency Andy could think of—drilled over and over, in fact. Andy had insisted on it. *We're going into dangerous waters here,* he had said. *We've got to be prepared for whatever might come up.*

Most of their scenarios had involved both of them being inside when something happened. Many of those—a disheartening number—seemed to end with Andy declaring that they were both screwed, and that suicide was preferable to becoming vampire meat.

In this particular case, the plan was that Marcus would turn around and run home as fast as he could. *Just stay the hell away,* Andy had insisted. *Pretend you were never here.*

If Andy was in trouble, though . . .

Marcus imagined himself sneaking up to the door, slipping inside, switching on the TRU-UV lights, and blasting a bunch of bloodsuckers into smoke and ash. Or if they were human, grabbing one of the automatic weapons hidden around the place—Andy had drilled him with those too—and opening fire, cutting down a bunch of sinister government agents where they stood. How hard could it be? The people, or vampires, had been inside for almost a minute already. There were a switch and a SIG Sauer right inside the door—he could have his hands on one or both in five seconds. In spite of everything he had done, Andy still thought of him as a kid—a smart kid, but a kid just the same. He could be the hero, though. He could save Andy's life, and all their work.

He could get himself killed too. Or he could blow away a bunch of people Andy had invited over for coffee and doughnuts. That last one didn't seem too likely—Andy wasn't a doughnut kind of guy, although he had been once, he said.

No, he had to do what Andy had told him to. He took one more look at the building, then turned around. Started jogging toward home.

He had taken two steps when he heard the first gunshot.

His jog turned into a sprint.

By the time he reached his front door, his lungs were seared, his heart thundering in his chest. He closed and bolted it, put on the chain lock, turned on the alarm system.

His dad hadn't budged from the couch. He snored softly. The movie had changed, some superhero thing on now. Marcus had always thought comic books were stupid, baby stuff, and didn't understand why people watched movies made from them. But having Dad asleep was good. It meant he wouldn't ask questions. Marcus went upstairs to his room.

Inside, he closed the door and locked it, too. All the locks in the world wouldn't keep vampires out. He would take whatever help he could get, though, and even a few seconds was better than nothing. His heart was pounding so hard it sounded like bass drums in his ears, and his nose was running and his eyes watered and he felt like he was going to puke. The things that had passed through his mind ever since hearing that gunshot—Andy dead, him dead, Dad dead—terrified him more than anything had since that last invasion, since Stella had appeared like an angel of God and torn the vampires apart.

Fuck it, he thought. *Andy treats me like a kid because I am one. I'm no hero, that's for sure.*

As long as it was all about machines, about tech and the web and manipulating data, he'd been fine.

But that gunshot brought it all home in a way nothing else had. They were dealing with life and death here—not just for him and his family, but for the whole town. Maybe the whole world. He wasn't equipped to handle that kind of responsibility. That was something that only came with experience, with maturity. His dad was a good man, a brave one, but Marcus wouldn't have trusted him to protect a town much larger than Barrow, because he hadn't been tested that way in a bigger arena. He'd never had to take on something like that by himself.

Maybe one day—if he survived—Marcus could be as gutsy as Stella and Eben, or Andy. Maybe he would be able to take vampires on, single-handed, and win.

For now? Now he just wanted out. If he was wrong, and Andy really had invited those people, then when he talked to him—when Andy explained that the "gunshot" was really someone dropping a heavy book on the floor (which didn't explain the second one he'd thought he heard as he ran home, although by then the sounds of his feet and his blood pumping in his ears had overpowered anything else)—he would tell Andy that he was glad he'd been able to help out, but he needed to start paying attention to his education, his future.

That much was honest, at least. He'd already missed out on time he should have spent learning about girls, trying smoking and drinking and pot—at least, if what he read about his peers online was true. He didn't actually know a lot of his peers. By the time he'd arrived in Barrow, a lot of the kids who had lived there had been shipped away—those who had survived the 2001 attack—and since the second attack, he hadn't made much effort at "normal life." There were some kids his age he saw on the streets now and again, texting on their cell phones, listening to iPods, sometimes even talking to each other, but for the most part he couldn't have identified them by name. It seemed like it was past time to start thinking about such things, before his teen years were behind him and he found he had become a lonely, miserable adult.

If he had a future at all. If whoever was in the War Room right now didn't come for him next.

If Andy was already dead, which seemed highly likely at the moment, then he wouldn't have to explain his decision to anyone. He would warn his father, and John Ikos, if he could reach him, and he would stay in his house and out of trouble and hope that it all blew over, whatever "it" was.

First, though, before he could back away from what he'd spent the last year or so of his life doing, he had one final task to accomplish. The laptop on his desk mirrored everything that went on in the War Room's network, so he could keep track of it and fix the occasional problem remotely. He flipped it open and started digging through the files, finding the data package that Andy had viewed most recently. He had told Andy where to save it if he was okay with the final cut of the video, and Andy had put it there. That meant it was good to go.

All across the globe, servers were waiting.

He just had to send it out.

Ten minutes of work, maybe fifteen. It would be done. What Andy called their crowning achievement.

He just hoped he had the time.

29

In the dark, even with night vision better than that provided by any technologically enhanced goggles, it was impossible to see where the line of low hills ended and the night sky began. There was blackness and then there was more of it, only interspersed by the occasional star glimmering between thick cloudbanks.

A few miles outside Barrow, snow still blanketed the ground, crunching dryly under Stella's boots. Had the moon been able to break through the cloud cover it would have gleamed off the snow, but instead the ground was just one more shade of gray. Color had abandoned the world, leaving only shades of gray and black. Or maybe that was just Stella's mood.

She knew she had blown it with Andy. She should have been more conciliatory instead of giving him hard-line attitude from jump. They'd been something like friends—allies, anyway—and she should have made nice. That had never been her nature, though, as human or as vampire. She had always been a person who demanded what she wanted, who figured she had to show that she meant business, rather than trying the "more flies with honey" approach. Then by the time she discovered that any given person would respond better to more gentle persuasion, it was too late.

Well, she had a long time to change her habits. Centuries, if she was careful.

If war came, though, all bets were off. Longevity would no longer be even remotely guaranteed, especially for those on the front lines. And she had a strong feeling, based on everything that had happened since 2001, that she and Eben would be on those lines. Somehow they kept finding themselves in the middle of things. She had often wondered if it was coincidence that they had been Barrow's law enforcement when it all began with that first invasion, or if there was some other force at work. Providence, fate, kismet. God. She supposed she would never know for sure—that was the point, wasn't it, of life's mysteries?—but when she looked at the pattern of events that had brought the two of them from being completely ignorant of vampires to where they were now, some sort of guiding hand certainly seemed to be at work.

If she knew whose hand it was, she would lop it off. She had never asked for any of this. Turning back the clock on it wasn't possible, but if she could she wouldn't hesitate for an instant.

If there was still a chance to call off the war, it would be by persuading Andy to pull back whatever data he had sent out. She couldn't do it herself, and apparently she couldn't convince him to. Which was why she was tromping through the snow looking for the cabin—

more of a bunker, really—that John Ikos had built smack into the base of one of those low hills. He had disguised it so well, with only a slit of a window showing, and the door, if you knew what to look for, that even though she had been there a few times, she always lost track of it.

Andy respected Ikos, though. More precisely, Ikos hadn't lost Andy's respect by becoming a vampire. Instead he had redirected his efforts away from hunting animals for their skins and meat toward hunting predators who lived on human blood. There weren't many humans Stella could think of who had destroyed as many undead as Ikos had. As a result, for Andy his credibility remained high.

If Ikos would listen to reason—and if she didn't start out by attacking him—maybe *he* could convince Andy. It was worth a shot, she figured, because it was the last shot she could think of.

When she found his cabin, however, the door stood wide open, a black mouth in the faintly more shallow blackness. She quickened her pace—leaving his home unguarded was not something he ever did. Usually when someone approached the place, it would be locked up tight, and Ikos would be in the window slit, drawing a bead with a high-powered rifle.

No light showed through the window, and Stella couldn't hear anything from inside. She approached the doorway cautiously. It wouldn't be unlike John, if he were to leave his door open for some reason, to set some kind of trap in case any vampires happened by.

The front part of the structure was Ikos's hunting blind—concrete wall, strictly utilitarian, with spaces for weapons, binoculars, night scopes, and the like. All seemed to be in its place. A steel door separated that part from the main cabin, but that was open, too. She leaned in cautiously, scanning for tripwires or other sensor devices that might trigger a trap.

All she saw from outside the door, though, was Ikos's customarily neat main room. The cabin was small and he kept it tidy, everything in its place, because otherwise he wouldn't be able to move around in it. The doors had apparently been open for at least a couple of days, because snow and twigs had blown in, and long tracks showed that a snowshoe hare had investigated and left again.

Her left hand brushed the jamb as she went in. The place smelled clean and empty, fresh air having blown out the usual scents of wood smoke, beans, and Ikos's musky sweat. "John?" she said, into the silence.

Only silence answered.

Stella went through the outer bunker, noting that a couple of slots in the gun rack were empty, and into the main cabin. It was cold inside, the stove in the corner that usually glowed with a gentle warmth dark and dead. Her first fear—that she would find Ikos dead inside, or else spilled blood and signs of struggle—was not realized. The place was as orderly as ever except for the debris that had blown in from outside.

She tried to take a quick mental inventory, but decided she hadn't been here enough times, or paid sufficient attention, to achieve any accuracy at all. The missing rifles made her think he had gone hunting, but he wouldn't have left his doors open in that case. If someone had broken in, they'd left no sign of doing so. She was about to give up and leave when her gaze fell on a slip of paper on his rough-hewn dining table, anchored there by a blue enameled coffeepot.

She picked up the paper. She had only seen Ikos's handwriting a few times, but this looked like it to her—unschooled but neat, like everything else about him. "You," it began. *Could be for just anyone,* she thought. *But somehow I don't think it is.*

She kept reading. "I'm gone. Decided it was time to move on. Don't try to find me. If you do, I'll fucking well kill you. Yes, you."

Short and to the point. That was John Ikos, all right. Stella put it back under the coffeepot. Not that it was meant for anyone's eyes but hers, she was convinced of that. But she didn't intend to take it with her. As seldom as anyone passed by here, it would probably sit there until it decomposed. The whole place would be returned to the earth—not soon, in this cold land such processes took longer than in more tropical climes, and those concrete walls and steel doors would last for decades—but as she was learning to measure time, it wouldn't take long.

She wouldn't be getting Ikos's help with Andy Gray.

Maybe in the long run—the very long run—whatever Andy had done wouldn't matter anyway. Maybe she overestimated his influence, or the power of cold hard facts in a world fueled by gossip, style, flash, and image. Vampires would continue to rule the dark hours, and humans the light, and even if war came it wouldn't mean total annihilation for one or the other. Wars were never as decisive as all that.

The distant horizon glittered like pewter in firelight. Time to get back to her own cabin, before the sun penned her inside Ikos's. She left his place, went back out into the still, quiet predawn air. A bird flapped by overhead, harbinger of spring and summer, when the sky would be thick with them.

War might come, but this moment? This moment was about peace.

Stella would take it while she could get it.

She hurried back to her cabin, hurried to beat the sunrise—but not so fast that she couldn't enjoy the last, fading moments of night.

Epilogue

"I WANT A Count Chocula shirt!"

The vast suburban Seattle store was brightly lit, its floors clean and its aisles wide. Over its public address system, a young employee insisted, for the third time, that the store would be closing—in five minutes, this time, having counted down from fifteen—and that all customers should bring their final purchases to the registers.

The kid who wanted a Count Chocula shirt wailed over the announcement, drowning out the young woman's voice. He was probably five and even though he was skinny he barely fit into the little seat of the shopping cart his mother pushed. She was in her late twenties, African-American, pretty but a little frazzled, with a lock of hair that had escaped from her scrunchy hanging down in her face (she blew at it, trying to move it away, but it kept falling back in the same place, and every time she released the cart with one hand it drifted toward the right, into the shelves, and the boy would grab for whatever came within his reach).

"I told you," she said, with that forced patience

parents reserved for their children when they were out in public, "not tonight. We just had to come to pick up a few things for the birthday party tomorrow. You want to go to Agatha's birthday party, don't you?"

"I want a Count Chocula shirt and a party!"

"No T-shirt for you tonight, Cayden."

"Count Chocula's a vampire! Like the Count!"

"I guess lots of vampires are named Count, aren't they?" She stopped the cart by the Sesame Street toys, maybe inspired by Cayden's declaration. "I don't know," she said, mostly to herself. "Are these too young for Agatha? Girl's going to be five, like you."

"Count Chocula, the Count, Count . . ."

"Count Dracula," his mother prompted.

"Right, Dracula! Chocula and Dracula! And Blacula! They're all vampires! I love vampires!"

His mother glanced up to see an employee in a red vest standing at the end of the aisle. "He's obsessed with vampires," she explained. "I really don't know why."

"I can see that," the employee said. "I'm sorry, but we really have to close."

"I understand," Cayden's mother said. "I just forgot that he has to be at a birthday party first thing in the morning, and he needs a gift." She gestured toward the cart. "We've already got some wrapping paper and a card. Just this one thing."

"You have about a minute," the employee said. Then he wandered away to roust someone else.

"Geez," the young mother muttered after he was

gone. "Must be anxious to get home." She still didn't know she was being observed, and had been for twenty minutes now. She was young and fit, and the blood that ran through her veins would provide powerful sustenance for a *nosferatu* who had far to travel before the sun rose.

"I want a T-shirt!"

"Cayden, don't make me say it again."

Cayden would need his mother as he grew up. But Stella Olemaun needed a meal now, and the young woman was so vibrant, so full of life, just watching her made Stella famished.

Besides, Stella told herself, *she's just a human. You're not. Once you were, but not anymore, and you can't let these emotions get in your way. Would the woman spare a hen because she had chicks? Or will she buy chicken nuggets for Cayden next time he asks for them?*

She would take the woman in the parking lot.

The kid was still a tyke; he would have to be strapped into a car seat. When that was done, the mom would go around to her own door. That's when Stella would grab her, hauling her quickly around the back of the car so the boy didn't have to watch.

She could almost taste the blood. She expected it would be sweet, with a slightly salty tang—everybody's blood tasted different, and this woman was so fresh-faced, her skin clear, practically glowing, that Stella just knew hers would be delicious.

She licked her lips.

Finally, the mother settled on a stuffed animal—Olivia the pig, from the children's book series. "Agatha will love it," she told Cayden, handing him the pig. "I know her mom reads her the Olivia books."

He gave the pig a hug, then pretended to bite it on the neck.

His mother's eyes went wide. Stella thought she would go off on the boy. Instead, she ran her hand across his scalp, lovingly, took the pig, and put it in the lower part of the basket. As she leaned over him, she kissed his head. "You're adorable," she said.

The boy made a kissing noise back at his mom.

And right then Stella knew she couldn't take the woman.

She wanted to, wanted it so bad. She'd fed on plenty of other parents. Maybe not in front of their children, but knowing that people had families had never stopped her before.

This time, though . . . she just couldn't. She could hardly believe her own reaction. She would rather go hungry than leave Cayden—an absolute stranger, someone she hadn't known existed twenty-five minutes ago—without his mother.

Was it because the kid's cocoa-brown skin reminded her of baby Dane's? Or just because the sheer humanity of their exchange tugged at strings she had thought were long since left behind?

"Does that mean you'll get me the shirt?" Cayden asked, brimming with hope.

Stella came around the corner and into their aisle. "Oh, let him have the shirt," she said with a friendly smile. "He's only going to be young for a little while."

"You promise?" Cayden's mother said.

"And besides," Stella said, "he's right . . . vampires *are* cool."

"I suppose."

"So you'll get me the shirt?"

His mother blew out a sigh. "If they don't kick our tails out of the store before we get back there."

"Hurry," Stella said. "I'll stall the store Gestapo."

"Thanks, lady!" Cayden called. His gap-toothed smile was one of the most adorable sights Stella had ever seen. Certainly since she had lost little Dane.

"Enjoy it," Stella said to their backs as Cayden's mother wheeled him away. "Wear it in good health."

She stayed long enough to watch Cayden's mother pick up the shirt and hand it to him, then she left the store.

There would be other meals.

She could still travel some tonight, back toward Arizona. Toward Eben. Maybe she'd find dinner at a truck stop or a roadside diner.

They would have a lot to talk about, as usual.

Just now, she had added an item to their agenda. She had thought she was a posthuman, but it seemed she had been wrong. Maybe she never would be, not completely.

Or maybe she and Eben were part of that evolutionary step in the direction baby Dane had pointed in—a blending of vampire and human, instead of a branching off.

One event, however surprising, didn't necessarily signify a trend.

But it might point that way.

Lots to talk about.

She wondered what Lilith would think. She wondered if she would remember, when she told them, why she had decided to spare Cayden's mother in the first place. She thought she would, probably.

But as she passed beyond the store's parking lot lights, she still had plenty of questions about her place in the world, and Eben's, and how they would negotiate day and night, darkness and light, the call of blood and the still-human hearts that kept beating in their breasts and always would.

All she could say for certain was that they would make that journey together, wherever it might lead. The destination would make itself clear in time, she supposed.

Walking into the dark, toward whatever that destination might be, Stella Olemaun caught herself whistling a cheerful tune through a mouthful of razor-sharp teeth.

ABOUT THE AUTHORS

STEVE NILES is one of the writers responsible for bringing horror comics back to prominence, and was recently named by *Fangoria* magazine as one of its "13 rising talents who promise to keep us terrified for the next 25 years." Among his works are *30 Days of Night, Dark Days, 30 Days of Night: Return to Barrow, Criminal Macabre, Wake the Dead, Freaks of the Heartland, Hyde, Alistair Arcane,* and *Simon Dark. 30 Days of Night* was recently released as a major motion picture. *Criminal Macabre, Wake the Dead, Hyde, Alistair Arcane,* and *The Lurkers* are currently in development as feature films. Niles got his start in the industry when he formed his own publishing company called Arcane Comix, where he published, edited, and adapted several comics and anthologies for Eclipse Comics. His adaptations include works by Clive Barker, Richard Matheson, and Harlan Ellison. Currently, Niles is writing *Batman: Gotham After Midnight* for DC Comics. Niles resides in Los Angeles. Visit him at www.steveniles.com.

JEFF MARIOTTE is the award-winning author of more than thirty novels, including *Missing White Girl* and *River Runs Red* (both as Jeffrey J. Mariotte), *The Slab*, the *Witch Season* teen horror quartet, and many more. He also writes comic books, and his horror/ Western series *Desperadoes* was named the Best Western Comic Book of 2007 by *True West* magazine. He's a co-owner of specialty bookstore Mysterious Galaxy in San Diego, and lives in southeastern Arizona on the Flying M Ranch. For more information, please visit www.jeffmariotte.com.

30 DAYS OF NIGHT
GRAPHIC NOVELS BY IDW PUBLISHING!

30 DAYS OF NIGHT: RETURN TO BARROW

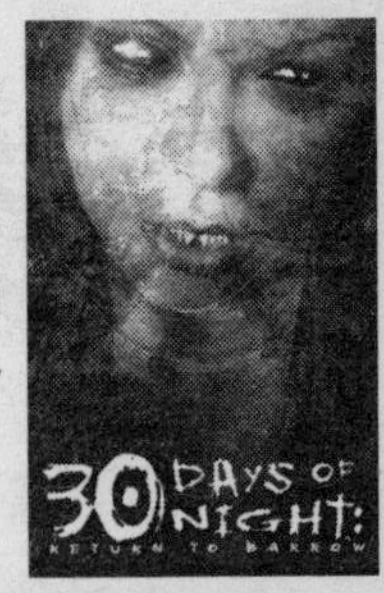

Revisit Barrow, Alaska, the town where it all began, as the long night creeps once more over the tundra. Some things may have changed, but the horror remains...

"Will Barrow's new sheriff coax the secrets from the frosty Barrow survivors? And what's with the gory headless vamp? It all plays like the Wachowskis taking on Anne Rice... without all the lame-ass philosophy. A-"

—Tom Russo, *Entertainment Weekly*

ISBN: 978-1-932382-36-5 • $19.99

30 DAYS OF NIGHT: BLOODSUCKER TALES

The world of the undead is a vast one, with many stories remaining to be told. In ***Bloodsucker Tales***, **Steve Niles** continues the saga of ***30 Days of Night*** with the bloody and terrifying story "Dead Billy Dead," illustrated by talented newcomer **Kody Chamberlain. Matt Fraction** joins in with "Juarez," introducing Lex Nova, private detective and free-range madman, illustrated by **Ben Templesmith**.

ISBN: 978-1-932382-78-5 • $24.99

30 DAYS OF NIGHT: THREE TALES

This ***30 Days of Night*** graphic novel collects three tales of terror. "Picking Up The Pieces," by **Steve Niles** and **Ben Templesmith.** "The Journal of John Ikos," by **Steve Niles** and **Nat Jones.** "Dead Space," written by **Steve Niles** and **Dan Wickline** with art by **Milx**.

ISBN: 978-1-933239-92-7 • $19.99

www.idwpublishing.com